The Catfish

By

David Hatton

Front Cover Design by Warren Designs

Edited by Julia Gibbs

Feedback for David Hatton

Taken from Amazon, Facebook & Good Reads

******

"Utterly compelling. I am very much looking forward to reading more from this author."

*****

"David Hatton is one of those natural story tellers who keeps you guessing what's coming next. Can't wait to read more from this author."

*****

"Looking forward to the next novel from this new and exciting author."

*****

"David has an exceptional writing style that is easy to read. I can't wait to read the next one."

*****

"I feel David Hatton is really getting into his stride as a newly published author. I am very much looking forward to David's next book along with others in the future."

This book tackles very emotional and disturbing subjects.

This story is for anyone.

But it won't be for everyone.

"Justice cannot be for one side alone, but must be for both."

Eleanor Roosevelt
(1884 – 1962)

Prologue

Welcome to TeenTalk, the UK's leading Chat Room for Teens. Please review our terms and conditions, select a username and click enter.

Hello Charlie! Welcome to the room! Select someone to talk to or speak to the group.

Charlie: Hi everyone. I'm Charlie.

NEW CHAT REQUEST FROM ANNA

Charlie: Hi Anna

Anna: Hi Charlie. ASL?

Charlie: 19, M, Horwich, you?

Anna: 11, F, Farnworth

Charlie: I've been to Farnworth.

Anna: Cool, we're not far away from each other. What do you like to do Charlie?

Charlie: I like computer games and ice cream.

Anna: I like ice cream. What's your favourite flavour?

Charlie: Pink

Anna: Strawberry?

Charlie: yes, what is yours?

Anna: I like pink too ☺

Charlie: Would you like to meet?

Anna: Woah, Charlie, I've only just spoken to you, let's get to know each other first.

Charlie: OK.

Anna: Do you go to college?

Charlie: No I stay at home with my mum. You?

Anna: I go to St Mary's.

Charlie: Mark went there.

Anna: Who's Mark?

Charlie: My neighbour.

Anna: Where did you go to school?

Charlie: St John's near my house until I was too old.

Anna: Did you like school?

Charlie: No, they bullied me.

Anna: I get bullied too ☹

Charlie: Would you like to come to my house?

Anna: I think we should meet somewhere neutral first. I need to protect myself, Charlie.

Charlie: Neutral?

Anna: Yes, maybe in Farnworth. My mum wouldn't let me on a bus on my own anyway, you'd have to come and collect me.

Charlie: I can come meet you and bring you home. We can play computer games and my mum will get us some ice cream.

Anna: Maybe you could buy us beer?

Charlie: Why?

Anna: Because you're over 18. You're allowed to buy beer. You can buy me beer. We could drink it and play your games.

Charlie: If you'd like that.

Anna: Where should we meet?

Charlie: I don't know. At the bus stop?

Anna: It stops outside the cinema. Shall we meet there?

Charlie: Yes.

Anna: How will I know it's you?

Charlie: I'll wear a hat.

Anna: Haven't you got a photograph?

Charlie: <JPEG File Upload>

Anna: Oh wow, you're handsome. Got any more photos?

Charlie: <JPEG File Upload>

Anna: Nice. Anything more revealing?

Charlie: Like what?

Anna: I want to see you naked, Charlie.

Charlie: Why?

Anna: I'd just like that.

Anna: … Charlie?

Charlie: One second.

Charlie: <JPEG File Upload>

Anna: Ah nice, I can't wait to get my hands on that

Charlie: And play computer games?

Anna: Well some kind of game ;)

Anna: Do you want to see a photo of me?

Charlie: yes.

Anna: <JPEG File Upload>

Charlie: You're very pretty. Do you not like clothes?

Anna: Not when I'm hot. I'm hot for you Charlie

Charlie: You're funny.

Anna: So shall we meet?

Charlie: At 2pm? Outside the cinema?

Anna: I'll be there.

Charlie: Bye.

Anna: Oh OK, see you soon! Bye xxx

He closed the lid on his laptop and glimpsed at himself in the mirror. How could he go and meet this girl? No wonder the other kids called him *Fatso*. His blue and white Bolton Wanderers t-shirt barely covered his belly. The tracksuit bottoms were worn at the knees; black with a white pinstripe down each leg. Red elasticated cheeks drooped, forcing him to wear a constant morose mien. Those distant eyes were also a source of mockery;

he was the *div-kid* to the others but he was smarter than he let on. For one thing he was excellent at maths. He'd held the record in school for reciting Pi to three hundred decimals. He took things in too. He could see their stares, their elbows jabbing and smarmy smirks.

Placing on the red hat, *Making Bolton Great Again,* a humorous stocking filler after the Trump Campaign, he stepped out of his chair and made his way downstairs. His mother was furiously whisking in the kitchen; she had a bake sale on at church later that day and she'd be busy for a few hours. Charlie glimpsed inside her handbag, helped himself to a crisp fiver and slipped it into his pocket before sneaking out of the front door.

The bus ride over was a bumpy one as the pot holes deepened. The bus kept stopping; that was the thing about Saturdays, everyone wanted to go into town. A frail lady got on, pushing a trolley-bag, and the bus driver waited until she sat down before moving on. Charlie kept looking at his watch; he only had fifteen minutes. He sighed loudly to ensure everyone, including the driver and the elderly woman attempting to safely sit down, knew of his impatience.

They passed a line of stone terraces and a row of pubs before escaping into the hills. He gawped over at a mansion. It was white with large bay windows looking out over Rivington Pike and a reservoir at the end of their garden. The front door opened and its inhabitant walked out towards his midnight blue Porsche on the driveway. Charlie banged on the window.

'Dad! Dad!' he called and the passengers turned around, giving him a fierce stare, before his father was out of sight. Charlie stared on, his fists resting on the glass as the mansion shrank in the distance. 'He didn't see me!'

The bus rolled into Farnworth. A burnt-orange stone building sat on the left with arched gothic window frames. A

Moorish cupola was raised high above a sign advertising the cinema complex. Charlie pressed the red button to alert the driver. The vehicle came to a halt and he stepped off. He looked at his silver Rolex watch, a gift from his grandfather before he died. With three minutes spare, he walked to a convenience store next door and grabbed two chocolate bars using the remaining money from his mother's purse.

A poster advertising the latest superhero release formed the entrance of the cinema. He hovered next to it amongst the smokers and the abandoned dates as he counted down the seconds on his watch. As the big hand landed on the hour, he glanced up and sought out his new friend. She wasn't there. He sighed and looked back at the watch. *She's late.*

The village was flooded with locals rushing to the market precinct, collecting their fresh produce and bargains for the week. Across the street, a library advertised its latest local exhibit. It was red-bricked with sandstone columns forming the entrance, and a dome rose high above the local residents flocking to return their borrowed books. A collection of bakeries, butchers and florists snaked around the main road leading to a leisure centre, where Charlie once had his swimming lessons with school.

A red Honda pulled to a halt outside the cinema and three people stepped out, leaving the doors wide open as they approached the entrance. The girl took the lead, marching towards the entrance carrying what appeared to be a microphone. She had a pierced lip, long pink hair and a ruffled black dress. Behind, two skinheads with black leather jackets followed, one carrying a video camera, the kind Charlie hadn't seen since he was on an all-inclusive package holiday when he was five; a fellow resident of the hotel spent his evenings filming the buffets, leaving Charlie bemused as he waited in line for a slice of pizza.

'Are you Charlie?' The girl approached him and held the microphone towards his mouth.

'Yes, am I going to be on television?' Charlie held up his hand to his face and squinted his eyes, as if the sun had pelted its rays down on a frazzling Farnworth, when in reality the town nestled behind a cloud allowing for an ambient afternoon in Bolton's suburbia.

'You sure are, Charlie. Are you waiting to see Anna?'

'Yes, she's my friend. Do you know where she is? She's late.' He looked back at his watch. *It's almost five past now.*

'Anna isn't coming, Charlie. She isn't real. Do you know who we are?' The cameraman zoomed in to Charlie while his mate stood behind, towering over the interviewee who was of average height.

'Are you on that media course at UCLAN? Barry does that course.'

'Who's Barry?' the girl replied with a confused stutter, before shaking her head. 'Never mind. No, Charlie, we're The Predator Hunters. We're here today to reveal to the world what a sick freak you are! You entice young girls, sending nude selfies of yourself online and then ask them to meet. You offered to ply her with beer before you could have your filthy way with her, didn't you, you sick fuck?'

'That's not true.'

'What's this then?' The interviewer lifted out her phone and displayed a photograph of Charlie in his birthday suit. 'Is this you, Charlie?'

'Yes, Anna asked me to send it.' He turned away, unable to look at himself in such an undignified manner. A rush to the head brought on a spurt of nausea for a confused Charlie, who continued to look around for Anna.

'You thought Anna was eleven years old, didn't you, you sick freak.'

'She told me she was eleven.' Charlie scratched his head and stared glumly at the girl before him. 'Where is Anna?'

'You're going to come with us, Charlie, and we're going to call the police.'

'I need to go home.'

Charlie dashed from the view of the lens, but a hard grip ripped his t-shirt. He felt himself fall backwards onto the floor, where he lay with his belly on display. Placing his hands over his face, he yelled a muffled *no* and grasped on to the lamppost beside him. The skinheads put down their equipment and lifted him off the ground, throwing him into the back of the car while the girl shouted a pre-prepared statement in line with a citizen's arrest. In the car, Charlie fell flat onto a dusty seat. A collection of beer cans filled the foot-well, which he crushed as he attempted to sit up just as the door closed behind him. He furiously pulled at the handle but it wouldn't open.

'Why can't I open this door?' Charlie's voice was muffled through the window.

'They're child-locked. Just like you should be.' The girl turned around and glared at her prisoner.

'Where are you taking me? I need my mum. Are we going to see Anna?' His voice began to break with his panic-stricken pleas. He banged on the window, forcing the car to shake.

'Sure, Charlie, we're going to see Anna.' Away from view, she rolled her eyes and smiled at her colleagues, before entering into the car. One of the skinheads took the driving seat and once they all had their seat-belts on, the engine rumbled and heavy metal blasted out of the speakers.

Charlie calmed down, comforted by the thought of seeing Anna, and the car sped off away from the cinema. They drove further out of the town and the sights became less familiar to Charlie, who quivered in the back. He wondered how he would find his way home. He calculated the route, retracing his steps to the bus stop, but with every turn, his memory faded. The shops disappeared and the buildings grew into tower blocks. A crowd poured out of a pub, its windows boarded up and St George flags flew high above the car park. *Free Tommy* was chalked onto a sandwich board nearby the entrance.

The car drove into a cul-de-sac and they pulled up outside a grey pebble-dashed house. To the right, a garage awaited with its entrance open. The skinheads opened the passenger door and pulled out their hostage and led him towards the garage.

'Where's Anna?' Charlie called.

'She's in there,' the former cameraman said, before spitting on the floor. 'Now sit here.'

They threw him onto the concrete ground and pulled down the garage door behind them with a hanging cord. Light filled the room from a lone hanging bulb with no shade, exposing a collection of tools, metal chairs and a pool table, which had nets around each hole to collect the marble-sized balls. Damp oozed into the outer wall and the wooden beams above them had begun to rot. The skinheads paced the room while they calculated their next moves, before one of them, who was wrapped in neck-tattoos, picked up his camera and continued to film the star of their short film.

'I'm going to call the police.' The girl lifted out her phone and walked out of a side door into the house, while the third wheel looked in a black toolbox, placed on a shelf above his head. He pulled out a rope and tape and turned towards Charlie.

'I need to go home.' Charlie stood up. He had grown pale and he began to shiver.

'You're not going anywhere, mate.'

Without a moment to think, Charlie charged at the cameraman, knocking him over. The pair thumped onto the floor and his captor's back cracked as it made its impact with the hardened floor beneath. His peer ran to his aid, rolling Charlie off. Gasping for breath, Charlie glanced around him and found a hammer resting on the floor beside a half-empty tin of white paint. He lifted himself up and limped towards the tool. The cold palm of the cameraman gripped on to Charlie's shoulder, who turned around and launched the head of the hammer into his skull. The instrument formed a dent into his forehead. He dropped the camera and his pupils disappeared beneath his lids, before falling to the ground. Blood poured from the wound onto the grey concrete ground.

Charlie dropped the weapon. His flustered face grew pale as he turned towards the garage door. He'd seen the same lock at his granddad's house where he used to help him work on his woodwork in the last years of his life. Clicking the lock, he lifted the door and made his escape.

'Get him!' screamed the injured cameraman, who lifted his woozy head and squinted his eyes towards the escapee. His colleague lifted himself off the ground and ran after Charlie. The girl returned from the house and saw the chaos unfolding before her. She grabbed the camera off the floor and ran after Charlie, recording every second.

Charlie ran out of the cul-de-sac towards a main road. His weight pulled down on his lungs and he grew breathless. Approaching a set of traffic lights, he prayed for a space between the speeding vehicles. He turned around and saw his interrogators getting closer. Before him, a red lorry carrying a double trailer headed towards the crossing at fifty miles per hour.

Charlie looked both ways and stepped out.

Screams echoed across the street. The girl holding the camera said an expletive before the footage turned to black.

Chapter 1

The office of Rachel McCann sat in a small terrace on the high street between a pub and a bank. Across the road, a former railway station now formed a children's play area, however memories of the track and its historic locomotives remained embedded into the green space. A stone cottage formerly housed a local MP, but today was used as a commercial space. Ms McCann had the ground floor, and an accountancy firm utilised the upstairs.

Two maroon leather couches sat parallel, facing each other with a glass coffee table in-between. She took a seat on one and read through her text books, preparing a case for a client who'd visited her a week prior, while she munched on a jam-coated crumpet. The exercise was gratifying to the lawyer who, since setting up on her own after leaving a large international law firm, had had only one customer. The piling bills on her desk beside the window had multiple threats of shutting off her electricity and turfing her out of her office. But as she perused her books, she smiled, enjoying the ample time she could take to really embed herself in the case. She didn't have that sort of luxury at her previous firm. A team of assistants did all the leg work for her. Although she missed the paralegals' constant offer of coffee; now she had to make it herself.

What she didn't miss was the sleazy men who hovered around her desk. She was the eye-candy of the office, and despite the fact that she'd worked so damn hard for her position, there was no doubt as to why they'd taken her on. Her flowing hazel hair, her sun-kissed complexion, slim frame and yet large chest adjusted the necks of her colleagues who gawped as she walked the corporate corridors. They either accused her of sleeping her way to the top or said she was meeting a diversity quota; she could never win. It was surprising how many people who worked in law refused to abide by its basic principles. Then again, who would dare sue a lawyer?

The doorbell rang. She looked towards the window and watched the sun slowly rise. Winter was due and the morning had offered a crisp accompaniment to a robin's call. Anticipating the postman with yet another online delivery of books, she brushed the crumbs off her plain black A-line dress and made her way to the door. A trail of teal beads ran down her chest from around her neck and a silver pendant was wrapped around her wrist, covered in gems handed to her over several Christmases and birthdays.

Behind a heavy black door making up the entrance to the building, an agitated creature stood fidgeting. She was of average height but appeared short as she hunched over. Her short brown bob had white wisps and her skinny frame hid beneath a green cagoule. The years of strain poured from her eyes like a tree showing its age through its rings.

'Hi there, are you Ms McCann?' she asked with a Bolton brogue. The lawyer peered down at the lady before her. Her blue jeans hung loose and her white trainers were worn.

'The very same,' Rachel replied, holding out a hand to shake hers. 'How can I be of service?'

'I need legal representation,' she said, her eyes struggling to make contact.

'You should probably come inside then.' Rachel moved aside, allowing the potential client in, welcoming her with a slight nod. 'Can I get you a drink?'

'Water if you have any.'

She walked towards a cooler beside her desk and poured into a plastic cup, before handing it to the dishevelled woman before her, who was brushing down the seat before taking it. They

24

sat opposite each other and Rachel moved aside her books and dirty plate from the coffee table to make room for her guest.

'What's your name?'

'Karen Irvine,' she said sheepishly. She peered around the room as if she was weighing up whether Rachel's credentials were enough for her case. Her framed multiple degrees lined the main wall, and bookcases full of law journals filled the rest. A collection of abstract watercolour paintings from a local artist hung in white frames, placed seemingly slapdash across the white walls.

'How can I help you, Karen?'

'It's my son, Charlie. Charlie Irvine, you may have heard of him?'

'I can't say I have.' Rachel shook her head.

'You've not been in Horwich very long then?'

'No, I lived in Warrington before I came here. I've just moved here and set up on my own. My mum lives down the road. My dad died last year so it seemed like the fair thing to do. I did grow up here though.'

Build rapport, thought Rachel. *Give the client something of yourself.* It was discouraged in her last place but she wanted to provide a very different service in her new business. Her last job was all money, money, money. She had tougher targets than a cold-calling centre. Build it, close it, bill them and move on. It just wasn't *her*. They were overseeing corporate giants; she now wanted to help the man, or indeed *woman*, on the street.

'I see. Well I'm sure you'll hear a lot about him soon enough.'

'Is he in trouble?' Rachel put on a pair of glasses and picked up a brown leather-bound notepad from underneath the coffee table and began to write notes.

'He was what they call *'catfished'* by a local gang. They call themselves The Predator Hunters.'

'I see.' Rachel lowered her head, losing eye contact with her client. A churning sat uncomfortably in her stomach. 'When did this happen?'

'It was back in April. They chatted to him online. He talked to what he believed was an eleven-year-old girl and went to meet her. They cornered him and he's since been plastered all over social media. His name is mud around here.'

'Mrs Irvine, I'm not a defence lawyer.' Rachel replaced the cap on her pen and put down her notebook. 'I'd happily recommend someone more suitable to represent your son...'

'I need *you*. It's not a defence strategy that we need. Nobody's charging my son.'

'They're not?' She scratched her chin and pursed her red lips.

'No. Charlie is dead,' Karen replied matter-of-factly. Silence hovered in the air like a nasty smell.

'Oh.' Rachel tilted her head and mused over Karen's pain. The bags beneath her eyes drooped like a flag in a windless sky.

'He ran in front of a lorry.'

Rachel wasn't surprised. She was aware of these vigilante groups and their targets, they had a similar network in Warrington. Those that managed to escape the law couldn't escape the shame and ultimately ended their lives.

'What is that you want, Karen?' Rachel asked with an arched eyebrow. She lowered her black circular designer glasses to the edge of her nose and stared curiously at her client.

'I want to get those bastards… and justice for my son,' Karen replied with a raised voice. Rachel admired her transition from a timid badger to a feisty shark.

'On what grounds?' Rachel crossed her legs and gave her client a sceptical stare.

'I don't know. I need your help with that. But there must be something we can get them on?'

The lawyer sighed. She scratched her head as she considered the possibilities but nothing came to mind. But it wasn't necessarily the lack of lawsuit that bothered her.

'Ms Irvine. I'm so sorry this has happened to *you*.' Rachel sighed as she empathised the '*you*'. 'But I don't think we have an angle here. Even if I did believe there was a way that we could somehow fight this, I'm trying to build a reputation around here and I don't think representing a paedophile is going to help that.'

'He's not a paedophile!' Karen barked. Rachel's head flung back and her eyes widened.

'Well maybe not in *your* eyes, Ms Irvine, but you've got to admit, this doesn't look good.'

'He was catfished. He didn't know what he was doing.' Karen's eyes were pleadingly moist like an orphaned child on a Christmas charity advert.

'How old was Charlie?' Rachel stroked her chin.

'Nineteen. Why?'

'Then he was old enough to know better than to message young girls on the internet. Especially eleven-year-olds. What was he thinking?'

'That's the thing, he didn't know better.' A tear sprung from Karen's eye down her cheek, which was blemished with exhaustion. 'You see, Charlie had a development disorder. He was an innocent soul. Very child-like. He couldn't work. He sat at home all day on his computer games. No friends ever came over. He had no one to talk to, until these chat rooms became available. Suddenly he found people to engage with. He was happy. Or what only I could describe as happy. Emotion wasn't something we saw a lot of from him. But it kept him occupied and he seemed content.'

'I see. What did the police have to say about the matter, Ms Irvine?'

'They didn't have anything to say. They didn't really care. As far as they're concerned, The Predator Hunters are doing a great job of keeping this town free from monsters. And when Charlie died, there was nothing more to pursue. He ran out in front of a vehicle. It was declared as straight-out suicide and in their eyes, justice had prevailed. There was no investigation into Charlie or the vigilante gang. I offered up his computer and his medical records, but they said there was no case to defend. Charlie was dead. End of.'

'Ms Irvine, I'd love to help you. I really would. But I really can't see how I can. And for your own sake, I feel you should let this go as what are you really going to get out of this?'

'Justice for my son!' Karen bellowed. 'He's innocent and I want his legacy to be restored. It breaks my heart. I hear them everywhere talking about him. In the local café, down the pub. People turn and look at me with this look of disgust. I need this town to know the real Charlie and how *this* isn't him. And the

28

only way I can do that is to prove his innocence. They took advantage of this very vulnerable person.'

Karen lifted her pistachio leather handbag. On first glance, the bag appeared to be branded. One of those designer names even Rachel struggled to afford back when she was on the big bucks. But following a closer inspection, she could see the cheap cuts and the shoddy stitching inside. It was clearly purchased off a backstreet market or by a beach in a Spanish resort. Out of the counterfeit, she lifted a newspaper cutting filled with her son's shame and handed it to the lawyer, who read over the details.

'As a parent, I'm sure you want to see the best in your son. But there must be a reason they managed to get him to meet this girl in the first place. I'm just not sure what I can do for you.'

'He wanted a friend,' Karen replied, stress ripping from her vocal chords.

'Then why was he sending naked photographs to her and offering to buy her beer?' Rachel lifted the newspaper and pointed towards the evidence.

'They lured him into that!'

'And then attacked one of the group members with a hammer?'

'He needed to get away!' Karen protested. Rachel took off her glasses and folded them away into a white plastic case. She unfolded her legs and shuffled towards the edge of the couch.

'Ms Irvine. I'm touched that you came to see me today. I really am. And I understand that you want to fight for your son's innocence. But there is no case here to be had.'

'Miss McCann.'

'Please, call me Rachel.'

'Rachel, it's fine if you don't want to pick this up. Really it is. I'll understand. You're the third law firm I've approached this week. They all said the same as you. I hoped with you being new in town that you might take the case, or as a woman you might understand where I'm coming from.'

'If the others won't take it, I'm sure I'm no use either,' Rachel explained. 'And as for me being a *woman*... my gender does not in any way influence my stance on the law.'

'Do you have children, Rachel?' asked Karen.

'I do. A ten-year-old girl.'

'Wow, you must have had her young.'

'I'd just left college.' Rachel smiled and a red pigmentation shadowed her cheeks.

'Then you'll know what it's like to do anything for your children. And defend them to the end.'

'I do,' Rachel replied and her smile retracted. 'But I also know what it's like trying to keep her safe on the internet from people like your son.'

Karen's face evolved from a puppy-eyed plea to a disgruntled dragon. She snatched back the newspaper from Rachel's grip, forcing it to tear, and placed it into her bag. Rachel felt no guilt; Karen's son, whether she liked it or not, *was* a predator.

'I see. Very well then, I'll go.' She stood up and made her way to the door. As she opened it, she turned around to the lawyer. 'Listen, Rachel, I understand where you're coming from. I really do. I'd feel the same if I was you. But do me one favour. Do a quick online search for Charlie Irvine. You'll find him soon enough. The video is on The Predator Hunter's page on Facebook. Watch it, please. If you do nothing else for me. Just watch it.'

The door closed and Rachel laid her head back on the couch. Karen Irvine had exhausted her. She looked at the clock towards the lost time she could have spent on her only case. She picked up her textbook and recommenced her reading.

The case in question was a complex one. She was representing a local restaurant owner; he was suing a customer who'd left a brutal review on TripAdvisor. The customer had accused the restaurant of food poisoning, while her client assured her that during the evening, the customer had made a fuss as she attempted to gain a free meal and free drinks before ultimately ripping up her bill as they left, despite the service in the owner's eyes being above adequate. The review had been picked up and published in a local free newspaper and damaged the restaurant's reputation, leading to them losing bookings and ultimately closing its doors the month prior. She scratched her head as she read the mounds of arguments. In a world where anyone can be a critic and free speech is a constant dilemma, she wondered how far she could really take the case, but she would damn well try.

Lunchtime called and she took herself off to a local café in the centre of the village. She sat amongst the chaos of the lunchtime rush as local businessmen queued for a quick sandwich and a coffee. It was a small independent café which also ran as a deli. Weaved baskets filled with preserves and artisan handcrafts piled up beside the counter, whilst the scent of cinnamon brought a stark reminder that Christmas was nearing. Chalk boards showcasing the café's specials lined red walls, and a selection of cream cakes and jam sponges sat enticingly beneath glass stands.

She took a seat by the window, enjoying her latte and a cheese omelette. The café offered free Wi-Fi but she enjoyed being switched off from the world, if only for an hour, while she people-watched. A frail pensioner slowly meandered to the post-office, a butcher ran out wielding a knife as a hooded-teenager ran off with a packet of his finest steak, and a Pakistani lady stood by a local convenience store, handing out a copy of *The Big Issue*. Rachel sat in wonder as to how this poor young girl had managed to get lost within the system and whether her family knew she was out here begging for money. She reached into her purse to see if she had any change for when she passed her later on her way back to the office, but she'd just dropped her remaining coins in the waitress's tip-jar.

A green anorak distracted her curiosity; the same blend as the one in her office earlier in the morning. It was Karen, walking by with her head down, barely lifting it to cross the road. She looked broken. Sadness followed her like a rain cloud. As she aimlessly wandered, people would pass, nudging their friends' elbows and nodding their heads towards the infamous woman with the sinister son.

Rachel tilted her head and sighed. She took out her mobile phone and switched on the Wi-Fi, breaking her lunchtime rule. After a quick scan on Facebook, she found the video in question and pressed play. Fifteen minutes of footage played; the vigilantes read out the exchange of messages between the supposed victim and her groomer, all the way through to Charlie's horrifying end. Her heart pounded as the video stopped.

Grabbing her belongings, she threw a note down on the table and ran out of the café. She paced up the road in the direction towards where she'd seen Karen shuffle to until she came to a crossroads. She looked up and down and took a hunch to turn right towards the shops. Turning her head from left to right, she scanned the locals for anyone who would resemble the woman who occupied her office hours earlier. It was a small village and only a handful of people were scattered across the hamlet. She approached a florist and spotted the familiar green coat which had passed the café, its owner eyeing up a bouquet of white lilies.

'Ms Irvine!' Rachel called.

She turned around and her eyes widened as she saw the sweaty lawyer running towards her, furiously exhaling and holding on to a pain in her diaphragm. She leaned on a stone wall while she grabbed a breath before turning to Karen.

'Thank God I found you. I think we have a case.'

Chapter 2

A small terraced house just off the main road was the home of Karen Irvine. A typical two-up, two-down red-bricked building made up part of the original estate of the former mining town. A small extension eating into a paved yard out of the back was transformed into a kitchen with beige cupboards and a free-standing oven, while the rest of the downstairs was made up of a separate living room and dining space. Since its original occupants had left, Karen had modernised the abode and installed a log-burner to make up a centrepiece for the lounge. A cream sofa and a matching armchair surrounded it. A tabby cat slept in the armchair, which Karen shooed away as her lawyer approached. Rachel took a seat and got out her notepad and pen, reading through her notes, which she'd scribbled down the previous evening after meeting her new client at the florist. She'd turned up to Karen's in a cobalt blue bell-sleeve shift dress and bronze metallic strappy sandals with a heel. She slipped off her white leather coat and settled into the armchair.

'I do have an angle...' she called through to the kitchen as Karen made them a pot of tea. 'But I'm not sure if it's quite the one you're looking for.'

Karen returned to the lounge with a tray, filled with tea and biscuits. She served the refreshments and sat on the couch opposite her lawyer. White fluffy slippers covered her feet, and a woolly cream jumper wrapped around her arms and tartan pyjama bottoms made Rachel question whether her client knew she was coming.

'Oh right. Well anything is good, I suppose.' Karen smiled like the Cheshire cat for the first time since her son's passing.

'It doesn't necessarily exempt your son from the claims they made though.'

'Well what's the point then?' Karen shrugged and her smile faltered.

'Look, Karen, we need to establish your angle here. If it's just the case of exonerating your son, then I'd suggest you speak to the papers.'

'They won't speak to me. I tried all that, they're not interested. I couldn't even get a spot in the free paper that comes round once a month. That's saying something too… last month's headline had a story of the local council having to evacuate their office because someone had burnt their toast. Blimey, call *that* news?'

'Then you need to consider what your goal is here. Legally.' She pulled the frames of her glasses forward to the tip of her nose and threw a piercing stare at Karen.

'I want to stop this gang.' A tear formed in the corner of her eye and she gritted her teeth.

Despite her surroundings being bright yellow with abstract wall-hangings, the house felt dark. Sadness oozed from the walls as its inhabitant festered within her misery.

'But why?' Rachel smacked down her pen, crossed her legs and tilted her head. Her shoulders shrugged with an aloof air. 'Why would anyone close down a group which is out to protect children? It just doesn't make sense.'

'I thought you were representing *me*?' Karen folded her arms and leaned back, throwing her head against the soft headrest. 'Why are you interrogating *me*?'

'Because if *I'm* asking it, so will the courts, the defence and the judge. At the moment you appear to be simply attacking this group because it exposed your predator son.'

'He's *not* a predator! If you think that, then you need to leave.' Karen stood up and pointed towards the door.

'Actually I don't believe that. I've seen the exchange of messages between Charlie and that girl, and I've watched the video. But the courts, those who will be making these decisions, will want to know what you're getting out of this. And I'm sorry but they'll side with these vigilantes. They're protecting our streets. While they'll just think you're in it to clear your son's name and what mother doesn't see the best in her only child?'

'I can't let them do this anymore!' She returned to her seat and placed her head in her hands.

'Ms Irvine, if your son was say… eleven… like the girl he believed he was messaging. And some grown man was messaging him, trying to groom him, wouldn't you want to know that there were people out there trying to stop them?'

'Well of course.' She threw her hands up in the air, palms up towards the ceiling.

'So why is this different for your son?'

'He wasn't well.' Her voice crumbled.

'Predators never are.' Rachel turned her head and offered a sceptical glance.

'He had mental challenges.'

'Right… we're getting somewhere here. Your son was a vulnerable person.'

'He was… my Charlie didn't know what he was doing.' Karen picked up a tissue and dabbed her cheek. She placed it down over a plastic DVD case for *The History Boys,* hovering on a nest of coffee tables. Based on a play by Alan Bennett, the film starred a predatory teacher named Hector, who despite his seedy ways, continued to be regarded fondly by his pupils. *Oh the irony,* Rachel considered.

'And so this group targeted a man who was vulnerable and not accountable for his actions. They didn't know this though. So what should they have done?'

'Left it to the professionals?' Karen suggested.

'Right, but government cutbacks mean the police don't have the resources to cover the scale of these crimes. So they almost rely on groups like this to do their work for them. Publicly they wouldn't approve it, but at the same time they haven't condemned them either.'

'But did they have to upload it to social media?'

'Exactly! I've researched these groups, Ms Irvine, and they allow the general public on social media to be the jury without a court case. My God, if Charlie hadn't killed himself, one of your neighbours would have killed him instead. They put him in direct danger and didn't allow him to have a fair trial. In fact actually, just work with me here for a minute. If we say… *hypothetically…* stay with me…your son was exactly what this group claim he is.'

'Mmm?' Karen offered Rachel a concerned glance.

'He's arrested by the police. He's charged. If I was his lawyer, I'd sure as hell ensure that his case got thrown out of court based on the fact that he couldn't possibly have a fair trial. He was lured into this meeting and he hasn't actually committed a crime as he hasn't actually groomed a child. And then how can a jury possibly, under any circumstances, be allowed to make a decision on someone based on the information in court alone when there's so much public opinion and apparent evidence on the internet, which could prejudice their decision?'

'Hey presto!' Karen rejoiced, for what Rachel assumed must have been the first in months.

'It's not as simple as that though, Ms Irvine.'

'Oh?'

'Most of these cases do go to trial even if these videos are all over the internet. But most of the time it's because the police then raid their houses and find inappropriate images on their computers. They also find evidence that they've met up with children plenty of times before. That's where your crime comes in. And The Predator Hunters have simply pointed the police in their direction.'

'But what about the fair trial? Because of the social media... thing...'

'Well if it's dropped, the accused go home and then either kill themselves or another vigilante does the work for them. Do you think this group care about legal justice? They're after social justice and nothing more.'

'I know they don't care. They treated Charlie terribly.'

'So there you go... the police aren't bothered either. Their work is done. One less person on the streets to worry about.'

'But my Charlie *isn't* a predator. He was a vulnerable person. That would have come out in court had he had a chance to defend himself.'

'And that's where I come in. If your Charlie had been taken through the appropriate authorities, legally, without social media, he'd have been provided legal representation. He'd have had an appropriate adult to support him, he'd have been ensured full protection on behalf of the law, and he would have been fairly treated without these social justice groups ever coming into it. His name would have been blocked from the newspapers. He'd have been treated like a child would have. And he'd have been able to be defended within a court of law and likely let off and looked after on the other side. And, as long as his computer was clean, they'd have dropped the charges as no crime would have been committed in the first place. They may have kept an eye on him for a while, given him an education in online safety and what's appropriate…'

'I would have banned him from the internet,' Karen interrupted.

'Exactly! But what's important is that your son would have been alive and given the protections which any person who has a disability rightfully deserves.'

'So we can ban them?' Karen asked with an optimistic flutter in her voice.

'I don't know if an outright ban can be had, but I think we can certainly open the judge's eyes, and the public's, to how dangerous these groups can be to vulnerable people. We can explore petitions later but first we need to clear your son's name.'

'So there's our angle?'

'I'm afraid it's not enough. Charlie won't be the first person to be a victim of this group and sadly no one has ever been able to ban these vigilantes. So we need another angle. A crime that they have committed. Something which shows they took advantage of their vigilante privileges.'

'Well what do we have?' Karen scratched her head and her eyes appeared lost as she scrolled through the legal maze which Rachel had carved out for her. As someone who had barely finished high school with as much as an O-Level, she struggled to keep up with the intelligent Rachel Walker, whose mind ran at a thousand miles an hour with endless loopholes to legal barriers.

'I saw that video, Ms Irvine. They kidnapped your son. They held him hostage, locked him up in a dirty garage and his only chance to escape meant he had to attack them. And, in his escape, he ended up killed.'

'He killed himself.'

'Are you sure?' Rachel leaned her chin on her palm before edging closer to her client. 'Ms Irvine, watch that video again. Your son was running away. He didn't know what they were going to do to him. He was frightened for his life. He saw a small gap in the road and ran out. I'd argue whether Charlie, and excuse my ignorance towards his condition here, would have had the social aptitude to consider suicide as a way out.'

'Maybe, I never knew what was going on in his head half the time.'

'No but a psychologist would. Besides that, regardless whether it was suicide or misadventure, your Charlie was forced into a car and locked up in a garage against his will. There's no law against approaching your son, or questioning him. Nor is it really against the law to upload these videos, although I'd argue ethically otherwise. But I tell you what, kidnapping and holding someone hostage is certainly a crime. And I'll ensure this group suffers as a result of that.'

'What are you thinking?'

'We'll sue them.' Rachel bit the top of her pen, smiled and wrote it down. 'Making them responsible for your son's death.'

'I don't like that...' Karen shook her head. 'No. They'll think I'm in this for the money and I'm not. I just want justice for my boy.'

'And you'll get that. You'll have your day in court, Ms Irvine. You'll have doctors, psychologists and computer experts to showcase your son's lack of awareness, his lack of responsibility, and the fact that there is no proof that he was in any way what they claim he is. You'll get the respect back from your neighbours too.'

'But I don't want any money. I'll look greedy.'

'Suing them ensures this group is put out of business. It costs money to do what they do. I've seen their videos. They're professional. They rely on donations from the public. It's also quite a slick operation that they have there. It takes time, patience, and it's a full time job to be able to operate at the level they do. Charlie was easy, I've seen the messages they exchanged; he was ready to meet that day. Real groomers take weeks, months. All that takes time, money and resources. And we'll put a stop to them and ensure that any future victims, like your Charlie, will be forced to go through appropriate channels, rather than a social hanging. Groups like this around the country will have to stop and look at their own practices before acting on future potential predators.'

'But the money... seriously, I couldn't ask for it,' Karen replied as she moved her hand around her belongings. 'I'm a humble person, I've never needed much and I never will.'

'We need to go on something. It might look like you're financially motivated at first, but once we're inside the court they'll soon see the real you. And this court case won't come cheap. I need a salary, Ms Irvine, I'll need to pay for experts, IT forensics and psychologists. That all comes at a cost. We won't have much left at the end. And you? Do you work?'

'Yeah, I work down at the local supermarket on Lee Lane.'

'And you think you'll be able to work full time while we have the case? You'll be taking unpaid leave. You'll need to live, to pay your mortgage and your bills.'

'This place is rented.'

'Even better. You'll need to have a roof over your head, Ms Irvine, and while you're out of work, you'll need some kind of income, or at least a rebate. We need to go hard or not at all. And if there's any money left at the end for you, you can give it to charity if you want. A children's charity feels quite fitting. That'll show them that you're not in it for the money and that you do care about the kids after all.'

'Thank you, Rachel.'

'Look we've got a long way to go yet. I can work on this over the next couple of days and I can file a case, but I'm afraid I will need an upfront payment. I could lose my office and I need somewhere to work. I'm happy to personally work for free for now, but what I don't have is money to begin to start paying for experts and everything that we'll need to ensure that one, we have a case, and two, that we can prove it in court. That's going to cost a hefty sum.'

'But I don't have anything to give,' Karen pleaded.

'Then I suggest you go to one of the no-win, no-fee lawyers. They have the funds to do everything up front and recover their costs later from the other side. I'm afraid I don't have that kind of capital.'

'I've tried and they turned me down.'

Rachel sighed. She looked over her notes and scratched her head. She wanted to help this woman who appeared as vulnerable as her son.

'We need to get our hands on something. Does Charlie have any relatives whom we can approach?'

'There's Charlie's dad, he's a wealthy man, but he's never had much interest in him. He left us before Charlie was born. They didn't have a relationship.'

'Then isn't it time he started making up for it?'

Chapter 3

A long private drive led up to the entrance. Outside a Porsche slept peacefully beneath a cherry tree. Karen's fifteen-year-old black Skoda with a fresh white scar across the side broke the ambiance of the idyllic home. She stepped out and knocked on the red door with a silver 43 pinned to the front.

'Hi, Karen,' Josh answered with an unwelcoming tone. He ducked beneath the doorframe, designed for those who were a foot shorter than himself. His black locks held a streak of white and were gelled back. His white polo-shirt had a designer name and his jeans were fresh out of Macy's following a business trip to New York. 'What are you doing here?'

He contemplated her anorak, jumper and cords with a mourning for the person she used to be. When they met she was full of life, confident and stylish. Today she looked like the *before* image in a Gok Wan transformation show.

'I'm here to talk about our son.'

He stepped aside and she walked into his home. A large open-plan space welcomed her with huge windows giving the inhabitants a glimpse out over the Rivington hills. Large wooden beams stretched across the home. Beneath, two brown leather couches sat parallel, facing into an oak coffee table; a book on vintage wines rested on top. A glass dining table separated the living space from the kitchen, and dark blue cupboards with sparkly white tops curved around an island.

'I'm sorry I wasn't there at the funeral. I was in Singapore.'

'Jennifer told me,' she said with a sadness in her voice. 'Where is she today?'

'She's in London at a Women's Leaders conference,' Josh replied. Karen raised her head and her eyes dropped to her knees. 'Why are you here, Karen? Charlie died six months ago, I can't possibly see what I can do for you now.'

'I've instructed a lawyer to represent our son's legacy, trying to clear his name, and sue those who lured him into this awful situation.'

'Clear his name? He was never charged. He's dead, Karen.'

'And his name was thrown in the mud. By suing those who led him into this, we can assure his name is cleared in the press.'

'Again... he's not here. If he was alive it would be a different situation, but what possible difference could this make?'

'Well for one, people will stop looking at me like I'm some horrendous mother who raised a predator son,' Karen replied, the hurt almost retching out.

'So it's for your own ego?' Josh replied.

'No!' Karen screeched. 'How can you accuse me of that? No, I can't stand to know what they're thinking about our Charlie. People need to know the facts.'

'So what can I do?' Josh folded his legs and lay back.

Karen took a deep breath and glanced towards the green hills. 'I need money.'

'And you think I'm going to give it to you?' Josh cackled a lone laugh. 'You can think again.'

'I can get it you all back, once we've sued them!'

'And what if you lose?'

She stood up and walked towards the window. A trampoline sat in the centre of the garden and a swing swayed gently in the wind to the side.

'After you left, I never asked for anything. You made it quite clear you didn't want to raise him. You never visited, or even bought him a present. You got away with nineteen years of avoiding paying for anything while you sat here raising your other kids in this mansion. You had everything while we struggled by. The least you could do is help me with *this*.'

'I didn't do anything for him because he wasn't *mine*.'

'He *is* yours, Josh! You've always punished him for my mistakes. You'll never let me live down that mishap.' Her eyes welled and she bowed her head, avoiding his eyes which offered a mirror into their past.

'That *mishap* ruined our relationship.'

'It was a mistake. A drunken mistake. You knew how depressed I was and you were always away visiting other countries.'

'You mean I was working...' Josh raised his right eyebrow. 'You certainly enjoyed the benefits of my job.'

'That may well be the case, but I was lonely. Each night finishing a bottle of wine to myself, crying in the bath. And I did something stupid one time after a night out.'

'And you got pregnant...'

'And I told you the dates didn't add up. Charlie was always yours. He had your eyes. I saw you in him every day for nineteen years.'

'That *retard* was never mine.'

Karen gasped and fell back. Silence hovered over them as they soaked up the sting of his words. She pulled down her lilac cardigan over the waist of her jeans and made an approach to her ex, towering over him as he sat on the couch.

'I'm sorry.' Josh lowered his head. 'I didn't mean that.'

'Yes you did. That boy, whether you liked it or not, *was* your son. I never asked for anything from you, not even a DNA test. I loved you and I knew I did you wrong, so I let you walk away from it all. For years I regretted it as I worried our son was losing out on a father. But it's quite clear that Charlie and I had a lucky escape. God help your children if they ever grow up to be anything other than the dullness of normal.'

She stormed towards the front door and opened it.

'Karen, wait, I'm sorry!'

She turned around.

'Oh just piss off, Josh. You have this life now. This wonderful life. Just be a good dad to them, eh?'

He nodded and she left.

He spent the afternoon working and fiddling with his acoustic guitar between conference calls. His office was a shrine to his and Jennifer's achievements. Certificates, awards and magazine articles detailing their projects that made up their successes, all framed and spread across the eggshell walls. A television screen hung on one side, video conferenced into the Sydney office.

'Josh?' an Aussie voice called. He looked up and mumbled a reply. 'Are you with us?'

On the screen five suited delegates stared into their cameras, all blond and tanned and about a decade younger than him. He shuffled and sat up straight.

'Yes, sorry, I just had something on my mind.'

'Well pull yourself together, we stayed up for this so you could join us.'

'I'm sorry, can we take a rain check? I'll dial in when it's convenient for you guys tomorrow.'

They cut the call and he sank down back into his chair, chewing on the cap of his pen and tapping his foot. He loaded a search engine on his tablet and typed in Charlie's name. Hundreds of articles celebrated the death of a dangerous monster and praised the team of people who ensured that Horwich's streets remained safe for the local youth.

A photograph of Karen weeping beside the road that Charlie took his last breath upon made up the front of one of the tabloids. He remembered those tears; when she sobbed into the late night when her mental health took its toll, when she broke down and told him about her *mishap,* and when he told her he wasn't going to stick around to raise a child which wasn't his. But this photograph of her before him was far, far worse. Her eyes held an emptiness which he hadn't seen before. True, raw loss.

He stepped away from his desk and opened up a safe, hidden within a wardrobe beneath a pile of clothes. He twisted the dial several times until it clicked and he opened the door. Inside were boxes of jewellery, handed to Jennifer over countless birthdays and anniversaries. Their passports and birth certificates and a thousand pounds in cash piled up. At the back was a brown envelope; he lifted it out and returned to his desk, pouring the contents out over the table. Inside there was a photocopy of Charlie's birth certificate and several photographs of the boy Karen claimed was his son; each image showing him a year older

49

than the previous picture. Karen posted them every year on his birthday. He'd never once replied with a card or a present.

Into the late evening, he'd continued to stare at the pictures downstairs on his couch, trying to capture a glimpse to see any resemblance to himself. He struggled. The problem was Charlie resisted looking into the lens of a camera and he rarely smiled.

A rattle of keys and the squeak of the door broke his trance. He looked up as Jennifer walked in. Despite the two-hour train journey from London and her hour's drive from Manchester Piccadilly train station to Horwich in the rush-hour traffic, she appeared as radiant as the day they met. Her long flowing red hair, her slim physique and her tall stature made her a likely fashion model had her academic success been overlooked. Her skin was pale without as much as a blemish and her blue eyes were as rich as a Caribbean sea. She walked into the house in a red empire dress and a navy blue jacket. She threw down her designer handbag and keys onto a side-bench and wrapped her arms around her husband, climbing onto his knee.

'What are you doing with them?' she asked, lifting the top picture and gazing over the boy. 'It's not like you.'

'Karen came over today to talk about Charlie and it just got me thinking.'

'It's a good job I kept onto them then, isn't it? I always said you'd regret throwing them away.'

'Thank you.' He offered her a small smile and kissed her arm, breathing in her designer scent which he'd bought her from the duty free shop at Manchester Airport on his way home from his latest business trip.

'What did Karen want?' she asked without a glimpse of jealousy.

50

'She's suing the gang who entrapped him. She wants to clear his name along the way.'

'I see.' Jennifer stroked her chin and placed her head on her husband's shoulder. 'I take it she needs money?'

'Naturally. I don't know what to do. I said some horrible things.'

'Yeah your tongue can be quite loose when you're angry. What do you think you'll do?'

'I don't know.' he sighed. 'What if he is everything they claimed he was? I mean they had evidence…'

'But at the same time he wasn't like other kids. He had challenges and he didn't think like the rest of us. I think in his heart he was still a child. I'm not defending it, but who knows? Regardless, I know if it was Molly or Seb that we'd be right there defending those two to the death.'

'Me too. But what if Charlie isn't my son?' Josh looked at his wife with moist eyes. She leaned in and placed her forehead on his, kissing his nose as she approached him, before shrugging.

'But what if he is?'

Chapter 4

Rachel returned to the house which she grew up in. It was a semi-detached stone cottage just off the Blackrod bypass. Her old bedroom was transformed into a guestroom, which she had now returned to. The third bedroom, a box room, once used as a study by her father, now fitted a single bed and posters of Justin Bieber lined the walls. She could hear her daughter singing his songs and practising her dance moves before her mirror like she did every night.

'Homework!' Rachel called through the door; a groaning replied. She returned to her room and slipped out of her work attire and into a white strapless dress. A silver chain with a diamond in the centre hovered down onto her exposed breasts and she straightened her hair in a full-length mirror built into the wardrobe. Peering at her watch, she quickly threw on a pair of black polka-dot heels and made her way downstairs, taking one last glimpse into the mirror in the hallway and spraying herself with CK's latest offering.

In the lounge, her mother sat staring at the television in a maroon armchair. The wooden floors held a white fur rug, and photographs of their family were spread across the walls. Taxidermy lined the sideboards, a hobby of her late father, who stood proudly in his mayoral robes in a framed newspaper cut-out. Dorothy looked up and smiled at her daughter with a frosty glaze over her eyes. Her short white hair was neatly combed back and her red woolly jumper had one of her husband's medals achieved in the army attached to the breast pocket. Rachel always found it remarkable that her mother could keep trousers so white without a single blemish, even when she used to go out walking in the countryside, which was a rare treat for her these days.

'Right, Mum, are you going to be OK with me going out?'

'You're going out?' she asked with an air of surprise.

'Yeah, we talked about this last night, remember? And then again this morning. You agreed to look after Matilda. Are you sure you'll be OK?'

'Oh yes, of course,' Dorothy replied, but her face said otherwise. 'We'll be just fine. You go and have fun.'

'Thanks, right well I've prepared a meal for you both. It's a curry and it's in the fridge. All you have to do is heat it for five minutes in the microwave and serve it up, OK?'

'We'll be fine. I know how to make curry.'

'Well I've put instructions on the front anyway. Matilda will tell you when she's hungry.'

'Yes, yes,' Dorothy replied, shooing her daughter out of her view of the television.

'Anyway, bye, Mum.'

'Are you going out?'

Rachel smiled, stroked her mother's hair and left. She was already running late and had no time to explain herself again. It was a dry, crisp evening and she felt a walk could do her good; it was when she was the most creative when it came to forming a case for her clients. Her biggest light-bulb moments had sprung up on these country lanes. It was a short stroll downhill to the restaurant; at least this way she could enjoy a drink. As for her getting home, it would depend on how well her night went.

The red-bricked fortress stood beside the train station and the bar served those who impatiently waited for their delayed trains. At the back, a restaurant peered over a former bowling green and offered a glimpse of the hills which the establishment was named after.

She was greeted by a waitress, who asked if she had a reservation. She explained who she was meeting and was escorted to a table in the corner beside a window. A candle in the middle lit up her date who sat behind perusing the specials. He was handsome for a man in his forties. He had mousy hair, which had been styled with gel. He was white, not her usual type, and had a goatee which had sprigs of ginger. Rachel considered him well-dressed; a white shirt, which showed off his toned physique, over designer blue jeans. A diamond encrusted Cartier watch wrapped around his wrist and a platinum ring sat beneath the fourth knuckle on his right hand. He smiled as he caught his date's eye, stood up and kissed her on the cheek, before placing his hand towards the empty seat before him.

'Sorry I'm late, Carl.'

'Don't worry, I haven't been here long myself. How's your day been?'

'Oh eventful, but I won't bore you with the details. How are you?'

'Oh the usual. Never a dull moment when you're on the beat.' He picked up a bottle of red wine, which he'd pre-ordered, and poured some into her glass.

'I should really get you to refer your suspects to me! God knows I could do with the business.'

'Still going slow then?' he asked as he perused the menu.

'I think it's picking up. Had a new one today which could be fairly juicy but we'll see. I don't know if she can afford me.'

'Well here's to new business, fingers crossed.' They clinked glasses and decided on their order, before relaying their choices to the waitress.

'I'm sorry I haven't been in touch the last week or two, my world has just been a little mad. It's tough having a ten-year-old who think she's sixteen, and a mother who forgets where she is half the time.'

'Hey, don't worry. I was worried you'd gone off me. I even went on the app to see if you'd been looking for other dates.'

'Oh God no, I don't have time for that.' Rachel offered a lone laugh. 'Besides, I like you. Finally found a good 'un after all that searching. Christ, I had some terrible dates.'

'Me too!' They both laughed as they reminisced over the no-shows, the ones they wished hadn't turned up, and those dates which they'd hoped would have led to more but were instantly blocked as soon as they got home. Rachel then went on to discuss the struggles of being a single mother and a carer at the same time.

'You should really let me help more,' said Carl.

'Help?'

'Well you don't have to wait until you have a free night. I could always come round and make tea for you and your family. If I met Matilda, maybe I could be of use, pick her up from school now and again. Everyone knows the hours of a lawyer, while I'm usually finished early afternoon or have a day off in the week to be able to offer my assistance.'

'That's very sweet, thank you. And I'd love you to meet Matilda, I just haven't introduced her to a man before so I'm a little nervous. I'm her whole world. The idea of her having to share *me* might not be the most appetising to her. So if I'm going to do all that, I need to know that we're in this for the long game.'

'I get that. And you would be a terrible mother if you didn't do some due diligence.' He smiled and she mirrored it. 'Look I know you need to get your head around all this first, so in

56

the meantime I'll just lay my cards out on the table so you know where I am. I like you, Rachel, a lot. I know we've only been meeting like this for a couple of months, but I really like you and I see you being in my life for a long time. As soon as you feel ready to take our relationship to the next level, you just need to say so. I'll be there.'

'Thank you.' She smiled and brushed her fringe in front of her eyes, embarrassed by his words. 'You're not too bad yourself.'

'So where is Matilda tonight?' As he spoke, their meals arrived, disrupting their conversation. They partook in the restaurant dance of salt, pepper and parmesan, before nodding an awkward agreement that they were enjoying their meals to the waitress while their mouths were full of food.

'What were you saying?' she finally replied once they were free to continue their conversation.

'I was asking where Matilda was tonight.'

'Oh she's with my mum,' Rachel replied.

'Is she safe there?' he asked and Rachel stared up in surprise. 'Oh, it's just with you saying with your mother not being well…'

'Wow, you really are a cop. I'm getting the full interrogation.' She laughed and dabbed her chin with her napkin.

'No sorry, that was rude, ignore me. You know what's best when it comes to your daughter.' He turned red and stared down at his food.

'Oh no, you're right to ask. They're fine. Mum is forgetful but she's safe at home. They have meals to microwave and Matilda is a good girl. To be honest, they look after each other and they enjoy each other's company. They'll be OK.'

'I'm sure they will.' He nodded his head and smiled.

The tables were covered with white linen. The floor was chequered like a chessboard. An open fire roared to their right and, as the sun set, the bowling green disappeared and the windows mirrored the diners, which Rachel used to adjust her hair every time her date glanced away.

They consumed their meals and shared a dessert. They hovered over the bill, each attempting to pay it before Carl snatched the receipt and ran to the waitress with his card. The feminist within her tutted with frustration, while the old-fashioned gal deep down was warmed by his desire to look after her. There was a time when she would have insisted on paying; there was no doubt her former salary would have outweighed his policeman's wage, but today she barely had what was even considered a wage as every penny kept what was left of her business alive.

'Can I give you a lift home?' he asked as they entered the car park, pointing towards the black Lexus saloon in the car-park. She was impressed by his vehicle and wondered how he could afford such a luxury on an individual wage, but she wasn't brave or impolite enough to ask.

'Well why don't we go to yours?' she winked and followed him to his car.

They drove along the bypass, the hills disappearing within the night, with only Carl's headlights providing any glimpse into their path. He turned right onto a street familiar to Rachel, who spent her nights in the company of the neighbouring houses.

'Do you need to collect anything before we get to mine?'

'No I'll be fine, I have everything I need in here.' She lifted her black polka-dot handbag, which matched her shoes, and tapped the front. 'Just slow down as we pass my house, I just want to make sure Matilda's light is out. She's a nightmare for watching late night TV, especially when I'm not home. She has my mother wrapped around her little finger.'

As they drew closer to her house, alarms began to ring. The lights were all on and the front door was open. Dorothy stood outside on the street waving at oncoming traffic, dressed in only a white nightie, which she held down as a gust of wind blew past. Rachel called for her date to pull over as she saw smoke seeping out of the front door. Carl slammed on his brakes and they both ran out of the car.

'Mum, what happened?' she asked and shook her shaken mother.

'I don't know. I was on my way to bed and I could smell burning. I went back and the pan was burnt to a crisp and the kitchen was full of smoke.'

'Why was the pan on? I told you to microwave dinner!'

'You did?' Dorothy asked with a confused tone.

'Where's Matilda?' Carl shouted, looking up towards the windows.

'She's inside.'

Rachel paced towards the door but her date placed his arm in front of her. 'No, I'll go.'

He ran indoors and up the stairs. In the distance, Rachel could see his silhouette behind the curtains, while she wrapped her arms around her mother. She closed her eyes and rested her forehead on her shoulder. Moments later, Carl returned with Matilda in his arms. Her frizzy-black hair was glued down to the side where she'd slept, and her usually brown skin grew pale. She rubbed her hazel eyes, confused by the disturbance.

'Oh thank God!' Rachel ran over to Carl and grabbed her daughter, sobbing into her soft black hair. 'Never again, never ever again!'

The fire brigade arrived minutes later and quickly extinguished the small blaze in the kitchen. No damage had been done but the house reeked of smoke.

'She's asthmatic,' Rachel said, nodding her head towards her daughter. They located her inhaler and asked her to take a few puffs before reassuring her mother that she would be alright.

'Come and stay with me,' Carl offered. 'I've got plenty of space for all of you. Just grab what you need here.'

They collected a few belongings and stepped into the car. They arrived fifteen minutes later at Carl's house; a detached four-bedroom new-build on an estate just outside of Lostock. He took their belongings and showed them around the house, dishing out a room each, including Rachel who feigned interest in a separate room, before sneaking her bag into the master bedroom.

While they recovered from the shock, Carl put together a bowl of ice cream for Matilda and a glass of port for his girlfriend and her shaken mother. He found some cartoons on his entertainment system and together they all huddled on the L-shaped couch beneath a throw.

'When did you move in here? It's very nice, Carl,' said Rachel.

'It was my parents' house. They died last year.'

'Oh, I see, I'm sorry, but I guess that explains… no sorry.'

'Why I can afford all this?' Carl laughed and wrapped his arm around her.

A bleeping from Rachel's handbag distracted her from further embarrassment. She lifted out her phone and read the first line of the text message.

'Well that's something anyway.'

'Hmm?' Carl peered over towards her.

'The client I was telling you about earlier. She's managed to find the funds to pay for my services.'

'Well that's great.'

'She wants to meet tomorrow, I'll tell her to postpone.'

'Don't be stupid. You go to your meeting. I can sort things out here with your mum and Matilda.'

'Will that be OK, Mattie?' She turned towards her daughter who was absorbed by the cartoons on the television and her multi-coloured ice cream; she appeared to be over the trauma they'd endured earlier in the evening.

'Oh yeah, Carl's alright. I'm sure he won't burn the house down anyway.'

Rachel giggled and placed her head on her boyfriend's shoulder, secure that he would do his best by them. 'I guess you got to meet my family after all.'

Chapter 5

They sat parallel like they had only two days prior in her office, however they both had a little more optimism for their meeting on this occasion. Rachel had already called the landlord and paid the rent and she'd waited outside a charity shop until it opened to grab something suitable as all her clothes were embedded with smoke. She found a grey jacket with a matching skirt, which she managed to style it out with a lilac blouse. Before her, Karen Irvine hovered on the mirroring couch in a purple fleece and blue jeans. The strain on her eyes had eased since their first encounter.

'Tell me about Charlie's condition.' Rachel began the line of questioning, chewing on the corner of a plastic pen cap.

'He had autism,' Karen said bluntly.

'OK, treat me like I'm an idiot, Karen. Like I don't know anything about autism. What is autism and how did it impact Charlie?'

'It's a developmental disorder. It means he had trouble with social interactions. He had crippling anxiety, he struggled to understand and relate to other people. He was obsessed with routine and rules, but mainly by his own; he sometimes struggled with other people's rules which got him in trouble.'

'When did you discover Charlie had autism?'

'Well I think I knew in my heart of hearts before his diagnosis. At pre-school he was difficult to discipline, especially as a single parent. He was a very lonely person and would react aggressively to other kids if they tried touching him. You know what kids are like, they're always touching toys and other children. Charlie didn't like that and he'd flip. I'd have to go in all the time and they threatened to expel him. Can you imagine that, expelled from pre-school?'

'What about the diagnosis?'

'That came much later, it wasn't as advanced as it is now. It was still somewhat of a new concept to some back then and only when he was at school did we finally get confirmation. He didn't have any friends as he was an odd kid. His only friend was the assistant they put with him to help him with his English which he struggled with. Always good at maths, but English, terrible.'

'Go on...' Rachel replied as she quickly scribbled notes down on her pad.

'Mr Pugh, Nick Pugh, was amazing. He knocked one night as he only lives up the road and said he'd observed Charlie and thought he might be on the spectrum. He recommended he was tested and arranged for speech and language specialists, paediatricians and a school psychiatrist to spend time with him. They all came back with the same conclusion. After that, we got Nick full time at school to sit with Charlie. He was amazing and they had a great relationship. Bless him, he even came bowling one year on his birthday as he had no one else to invite. It's sad really.'

'Where's Nick now?'

'Oh he still lives nearby. He had to distance himself after Charlie grew up. Charlie found it difficult that Nick didn't want to come over after he left school. He was really upset about it, but what could we do? Nick was always a professional and their working relationship was over.'

'Do you reckon we could get this Nick as a witness for Charlie's condition?'

'I suppose, I sometimes see him down at the fruit shop. I could ask him next time I bump into him.'

'That'd be good.' Rachel nodded, before looking over her notes. 'So Charlie's condition. How would I know if I met Charlie that he had autism?'

'Well you wouldn't really. He looked normal. He was just what most people would call a bit odd. He'd struggle to talk to you, but some would say he was just shy. He'd obsess over anything. Like the chain you're wearing. He'd fixate on it and would want to touch it. We had to warn people that he could be a little grabby. He meant no harm though, he was just obsessed with shiny things.'

Rachel grabbed her pendant and held it onto her chest, as if Charlie could have reached out and touched it then and there. She reminded herself that he was long gone and returned her palm to her notes.

'I need to consider the award you would receive should we win this case. Did Charlie work?'

'No, he couldn't work,' said Karen, shaking her head.

'Did he receive any benefits?'

'He was entitled to them but he never claimed them. We never needed much and my little job paid for what we needed.'

'So he had no income. Was there any other support?'

'No not really.'

'OK, so we're going to put in for a bereavement award. Without any income, this is a fixed amount of twelve thousand pounds. On top of that we can ask for funeral expenses, if you could dig out any receipts for that... we can contact the funeral home directly if you need...'

'I can get all that. I kept everything. Anything which was a reminder that he was once here.'

'And then there's the legal fees, psychological experts, and IT forensics on your son's computer. I'm going to put in a claim for an award of twenty-five thousand pounds in total. Are you happy with this approach?'

'OK, great, thank you. What about a prison sentence for any of those responsible?'

'I'm really not sure at this stage, we need to prove they were personally responsible for your son's death and that's going to be quite complex. We're going after their organisation, not them as individuals and it would be hard to establish who was responsible for his death as the video isn't really that clear. At the least though, if we win, this will significantly damage their financial ability to continue putting vulnerable people at risk like this. We can also set up a petition to try and change the law to prevent these groups operating in the first place.'

Their heads hurt from a morning of complex legal jargon and their bellies began to rumble. They made their way to a café, just off the high street, and Rachel treated her client to a sandwich and a pot of tea.

'You said you have a ten-year-old.' Karen broke the silence as they settled into their lunch.

'Oh, Matilda, yeah, she's quite a girl,' Rachel replied, her face lighting up whenever she considered her daughter. She lifted up her mobile phone and showed Karen a photograph of Matilda which made up her screensaver. It was taken just over a month before at Halloween; Matilda dressed up in a black onesie and a cat-ears headband sat over her frizzy hair. Whiskers were drawn onto her face with a stencil.

'And your mother you're looking after too?'

'Ah yes but that's fairly recent, sadly. She began to lose her marbles after Dad died.'

'How do you do it?'

'Do what?' Rachel shrugged.

'Bring up a family and still have the career you have. I'm guessing you don't have a husband as you still have *Miss* on all your documentation.' Karen picked up the client agreement, which Rachel had made her sign, and pointed towards her title.

'No you're right. I brought her up by myself. Her father was someone I went to college with, he was young just like I was. He was going out all the time and we were casual. He had his whole life ahead of him. I didn't want to ruin that just because I wanted to have the baby.'

'So he never knew?'

'I don't know really for sure. Rumours clearly went round and it was all over social media when I gave birth. Whether he connected the dots I'll never know but he certainly never got in touch to ask. I gave him an escape and I suppose he took it.'

'You never gave him the chance to be a father. You never know, he might have been there and still could be.'

'Well we'll never know now.' Rachel picked at her nails, avoiding the judgemental stare from the woman who had had no option but to bring up a child alone.

'There's always a possibility, have you ever thought of getting in touch?'

'He's dead,' Rachel said sternly and stared at her stirring tea, holding back the tears she'd shed nearly a decade before. 'He overdosed at uni a year later. So even if I thought he might be interested, I'll never have the opportunity to ask.'

'Oh I'm sorry. So how did you do it?' Karen asked, changing the awkward subject. 'Go to uni and start this amazing career?'

67

'I couldn't have done any of it without my parents. I was lucky. They looked after Matilda while I was in class or at my Saturday job down at the cinema. I'm so grateful, I really am, which is why I'm back at home now doing the same for them. I don't know how others do it without the help, I really don't. I admire anyone who is out there doing it.'

'Yeah, I didn't a chance to go to university.'

'No but you managed to hold down a job and for nineteen years provided a nice life for a boy who needed extra support. That's far harder to juggle. I'm so lucky with Mattie, she's quite independent. Don't overlook what you've achieved, Karen.'

'I couldn't look after him in the end though, could I?' Karen wiped a tear from the corner of her eye.

'No, but we all bear that responsibility. Just last night my house caught on fire because I left my daughter with my senile mother.' Rachel shrugged, shaking off the trauma she'd been delivered.

'Oh.' Karan raised a hand to her open mouth, before shaking her head as she considered the judgement in her tone.

'Yeah, smart, right? And I'm the one with the multiple degrees.' Rachel rolled her eyes and shook her head.

'Do you not get any help for your mother? A sibling or a family friend?'

'Not really,' Rachel replied and a sadness overcame her as she considered the one person who *could* help her. 'I have a sister, Lisa she's called. She doesn't speak to us, really. She fell out with Mum a long time ago, and me? Well she just doesn't want to know me anymore. Shame really.'

'It's a tragedy when families don't speak. Especially sisters.'

'Look I'll get the paperwork sorted.' Rachel changed the subject. 'If you can get hold of this Nick Pugh and dig out the receipts for the funeral, I can do the rest.'

'Thank you, Rachel. I couldn't do any of this without you.'

They parted ways and Rachel drove back home. As she entered the house, she was pleased to see that the building had aired out and only a light scent of smoke remained, mostly covered with a cinnamon scented candle.

'Mum!' Matilda called from the lounge. Rachel walked into the room and found her daughter dancing alongside Carl on a computer console, which she didn't recognise. Matilda was in her *One Direction* pyjamas and Carl dressed down in a pair of grey sweatpants and a white t-shirt taken straight from his gym bag. 'Look what Carl brought!'

'Oh wow!' Rachel's eyes widened and she nodded her head towards her boyfriend. 'Can I have a word in the kitchen?'

In the corner, her mother was blissfully napping, wrapped with a throw, which she recognised from Carl's house the previous evening. They escaped to the kitchen and Rachel shut the door behind her. Carl appeared as relaxed as his attire. He'd also brought along a pair of slippers to really make himself at home. She couldn't help but stare at his abs through his tight t-shirt, and exhale.

'What's with the console?' Rachel asked with a stern tone; she shook her head to distract herself away from his pecs.

'It's mine. I've just brought it round for a few days so she can play with it.'

'She doesn't need gifts, Carl. I don't like her being spoilt.'

'Don't worry, it was just something to play with while she got over the trauma. She knows I'm only lending it to her. I'll take it back with me later, I promise.'

Rachel opened the door ajar and spied her daughter who was having the time of her life. She shook her head and smiled. 'It's OK, you can leave it here if you want for a couple of days. She needs the distraction. I have some paperwork to do and then would you like some dinner?'

'I'll cook dinner, I've already been shopping. I just need to put it together. You go and put your feet up and get your work done,' said Carl, appearing pleased with himself.

'Thank you.' She walked towards the staircase and turned back, watching Carl and her daughter gleefully dancing together, her mother peaceful in the corner, and then headed upstairs feeling a shiver of bliss.

Chapter 6

A little stone church sat high on the hills, its steeple competing with the transmitting station nearby. Inside, a red carpet led from wooden arched doors up to an altar covered in a green and gold cloth. Above it a gold cross stood in the middle of two chalices. Before the altar, a priest dressed in a white gown closed the prayers, and the choir sang as the congregation walked out of the ceremony. It was Sunday Mass and the church was full. Next door they gathered together for coffee, brewed and served by Karen and her friend, Sylvia.

Sylvia was a tall woman, towering over Karen who was of average height for her gender. A floral pattern rained down her blue dress and her long grey hair was tied back. She always carried herself with her a glowing smile, contrasting with the aura of sadness which followed Karen.

The hall was an extension to the church and included a kitchen, a stage and a large open space in the middle, which was used for a variety of functions. The congregation stood on an olive green vinyl floor, covering their eyes from the morning sun, which burst through the windows between dusty red curtains. Posters surrounded the stone walls of the hall advertising the next fundraiser which would pay for a refurbishment for the room. Tables and chairs were pulled into the centre to allow the gatherers to discuss the ceremony. In the corner, a parishioner sold lemon meringue pies, which he'd freshly made from his bakery business around the corner, with the profits offered to the church fund.

Karen and Sylvia made their acquaintance nineteen years before; Karen had walked into the church with Charlie in hand, who was no more than a few weeks old. A ghostly shy young thing, Karen quietly sat at the back. She was waiting to speak to the vicar about a free childcare offering she'd seen advertised on a chalkboard outside the entrance of the hall. Sylvia at the time was mayoress and wore a hazel perm and flounced around in red robes. She wore a hat which would've put Hyacinth Bucket to shame. Spotting the feeble new parishioner, she marched over and invited her to sit with her. At first, Karen nervously shook her head and suddenly found she was being dragged closer to the pulpit. She was introduced to the other attendees of St Michael's and taken under the wing of Sylvia, who took her into the kitchen and showed her the ropes. "You do your bit here and anyone will help you,' said Sylvia.

And she did. She spent every Sunday for nearly two decades making coffee and washing pots. And in return, she got free childcare three times a week while she worked at the local supermarket and the other parishioners offered to help her out, giving her a night off here and there to regain something of what was once her personal life.

'You're quiet today, Karen, quieter than normal. Are you OK?' Sylvia asked as she poured tea into a dozen mugs. The clink of change being thrown into the collection and the mutterings of local gossip drowned out their conversation from nearby eavesdroppers.

'It would have been Charlie's birthday today.'

Sylvia tilted her head and rubbed her friend's shoulder. 'I didn't realise. Are you doing anything for it?'

'I'll probably wander and visit his grave later.'

'Would you like me to come with you?' Sylvia offered.

'Thank you, that'd be really nice. It's only me who mourns him. His name's still mud round here. You're the only person I can mention him to these days. You're so understanding. I really appreciate it.'

'Karen, I saw Charlie every Sunday in here for all those years when he was growing up. I looked after him every Friday night. I loved that boy like he was my own. I never got the chance to raise a child, it's the only thing Alfred and I never managed to do. We were so lucky in many ways but not in that department. But having an impact on Charlie's life was an honour for me, no matter how small or insignificant it was. Believe me when I say this, that I mourn him too. Those little moments on a Friday morning when he'd come down from his room and sit and talk to me.'

'He never did that with anyone,' Karen replied.

'Well exactly, that's how I know it was special.' A warm smile radiated from Sylvia.

'I couldn't be without your friendship, Sylvia. I just wish I had these other ladies' support.' She peered up and nodded at the side-glancing pensioners who continued to nudge their friends' elbows, despite the fact that Karen's presence in the hall was anything other than unusual.

'Now come on, these cups aren't going to fill themselves.'

*

Four weeks passed before a court date was provided. Karen and Rachel arrived at the Crown Court in Manchester in a bitterly cold January. The grey stone fiercely stood amongst the glass skyscrapers and cocktail bars. They dressed in matching black suits and white shirts, freshly bought for Karen off the back of the invitation to the judicial review. Inside the court, the judge sat before them dressed in a black cloak. He peered over the wooden tables which the claimants sat behind, parallel to the coroner, who'd determined the cause of death for Charlie Irvine as suicide.

'Miss McCann, talk me through what brings you here today.' Judge Byron began the proceedings. He had a large bulbous red nose, thick brown bifocal glasses and thin white hair which was gelled back.

'Your Honour, I'm here today to review the conclusion made by Dr Patel over the death of Charles Irvine. He ruled his death as suicide. I'm here under the Coroners Act of 1988 to challenge that decision.'

'If you'd read the act thoroughly, Miss McCann, you'd know that you have up to three months to challenge the decision of the coroner and having reviewed the paperwork, I can see that it has been at least six months since Mr Irvine's death.'

'I understand that, Your Honour, however there are grounds that we can still challenge the result afterwards. We only need to look at the Hillsborough Disaster to see that this can still be challenged even years after a death. A few months, I'm sure, would not be undermining the process.'

'I see. And I assume you have the Attorney General's consent?'

'I do. It's all in the paperwork before you.'

'Have you made an attempt to turn over the decision directly with the coroner?'

'I have.' Rachel nodded. 'He stands by his decision.'

'And on what grounds are you wishing to challenge the decision made by Dr Patel?' He turned to the coroner to gauge his response, but he remained emotionless.

'Dr Patel is a respected coroner. I know, from my own experience of his work, that he is very thorough. However I've read the Coroner's Report and at no point were Mr Irvine's developmental disabilities considered, despite the fact that this was raised to the police at the time. He made no reference to any review of the video which showed Mr Irvine's capture and ultimate attempt to escape. I believe Charles Irvine died because he panicked and escaped a kidnapping. Charlie ran out into oncoming traffic in attempt to free himself from his captors. Your Honour, The Predator Hunters group is responsible for this man's death. Maybe indirectly. I'm not saying they drove the vehicle or threw him in front of the car, but there's no doubt had they not acted illegally that day, and had they not kidnapped this very vulnerable teenager, he would be still with us today. I need this overturned to ensure that those responsible are brought to justice.'

'And, Dr Patel, how do you respond?'

Dr Patel stood up. He dressed in a pinstriped black suit. He had a shaved head and spoke with a subtle Indian accent. A large gold ring was on his wedding finger. Despite having worked for over two decades in his profession, he maintained his youthful looks.

'Your Honour, I've been a respected coroner for twenty years. Never have any of my decisions been challenged before. I take a very scientific approach to my work. I've seen the video and Charlie very clearly looks towards the traffic and steps out. You'll see that today. If you also take into account that this group had publicly made very serious claims against Mr Irvine, in my opinion, he chose to end his life that day to escape the repercussions of his crimes.'

'Thank you.' Judge Byron asked him to take a seat. 'Miss McCann, what do you have to present to us today?'

'I have Mr Irvine's school assistant who worked with him for many years and a psychologist who will confirm the mind-set of a typical teenager with autism, as well as Charlie's mother, Karen.'

Nick Pugh took to the platform and gave his account of his history working alongside Charlie. He talked about his troubles, his routines and his inability to connect dots as easily as his classmates. How his mind worked was at the forefront of his argument, bringing examples to the judge of where Charlie had struggled to adapt as quickly as other children. As he talked, sweat poured down his pale freckly skin, leaking from the few ginger wisps which sprouted across his exposed scalp. He wore a beige suit, a white shirt, red tie and a pair of brown shoes to match. At times, he became tearful as he reminisced about the boy he spent six hours a day with for over twelve years.

'I remember on one occasion…' Nick continued. 'One of the other kids was bullying Charlie. He got him into a corner and pushed him. Charlie pushed him back and he fell over and Charlie just ran out of the playground. He didn't stop running. We found him an hour later shivering on a neighbour's garden wall in the rain; she called the school as she recognised the uniform. That was the mechanics of Charlie's mind right there. He just kept running until he could run no further and I personally believe he would have done the same had there been no traffic on the day of his death.'

A psychologist took the stand after Nick and talked about her experience with autistic teenagers. She described autism as a comorbid intellectual disability, in which connecting suicide as escaping their responsibilities would be unusual. She was a short woman with long black hair and her jowls gave her a constant aura of disappointment.

The video of that dreaded day was shown to the court. Karen walked out of the courtroom as she struggled to face watching her poor boy in a blind panic once again and his ultimate fall beside the lorry, while Rachel, with a laser pen, paused the video and circled the moment he ran out, arguing that he simply wanted to run away from his captors.

Rachel switched off the television and turned to the judge. "I'd like to bring in my next witness who is Charles Irvine's mother, Karen.'

She turned to Karen who reappeared in the court as white as a ghost, shaking like a leaf. She shook her head and hovered back. The lawyer walked up to her client and whispered.

'Come on, we need you right now. Charlie needs you.'

'I can't, I'm sorry.' A tear sprang from her eye.

'Miss McCann?' the judge called.

'One second, Your Honour,' she replied before turning to her client. 'Please, you need to do this.'

Karen continued to stare down at the floor.

'Miss McCann? Is your witness joining us or not today?'

Rachel hovered a stare over her client before giving a resigned sigh.

'No, Your Honour. That's all from me,' she said before returning to her seat, offering a judgemental glare to Karen.

Dr Patel provided his own expert witness; a psychologist whom he'd worked alongside for many years, arguing that recent studies showed that there was an increased likelihood of suicide attempts within an autistic population. Patel then borrowed Rachel's laser pen to highlight Charlie's head looking towards the oncoming traffic, clearly seeing the lorry, before stepping out.

'It was a quick but informed decision that he needed to leave this world where he would have potentially served a prison sentence.'

The judge asked Dr Patel to stand down and he read over his notes before turning to his subjects.

'I've listened to all your arguments and I thank the experts for coming here today. This is a very complex debate but I've come to a decision. Miss McCann, it is very clear that Mr Irvine could see the oncoming traffic and made the decision to run out that day.'

Rachel bowed her head and sighed. Karen's eyes watered as she took in the reality of their result, while Dr Patel smiled.

'However...' the judge continued. Karen and Rachel looked up and Patel's smile faltered. 'There is no doubt in my mind that Mr Irvine ran out that day as he had no choice. Not because of his future impending arrest, but to ensure that he escaped a clear kidnapping. I determine that Mr Irvine did not commit suicide but instead died by misadventure, attempting to escape a very frightening situation, especially for an autistic teenager. I therefore overturn Dr Patel's decision of suicide.'

Karen cheered and Rachel placed her arm around her. Dr Patel shook his lowered head and clenched his fists.

'We did it!' Karen rejoiced. 'Well you did it. I'm sorry, Rachel, I just couldn't stand up in front of those people. It's just not within me.'

'That's the first step done,' Rachel replied. 'We now need to find The Predator Hunters and bring them to justice. And next time you will have to stand up in court and speak.'

Chapter 7

The fifteenth floor of a tower block housed The Predator Hunters' operation. Multi-coloured cladding formed the outside. Stone balconies were filled with washing, discarded bikes and St George's flags. Inside the corridors, posters promised the removal of the flammable cladding after a catastrophic fire at Grenfell Tower in London two years before but the council had yet to fulfil its duties, causing some distress to those living within the death-trap.

Stephen Fletcher sat in his smoke-filled flat amongst the multiple computers, cameras and televisions which helped him capture his victims. For the first time in a while, he was alone. His colleagues, Alison and Simon, were out on a hunt having lured another unsuspecting predator into their trap. He'd usually join them but today he was distracted. Amongst the bills and cheques donated by the public, he had a formal letter from the law firm of Rachel McCann, outlining that he was being sued for a bereavement award for the death of Charlie Irvine. The bereavement award alone was for £12,890, on top of the solicitor's fees, experts and funeral costs they were considered responsible for by the Irvine family.

He looked amongst the donations, some of which he'd have to utilise towards paying bills, the upkeep in technology, as well as paying whatever he could towards his colleagues, and wondered how he'd face this uphill battle if the Irvine family won. The cheques he received were typically between fifty to one hundred pounds at most, his supporters being typically lower on the salary bracket, if indeed they earned at all. Despite their global support for their duties, they weren't fortunate to receive the big bucks like some of the other charities despite several national celebrity scandals bringing a flavour for his type of work.

If only he'd been in America, he mused. They had their own television show dedicated to this type of production, with millions being pumped in from advertisers to support the work. It was dramatized of course, they always were in America, but still, they got the job done. He'd had some local success on *North West Tonight,* a local news programme, and a documentary on Channel 5. They had an influx of donations after it aired but the documentary also showed the grittier side of their work, leading social media to divide opinion wider than Brexit had. His group's association with the National Front and his arrest for his graffiti on a Yorkshire mosque gave him some poor publicity and many distanced themselves from his previously noble work. What they didn't cover in the press was that his actions were in response to a group of Muslims who groomed a group of white teenage girls. He knew what he was doing and he knew that his actions were taken to make a change for the better.

He sat on the floor, petting his Pit Bull Terrier and puffing on a spliff. Despite it being twenty degrees outside, he sat in the dark, his curtains closed, dressed in a hoodie, sweatpants and a cap. Within a mirror opposite he could just make out his tattoo, a dragon sprouting across his neck. He took off his cap and rubbed his mousy roots which were slowly growing back, and he considered a return to his barbers to revive his skinhead look. A ring pierced his bottom lip and flesh tunnels scored his earlobes.

Reading over the letter from Rachel McCann, he sighed and rubbed his eyes. He'd had complaints before but he'd never faced this. He thought back on his years of success and wondered how far he could really take this group further if Karen Irvine was successful in her mission to bring them down. He peered around the room at the local newspaper cuttings stuck to the wall with tape, of where he'd had success. They travelled for the work; he'd established networks all over the country but everyone knew he was the go-to guy. They'd had some minor trouble from the police previously but mostly the authorities complemented their activities, they just preferred he didn't put it on social media so soon after their arrest, but he certainly wasn't risking that. The amount of times those perverts had got off based on a technicality; he knew oh so well.

The most unsettling part was how this solicitor had found his address. He'd managed to keep a low profile outside of social media. He even used a fake name publicly; only his family knew the name on his birth certificate, embarrassingly a Polish name passed down from his grandfather, which he knew would take some shine off his influence to ban immigrants from his proud country. He assumed she'd worked with the courts and the police to ensure she could raid his finances.

Whatever he did now, he needed money to defend himself. He had good cause to chase Charlie Irvine; he had the *TeenTalk* conversations and the nude photographs on his computer. The video of his brutal end was available for all to see too; he walked out in front of that truck. He wasn't the first to kill himself after being exposed by The Predator Hunters and he certainly wouldn't be the last. Good riddance, he said. He looked towards the newspapers who'd supported his organisation throughout the years and picked up the phone.

*

A convenience store sat in the centre of the high street, sleeping beside a pub and a charity shop. Karen, early as always, hovered outside the shutters, shivering as she watched the sun slowly rise beyond the hills. An orange neon sign rose above her. To her right, promotional offers on beer and stories of the company's community projects filled a window.

A jingle of keys around the corner brought her some hope. A man appeared, smiling with white pearly teeth and mahogany skin. His teeth mirrored his short-sleeved shirt; bright white like the washing powder adverts, and a stripy blue tie made up his uniform.

'Morning, Karen!' he called in a Lancashire brogue.

'Morning, Stanley.' Karen unzipped her purple branded fleece and bent down to collect the morning newspapers, delivered a few minutes earlier. The papers were covered in a beige sheet and wrapped in a plastic net. 'The papers beat you again! You expect me to carry these in at my age.'

'You're not a day over twenty-one, what's your complaint?'

She chuckled and blushed as she lifted the weight, which Stanley supported her with while they entered the store. Grabbing a pair of scissors, she clipped the netting and tore away the protective cover. Beneath a photograph of her and her son filled the front page. She gasped.

'Is everything alright, Karen?' Stanley ran over and placed his hand on her shoulder.

'I thought I'd have more time.' They read over the story together.

The Predator Hunters *are being sued by the family of Horwich paedophile, Charlie Irvine. Group leader, Stephen Fletcher, was horrified to be informed of the law-suit against his organisation whose aim is to protect the streets of the Bolton area. Irvine committed suicide in June after the group confronted him after he chatted up what he believed to be an eleven-year-old girl online, sending her nude photographs of himself and asking her to meet up, where he planned to fuel her with alcohol and ice cream. The Irvine family are now blaming Fletcher for his death.*

'This isn't good,' said Stanley.

'Can we throw these away?'

'Are you kidding? We still have sales targets. No one will take any notice, don't worry.'

Stanley's promise fell flat on Karen, who throughout the morning had customers query her involvement in the story. Some gave her a sympathetic smile, while others threw pity on her. A few regulars growled as they passed her. Eventually she moved away from the tills towards restocking beans in the canned aisle until a recognisable face approached.

'Oh, Karen, I'm surprised to see you in today.' She looked up and found a wrinkled, grey lady wearing a furry hat with a feather sticking out, glaring towards the shop assistant. She looked as if she'd discovered a bad smell. A dusty fur coat covered her and her brown shoes appeared fresh from a concentration camp.

'I'm here most days, Mrs Butcher.'

'Well with that said, I can't believe you've been digging up your son's sordid past all over again. Don't you have any pride?'

'I'm at work, Mrs Butcher, I can't talk now.'

She walked off and found Stanley in his office, who was writing up the rota for the following week.

'Can I go home, Stan?' she whimpered from the door. He walked over and embraced her, before hovering his hand towards the door, whispering *'go'*.

As she approached her little terraced house, just a few steps away from her employer, she saw her front door had been tarnished. A brown stain smudged her door handle and the frosted window offering a glimpse into the hallway. Shaking, she took out her keys and opened the lock, using a tissue to open the dirty handle. On the mat, faeces greeted her. She stepped over the stain, now etched into her mat, sat down on the stairs and cried.

*

Despite being a working day, Rachel decided to spend it at home. She needed to thoroughly clean the kitchen after their fire, which continued to tickle her nostrils. Despite most of the smoke now being fumigated out of her mother's house, the soot was embedded into the tiles and she was determined to restore the building to the country retreat which she once considered it to be.

The previous day, Carl, despite Rachel's protests, had brought Matilda a Beagle puppy to cheer her up following her traumatic experience. At first Rachel was furious—who the hell would look after said puppy?—until she saw Matilda playing gleefully with her new friend, which she'd decided to call Peppa, after her favourite cartoon. Peppa was white with brown and black patches across her fur. Despite the puppy's seductive eyes melting her heart, Rachel hated being undermined; Carl had brought it round and offered her daughter a pet without consulting her first.

'It was on the local Facebook group, it had been abandoned! I couldn't leave it there and I thought who could really need cheering up right now.'

The sob story and Matilda's glow when she was introduced to the dog swayed Rachel. She had to acknowledge the positive influence Carl appeared to bring to her daughter. Those puppy eyes of Peppa didn't help either; *manipulative bitch.* Rachel said Peppa could stay as long as Carl didn't pull any further stunts which would undermine her parenting authority.

Matilda had since returned to school and her mum had gone out for the day with a local charity which supported people who had dementia. This left Rachel to have the house (almost) to herself, allowing her to clean up and spend some time with her new adorable pet, which followed her around the house all day.

A shuffling echoed from the letterbox. She turned around and saw a mountain of envelopes and a newspaper; the same one which had been delivered daily for the past decade, still addressed to her deceased father. *The Bolton Times* covered news from across the region. Across the front was a photograph of Charlie Irvine, taken from the video which led to his demise. Beside him, a photograph of The Predator Hunters' leader, Stephen Fletcher, looking suitably angry as he revealed that his group were being sued for their heroic work.

Rachel sighed. Fletcher handed them the story, meaning he had full influence over the content. She thought of Karen reading the headline, labelling her only son as a *paedophile*. '*Why they couldn't have put alleged*,' Rachel wondered.

'Clever move. You can't sue anyone for defaming the dead.'

She picked up her mobile and dialled Karen. A quivering voice was on the other side. She'd read the story.

'How can they say all this? It's not true. They haven't even talked about how his cause of death was overturned. It was all their fault!'

'Don't worry, Karen,' Rachel replied. 'We'll have our day in court and we'll straighten it all out. I'll even respond to the paper on your behalf, they'll have to retract the suicide bit regardless. Unfortunately it'll only be a small print on the second page under their apologies.'

'It's already kicking off here, Rachel,' said Karen with a quiver in her voice.

'OK, stay strong, Karen, what's happened?'

'One of my neighbours has smeared dog shit all over my front door and posted it into my letterbox. The smell is horrendous. I don't know whether we should go through with this if this is just the beginning.'

'Karen, call the police, tell them what's happened. But surely this shows that more than ever we need to do this. We need to change people's perceptions of Charlie.'

'It's such a mess,' Karen wept.

'Karen, I'm coming over to help, OK? Just stay strong and I'll be there shortly.'

Rachel hung up and jumped into her car, a red Qashqai, once deemed ridiculously big for a single mother of one, which now didn't seem so unreasonable now she had a dog to transport too. She drove down the bypass. As she rolled into Horwich town centre, her phone rang and she answered it via the Bluetooth application on her stereo.

'Mrs McCann?'

'It's Miss.'

'Sorry, Miss McCann. Please can you come to the school? We've had an issue with your daughter, Matilda, today.'

Rachel sighed. *No, not now.* She banged her head on her steering wheel. She pulled over and sent an apologetic text to her client and drove back up the hill towards the school.

She arrived at St Peter's Catholic school for girls. She wasn't particularly religious but she couldn't deny the values and the grades, which they prestigiously promoted on their prospectus.

And she wanted, where possible, to keep Matilda away from boys. Rachel had survived perfectly well without them and so could her daughter. The stone building was small, with only two hundred kids across the seven years they accepted them for, before she had to endure the pressures of finding a suitable high school. She hoped she'd be able to afford a private school before then. The playground was filled with kids playing with skipping ropes.

Inside, she found Matilda in the head teacher's office. Mrs Dahl sat behind her desk with her glasses hovering above the tip of her nose, tied to a chain around her neck. A Celtic cross hovered above her chest, covered with a white shirt and lilac jumper. Rachel looked down at her own attire; she'd rushed out of the house in a baggy grey t-shirt and black sweatpants, hardly a look of a professional, but she'd planned to work from home and this call had been less than expected.

'Sorry about this, I didn't have time to change.' Rachel laughed off her clothing and brushed down her creased t-shirt.

'Miss McCann, please take a seat.' Mrs Dahl held out her hand towards the empty chair before her.

Matilda sat before her desk, dressed in her green uniform with a badge stamped on her left breast, which had recently began to form. *Please stop growing up,* Rachel pleaded in her head.

'What's happened?' Rachel looked towards her daughter before facing the head teacher, hoping one of them would fill her in on the disruption to her day.

'Matilda has been in trouble today. She was being disruptive in class and then she took it upon herself to punch Lauren Kelly.'

'Who's Lauren Kelly?' she turned to her daughter.

'She's horrible. She called me thick.' Matilda replied; she crossed her arms and pushed her bottom lip forward.

87

Rachel looked back towards the head teacher, who shook her head.

'I'm sorry but this isn't acceptable, Miss McCann.' Mrs Dahl held a hand out towards Matilda, in case there was any doubt as to what the issue was.

'No it's not. Matilda, you know better than this,' Rachel snapped and bit her bottom lip.

Matilda bowed her head. Her frizzy hair, wrapped up in pigtails, no longer appeared as cute as it did when she left the house earlier in the morning when Carl offered her a lift to school.

'Miss McCann, I'm sorry but I have no choice but to suspend Matilda for a week. I have some homework for her to do. When she returns next week, I hope she'd have learned her lesson and won't take such drastic action against her peers again.'

'Of course, I'm so sorry about this, Mrs Dahl. Can I ask what will happen to this Lauren?'

'It's her word against Matilda's, I'm afraid, and she denies saying anything to Matilda which would have wound her up. She's been sent home where she will consult a doctor for her eye. You're very lucky, her mother wanted to call the police but I've encouraged her to leave it be.'

'So that's the real reason she isn't being punished.'

'Miss McCann,' Mrs Dahl said sternly.

'No, don't worry. I'll punish my kid but I just hope in future you stop this bullying. Now come on, you!' She turned to Matilda, who slumped off her chair and followed her to the car. The drive home was a quiet one, beside the odd rant from Rachel. 'I can't believe you've done this, you have no idea how busy I am. Do you think I can afford to just spend the week at home with you?

You know better than this, you're grounded for a month, young lady!'

When they returned home, Matilda stomped up to her room with the homework set by Mrs Dahl. Rachel called Carl, who agreed to stay at their house over the following days and babysit Matilda while Rachel worked on her cases from the office. Relieved that she'd managed to sort this dysfunctional family out, she picked up the newspaper and continued to read the story of Stephen Fletcher.

*

A knock at the door disturbed a weeping Karen. She jumped and slowly tiptoed over to the window. Behind the net curtain, she spotted a familiar face and sighed. She ran to the door and answered.

'Sylvia. Thank God you're here.' She stepped out and hugged her. Glancing both ways, her eyes widened before lightly pulling Sylvia into her home, side-stepping the stain on her carpet. 'Thanks so much for coming round.'

Having locked herself in, Karen had dressed down into her lilac pyjamas and a white robe. Sylvia looked at her watch—it was mid-afternoon—and judged the state of her friend, before glancing at herself in a full-length mirror in the hallway; she'd spruced up in a light-blue floral ruffled dress, pink shoes and a matching pink homburg on her head.

'How could I not?' said Sylvia as she wiped a side bench with her white-gloved hands, before rubbing the dust off her fingers. They made their way to the lounge and found a seat. They did the usual diddle-daddle of tea offerings but Sylvia, as always, waved her hand; she drank enough of that stuff during the rest of her social calendar, which was as full as a royal's. 'How are you?'

'Awful. Just awful, Sylvia. They've vandalised my house. Even Mrs Butcher approached me in the shop today. I knew this might stir some feelings again, but I never expected it to be *this* bad.'

'Why didn't you tell me what you were doing? I was surprised to find out in the newspaper what you were up to. I thought we were friends, Karen.' Sylvia placed a hand on her round midriff as if Karen's secrecy had caused her physical pain.

'I couldn't face telling anyone. I felt sick starting on this journey and I didn't know how far I'd be able to get with it. It all happened so fast. But this lawyer, Rachel, she seems to think we've got a case.'

'Who is *we*?' Sylvia asked, her voice echoed with confusion. She peered over at the photograph of Karen and her son, wondering who else was in their life besides the girls at church.

'Me and Charlie.' A smile arose on Karen's face, a rare sight for anyone who had brushed past her for the last few months.

'Karen, Charlie is dead.'

The smile quickly retracted and Karen's eyes grew vengeful.

'So? He's still with me in my heart. And I want justice for him.'

'Is this really a good idea, Karen? You're opening doors which have been firmly shut for some time now and I felt we were getting somewhere with rebuilding your life. You're back at work and you are coming to church again. I thought we'd finally moved on from this mess.'

'Sylvia, I'm crying inside every day. Every time I see those ladies in church, I know they're whispering about me. I see the looks I get just walking down the street. I'm sick of not being able to mention my son without this overbearing feeling of shame. I couldn't even mark his birthday for God's sakes.'

'You marked it with me,' Sylvia said. 'We went to his grave and we lit a candle.'

'That's not the same, Sylvia. I'm so grateful I have you, but I should be able to celebrate my son's life with everyone. Look at Melanie's parents.'

'What about them?' Melanie was another parishioner of the church who once sang in the choir. She was diagnosed with a brain tumour on her twelfth birthday and died six months later.

'They are so proud of her. How many charity events have we had in her honour? We've opened hospital wards with her name on it. Her little face is in the newspaper for all the good which has come out of her death and her parents, whilst they are grieving too, are still beaming with pride that their daughter could help so many people from the beyond. They stand up in church and talk about her and all the lessons they learned from her life. I should be able to do that. I can't even put Charlie's name on the All Hallows Eve prayers list.'

'Who's stopping you?' Sylvia asked.

'The vicar! He said it wouldn't be appropriate given the circumstances.'

'Well he has a point…'

'I want to be like Melanie's parents. I want to shout from the rooftops about this person who was my entire life. Instead I'm not supposed to talk about him, like Charlie was some miscarriage that I should just try and forget. Well the only miscarriage round here is justice!'

'With all due respect, Karen, you're never going to change their opinion of Charlie. I think you're torturing yourself with this. There will be no winners on the back of this, believe me.'

'I still need to try,' Karen pleaded.

Sylvia scratched her head and glanced around the room as she collected her thoughts. She took a deep breath before approaching a delicate subject.

'I've never said this to you before, Karen, but what if they were right?'

'About what?' Karen's mouth gasped.

'About Charlie. What if this court case brings up some previously unforeseen evidence which goes against him? Something which proves he really was what they said about him?'

'Do you think there could be?'

'Who knows?' Sylvia threw her hands up. 'Look, I loved Charlie, he was a wonderful little boy. I'm not saying what happened was his fault. But he had a condition...'

'He was looking for friends,' Karen said with certainty.

'But was he, Karen? We all have needs. And I'm sure in his head he was the same age as that girl, but at the end of the day, he *was* a nineteen-year-old man, and had the body of one.'

'Are you saying you believe he was looking for sex?' replied Karen through gritted teeth.

'I'm saying he was capable.'

Silence settled between them and the atmosphere was unsettling. Sylvia tilted her head and shot Karen a sceptical stare, whilst her friend placed a hand over her mouth and trembled.

'If that's what you think, then you can go.'

Karen stood up and walked into the hallway towards the front door. Sylvia followed behind.

'Karen, please. I'm only thinking of your best interests.'

'Well this isn't about my best interests. It's about my son's. You'd know all this if you were a mother, but you're not.'

Her words pushed Sylvia backwards. She grabbed on to the stair rail for support, before strutting furiously towards the exit. Before she embarked out onto the street, she turned towards the rude host and said, 'God help you, Karen Irvine.'

Chapter 8

A knock on the door disrupted Stephen and his colleagues. They were reviewing the footage of their previous day's work, editing it before uploading it to the website and relevant social media groups. Alison stood up and peered out of the window.

'It's some Paki in a suit,' she said, pulling at her greasy pink ponytail. She chewed gum as she spoke, the stud in her tongue clicking against her teeth. She was dressed in tracksuit bottoms and a branded sports t-shirt, despite the fact that the only running she ever did was to chase predators. A paunchy belly poked out beneath her t-shirt with a silver hoop stabbing the button.

'Answer it,' Stephen replied and she opened the door. An Asian man stood there, dressed in a fine pinstriped black suit and a designer watch wrapped around his wrist. He had a thick head of black hair, sleeked back.

'Hi, is Mr Fletcher there?' he asked with a Yorkshire tongue.

'Who's asking?' she replied in her Manchester twang.

'That's really a matter for Mr Fletcher and me.'

'Let him in, Ali,' a voice shouted from behind.

She nodded her head inside and he followed her in. He looked around the room, squinting into the dark, and glanced at the screen where he spied the group's latest project.

'Still at it then?' He nodded his head towards the laptop. 'Despite being sued?'

'What's it to you?' Simon replied. He sat in the corner smoking a spliff, his head covered by a black hoodie. The only parts of his face that were visible were his pale cheeks and mouth with a couple of teeth missing in the front. Two piercing eyes with pupils like black holes hovered beneath the edge of his hood.

'Well I'm hoping I can be of help.' He tapped his satchel.

'I'm not being funny but the last person I need help from is you.'

'I'm a solicitor. May I?' He raised his hand towards the empty camping chair beside their television. Fletcher raised his hand towards the same chair, welcoming his visitor to take a seat and the lawyer obliged. 'I want to represent you.'

'I don't need representing,' Stephen replied, holding up the previous day's newspaper. 'I've got the public on my side.'

'The public won't be in court, Mr Fletcher. Miss McCann is a good lawyer and if you don't have representation, she will win. I've seen the video, she's got a case. A judge has already overthrown the cause of death, determining that the kidnap led to Mr Irvine's demise.'

'Well I'm not being funny, right,' Alison piped up. 'But we ain't having no muzzie representing us. You're as bad them.'

'With all due respect, Miss Sharples…'

'How the fuck do you know my name?' She marched over to him and placed her hands on her hips, which were thrust forward.

'I've done my research. I know who you all are. I know about your backgrounds as well as your arrests for racially motivated attacks. All that will go against in you in court. If you don't mind me saying, I think having someone exactly like *me* might go in your favour.'

96

Alison turned to Stephen, who waved his hand, encouraging her to back down and she retreated.

'Mr…'

'Iqbal. Mo Iqbal.'

'Short for Mohammed, I presume,' Stephen replied and raised his eyebrows.

'The very same.'

'How did you find my address?'

'I got your name and asked around. You're really not as anonymous as you like to think, Mr Kowalski.'

The other two gasped and turned towards Stephen, who shuffled shiftily.

'You're good. How much are you going to charge for this?'

'I'm guessing, and I don't mean to be rude, you have a low income.' He looked around the decaying room, trying not to pass judgement on the squalor which the group called their head office. Whilst the equipment appeared expensive, the carpet was warn, the lights remained off and the bins were overflowing with microwave-meal packaging and cans of cheap lager.

'You're quite correct. That degree paid off,' Stephen said sarcastically.

'Fucking ponce,' Alison barked. 'Coming here, judging us.'

'I'm trying to help, Miss Sharples. I can represent you and the government will pay me to do so. There's no need for any of you to pay me a penny. Are you really going to turn down free legal representation?'

'I'm not being funny, right. But why would someone like *you* help people like us? *Your* kind are usually the ones out there fiddling kids.'

'I'm a lawyer, I help people. I read about the case in the newspaper and thought I could be of service to you. As it happens I agree with you, Miss Sharples, some of my people have treated young girls horrendously, but we're not all like that. They are, I assure you, a minority. I represented those girls in Yorkshire myself and I'm here to represent you guys today. And I'm determined to also ensure that this world remains safe for my own daughter too. Believe me, I want your organisation around.'

'How old's your little girl?'

'She's eight and becoming more interested in the internet every day,' Mo replied. Stephen nodded his head and looked towards his colleagues.

'So where do we sign?'

*

The following morning Karen and Rachel, dressed in the same suits which they'd worn in court, arrived at Media City in Salford. The sun rose high over the peaceful waters of the quays, the tranquillity disrupted by the morning commuters rushing to get to their office jobs. The pair entered the television studios and after countless searches and identity verifications, they met a producer who talked them through their morning agenda. They had been up since the early hours preparing what they were going to say and they welcomed the offers of coffee from the runners. *'And make them large.'*

'Why have you agreed to this again?' Karen asked as she was powdered with foundation in the make-up room by a young girl, straight out of university, dressed all in black. 'I don't think I can do this.'

'Trust me on this,' Rachel replied. 'We need some damage limitation and this will help us on a national scale. You also need the practice. I can't have you shitting yourself in court again.'

They entered the main studio, where they were met by three television presenters. Two glamorous women dressed in colourful designer dresses gave the ladies a hug and welcomed them to sit beside the panel table where a plump middle-aged man with white hair sat between his co-hosts, drinking coffee, complaining about the latest celebrity who'd self-defined themselves as *non-binary*. The studio was bright, overlooking the quays which they worked beside. In front of them, cameras spun around with people carrying headsets counting down the clock until the ad-break ended.

A third chair was pulled up and a frumpy woman perched beside them; she had purple shoulder-length permed hair and wore glasses and a white apron dress. The three guests didn't have the opportunity for introductions before the director counted down before finally calling *'Action!'*

'Hello! The time is six AM and welcome to *Wake Up Britain*!' Sarah Capaldi began the show. She had bright blonde hair, a new, thinner nose, which she'd endured the previous year and a pearl pendant around her neck. 'Today we have the winner of *Britain's Got Talent*, Fudgey The Dog, and her owner to talk about what's next for them. We have Labour MP Gemma Richards, to discuss why immigration is good for Britain, and an opportunity to win a brand new car.'

'But first…' Nelly Simmonds took over. She was a tall brunette who had recently caused controversy by having a gastric band despite advertising a health plan, which was guaranteed to lose weight. The quick weight loss had caused her to carry a little extra skin and she wore a baggier dress to hide her excess. 'Karen Irvine's nineteen-year-old son was killed in a road accident trying to escape a group called The Predator Hunters. The group locked him in a garage after confronting him as he tried to meet what he believed was an eleven-year-old girl online. Karen is joined today by her lawyer, who is trying to sue the group for his death. Karen, you claim your son *isn't* a predator?'

'He was just a boy at heart. He had a development disability. He wouldn't have met her for anything sinister.'

'But how do you know that?' Peter Mansford chipped in. Despite his constant comments on his colleague's figures, he hadn't stepped into a gym for years but still managed to win the award for *Britain's Secret Crush*.

'I know my son. He wanted friends. He had autism, which meant he struggled socially. Just read the conversations which the group posted online, that wasn't someone who had a sexual interest.'

'With all due respect, Karen, but he sent naked photographs to her,' said Peter, almost laughing as he pointed out the facts.

'He was very receptive to what people asked of him,' Karen replied.

'He was catfished.' Rachel jumped in, saving her client from further scrutiny. 'They duped him into this.'

'Now you want to stop these groups from operating?' Gemma asked, turning to Rachel.

100

'Well yes, they are taking very vulnerable people, duping them into these conversations, getting them to meet up and humiliating them online. In this case, they kidnapped Charlie and he died trying to escape. Many commit suicide.'

'Now we're also joined by The Mothers Protection Group representative, Michelle Hellens. Michelle, you feel these groups are vital to ensuring our kids remain safe?'

'Definitely,' Michelle replied, speaking for the first time since she sat beside the ladies; they hadn't had time for an introduction. 'The police don't have enough government funding to operate these interventions directly, therefore they need people like Stephen Fletcher and his colleagues to do the work for them. I'm sorry, but they're protecting our children from dangerous people like *your* son, Karen.'

'My son was not dangerous!' Karen barked and turned her back on Michelle.

'I disagree!' Michelle replied and folded her arms, looking smugly towards the hosts.

The two women argued for five minutes before Peter jumped in and addressed the lawyer. 'Why would you stop this great group from operating, Rachel? You have children yourself. Can you not see the benefits of having The Predator Hunters looking after our internet space?'

'Before this case came along, I would have agreed with you, Peter, but having heard Karen's story and having seen the tapes, I can see that they are putting very vulnerable people at risk. Everyone deserves their day in court regardless of who they are. Charlie never got his day in court and we're fighting to ensure that people like Charlie do get the opportunity to tell their side of the story in the future.'

'Well he might have had his day in court had he not run in front of that lorry?' Peter replied, continuing to laugh as he pointed at his notes.

'He was trying to escape a group who kidnapped him! Besides, this is for the greater good. Forget Charlie for a minute. Michelle, you must have seen in the past that these predators get off on a technicality. It's vigilante groups like this who put it on social media, which gives these monsters the opportunity to get off any criminal charges as there is no way they could have a fair trial with a jury, who would have likely seen the videos on social media before they arrived at court.'

'But even if they get off, they can't do it again because everyone then knows who they are, the public are aware and know to keep their children away from them!'

'Well that's all we have time for,' Gemma interrupted. 'Now we're going for a quick commercial break and when we get back we'll be joined by Dr Lucy who will be telling us how your cereal could cause cancer.'

'Cut!' the director called and the women were hurried off the set.

'Well that didn't go well,' Karen groaned. 'I'm sorry, Rachel, but I certainly can't face court.'

*

Rachel returned home to find an empty house. She walked up to Matilda's room but her homework was sitting out on her desk and didn't even have any attempted markings, suggesting it hadn't been even looked at yet. In the master bedroom, she found her mother asleep and, just as she was closing the door, she heard the playful giggles of her daughter outside. She walked over to the window and glanced through the closed curtains.

Across the road from the house was a park. Beside a swing, Carl and her daughter were playing with a frisbee while Peppa chased it. Rachel's face grew red and she stormed down to the park to confront them. Their light blue jeans were covered in muddy paw-prints. It was a sunny day and despite the warnings of snow, it continued to be unusually dry and warm for the North West of England. Carl and Matilda had thrown off their hooded tops and ran around in just t-shirts.

'Matilda! Get in and do your homework!'

Matilda sulked off while Carl lowered his head, with a mixture of disappointment and shame, and called Peppa back to him.

'What the hell do you think you're doing, Carl?' Rachel growled as he walked into the kitchen.

'Hey, relax, she was working this morning and I felt she could do with getting out for some fresh air for a bit. It was getting stuffy in that room.'

'She is excluded and grounded. If she's treated like it's summer, she'll punch girls every week.'

'Listen, we had a chat and it sounds like she was being bullied by that girl. She was standing up for herself. Surely as a lawyer you can understand?'

Rachel sighed, suddenly feeling unreasonable. 'OK fine, but seriously for the rest of the week, she needs to learn her lesson. No more treats.'

'OK, Rachel. Listen, I'm really sorry. I've just never had kids, but always wanted them. I'm just trying to find my way around it. I really want to have her on side.'

'You're confusing popularity with respect, Carl. And believe me, I get that, I really do. I've been there. But we're going to have to work as a team here and I can't be the bad person all the time. I need your support if you're going to be in her life.'

He bowed his head and nodded like a naughty child, disappointed in himself. They returned to the house and Carl began to chop up ingredients for their lunch while she read over her paperwork. Rachel kept looking up and tutting at the distraction.

'I'm sorry, I'm really annoying you, aren't I? Why don't I be helpful and give Matilda a hand with her homework?'

'Yes please, that'd be great.'

He smiled, kissed her cheek and walked upstairs. His muscles stretched out of a tight black t-shirt and she grew red. Rachel was embarrassed that she could be so shallow as to forget all of his ridiculous behaviour by his distracting appearance. She returned to reading her papers as Carl disappeared. A few minutes later she heard giggling upstairs but was too exhausted to shout up. Instead, she opened up her laptop; the video from *Wake Up Britain* had done the rounds on social media with over thirty thousand shares and nearly fifty thousand retweets. Thousands of comments had already been added to the debate by the public.

I'm glad he's dead.

Lock them up!

Maybe this Rachel would feel differently if it was her own kid.

Rachel sighed as she realised that she really had her work cut out for her to change the public's mind on Charlie. In the meantime she just hoped that Karen wasn't on social media.

Chapter 9

A week later, Rachel knocked on Karen's door. Around the black door with a silver 51 on it, the remnants of faeces remained embedded into the stone and smudged onto a nearby windowsill.

'Hi, Rachel,' Karen said as she answered the door. She hadn't showered; her hair was greasy and she wore a white robe. She stood out of the way of the frame and allowed her lawyer to enter. Rachel tried not to breathe in as she stumbled past her client, who had clearly not showered for days.

'They came back then?'

'Yep! That TV show didn't help,' Karen said with a glum tone. 'Do you fancy a brew, I think the milk's gone off so it'll have to be black.'

'Black's fine but stick a sugar in it, will you?'

She followed her into the kitchen and found a series of dishes piled up. As Karen opened the fridge, Rachel spied a series of empty shelves. The remaining contents had rotted away and a stench of aging vegetables radiated from a nearby bin. Karen grabbed the bottle of milk and sniffed the contents before tearing her head away and scrunching up her face. Gagging, she replaced the lid and threw it in the overflowing metal bin.

'How are you?' Rachel asked with a tilted head.

'Not good, I'll be honest. I daren't leave the house without you. I've called in sick since.'

'It will pass, Karen…' But she didn't respond. 'You should've told me you were too scared to go outdoors, I could have picked some bits up for you from the shop.'

'I don't need anything.'

'You need to eat.' Rachel lectured her client. 'This court case is going to consume us all and we need to keep our strength up.'

'I'm not hungry,' Karen mumbled.

'Yeah well, I'll certainly want some milk in my brew next time I come over. Come on, you can't stay cooped up in here forever. You need to face the world one day. Be defiant, show them you don't care. You have nothing to be ashamed of.'

Karen sighed and nodded her head before escaping upstairs. Rachel took the time alone to browse around the downstairs communal areas, spotting photographs of Charlie and Karen together in a caravan in Wales. He didn't face the camera in any of them but a small smile escaped his lips in one of the pictures. On her return, Karen appeared fresher faced and forced a smile towards her lawyer. She'd dressed in a pair of jeans and a red jumper while her lawyer looked ready for a business lunch in her blue suit and matching designer handbag.

They made their way out to a supermarket in Bolton, at the request of Karen, who wished to avoid her neighbours in her local shop. They quickly swept past the news stand which continued to cover Charlie's story along with a local priest who had been accused of abusing his vulnerable parishioners.

'He was my priest,' Karen said, bowing her head as she passed. 'Did you read about him?'

'I saw something but tried not to read over it, they seem to be using that story to justify the vigilante group's existence.'

'He was a lovely man. Looked after all the arrangements for Charlie's funeral for me, not that anyone came. He put on a nice service and gave me support for a long time after my son's death. I don't know what to believe now, after all, Charlie was innocent.'

'They have witnesses and found dodgy porn on his computer, Karen, I'm pretty sure he's guilty.'

'Are you a believer, Rachel?' Karen changed the subject.

'I'm agnostic.'

'What do you believe will happen to your little girl when she dies?'

'I don't know, isn't that the great mystery?' Rachel shrugged.

'Do you not worry she'll go to hell if you don't raise her to believe in God?'

Rachel pondered that thought. She'd always encouraged Matilda to find her own path. She taught her about Christian, Jewish, Hindu and Islamic faiths, but she struggled to force anything on her herself. She put her in a church school for its grades and values, but figured that she could make her own mind up when the time came.

'I was a church girl for a long time,' Rachel explained. 'I was in the choir. It was sort of expected as my dad was a local MP and they liked to be seen as doing the right thing. But then I grew up and work took over. I guess I never really considered it again. In my line of work you do sort of hope for a higher justice system as the amount of people I see get off on a technicality infuriates me, but I suppose it's part of the job.'

'I hope Charlie made it to heaven.'

'I'm sure that if he's everything you say he is then he will be there.'

Rachel rubbed Karen's back and moved on through the aisles. They completed their shop and made their drive back to Horwich. They passed a little chapel on a hill and Karen asked if Rachel could pull up beside it. They stepped out and walked towards the back of the church where a dozen graves made up a yard. It was a crisp day and the sun brought a peaceful ambiance to the usually grim space.

'This is the chapel where that priest preaches. We've got a locum in until it all blows over.'

They walked past several graves until they found a patch of grass with a plant pot above it, facing down. Spiking out of a tiny drainage hole in the top, a small white daisy with a yellow centre danced within the breeze.

'This is where Charlie was laid to rest,' said Karen, staring at the lone flower.

'Where is his gravestone?' Rachel wrapped an arm around her client as she glanced around for any evidence of Charlie's presence.

'He had one when we buried him. The day after the funeral, I returned and it was full of graffiti. It said '*nonce*' over his name. It wasn't much of a stone anyway, we couldn't afford anything big. His dad refused to pay for anything or even come to the funeral. He never wanted a relationship with him. He's making up for it now, I suppose, helping us out with this court case, but his presence when Charlie was alive would've been far more valuable.'

'Oh.' Rachel bowed her head.

'I cleaned the grave stone up, but I came back the next day and it was tarnished again. I asked the funeral home to remove the stone after that, but he's still here. I brought the plant pot last time I visited on his birthday. I think enough time has passed now. I hope they'll soon forget about this place altogether.'

'I'm sure they will.'

'It's so sad, Rachel. He was bullied so much at school. When he went out people would mock him or stare. I hoped after he died people might finally leave him alone but they haven't. I just want peace for my boy.'

'We'll get it, I promise.'

*

Rachel returned home where she found Carl in the kitchen cooking a meal. His police hat was on a side bench; beneath, his uniform was folded neatly out of the way. The washing machine was on and she could see her clothes spinning around. He wore a pinafore above a plain red t-shirt and a pair of shorts which were cut at the knee. In the lounge, her mother watched *Countdown* and her daughter sat beside her reading *Charlotte's Web*, the latest reading task set by her school.

'Thank you.' She ran up to Carl and kissed him on the lips. She closed the door as her mother and daughter looked up in unison; they were eyeing up the smooch, which she'd planted on the man who had made her day. After shutting her family out of the spectacle, she embraced Carl and peered up at him whilst keeping her arms around his neck. 'This means so much to me. I'm so glad I have you. I've just spent the afternoon listening to someone who couldn't get her child's own father to take an interest in their lives, and here you are doing it for someone else's.'

'I care about you.'

'Yes but me and her come as a unit. You have to be there for her because you care about *her* as much as you care about *me*.'

'She's a nice kid and I want to be there,' Carl reassured her.

'Really?' Rachel's smile blossomed.

'Really.'

'Because this is it now, Carl. I need you to be sure. I can't have you just disappearing one day as I'm letting you into her life. I can't have her getting hurt. She needs consistency and support.'

'Rachel, I'm not going anywhere…. I love you.'

Rachel's white teeth shone out of her stretching lips. 'I love you too.'

Chapter 10

Twenty miles away in Preston, Mo Iqbal sat in his office watching the video of Charlie's demise. Before him his client, Stephen Fletcher, sat staring, puffing on his vape after the lawyer banned him from lighting up a cigarette. Beside him, Simon and Alison sat chewing gum, glancing around the room. It was small but modern office, with fresh white paint and blue carpets. Mohammed's credentials lined the walls and a bookshelf with a range of legal text books rested beside a filing cabinet.

The office sat in a small square in the centre of the town. The square had a patch of green in the centre with a hotel and luxury apartments, converted from old Victorian houses, surrounding the gated garden. The office overlooked a large park with a pavilion in the centre and an arch where a young couple declared their wedding vows beneath.

Despite the formal visit, the clients appeared anything but. They dressed in their black tracksuits. Simon had a cigarette rolled up and tucked behind his ear. Stephen had a new addition to his tattoo collection; a small star beneath his eye. While Alison, despite the cold, had decided that more flesh needed to be on display.

'It's well posh this,' Alison said. 'You've done pretty well for yourself. That's the problem with this country. Immigrants taking all the good jobs, like.'

'I'm not an immigrant,' Mo replied. 'I was born in Leeds.'

'Well your parents must be and you ended up with that top education while people like me go on without.'

'My parents came here with nothing and worked hard to send me to university. But please be assured I still had to work hard to get to where I am. But this isn't about me. This is about your case. You're being sued and I'm trying my best to get you out of this.'

Stephen turned to her and crossed his neck, shaking his head. She mouthed an *'oh'* and lowered her head like a scolded naughty child.

'You guys didn't help yourselves by putting this video online,' Mo began the meeting.

'We wanted to show what a pervert this guy was and how he attacked me!' Stephen barked, stroking the scar on his head, which continued to show many months on.

'I can see that. But you guys kidnapped him. You locked him up against his will. What were you thinking of? Why didn't you just let him go home and let the police deal with this?'

'Because they do fuck all. I needed the world to see what we're doing to keep these streets safe.'

'By kidnapping autistic teenagers?' Mo raised an eyebrow and chewed on his pen cap.

'Whose side are you on? You come over here fuckin' defending a paedo and havin' a go at us for trying to stop dick heads like this being on the street,' Alison barked.

'I'm trying to help you, Alison.'

'I don't need no muzzie with a briefcase helping me.'

Silence settled over the room as they absorbed her poisonous words. Mo clicked his pen repeatedly as he considered his next move. He took a deep breath and then stood up.

'Alison, can we have a word privately?'

'Wha …? Why me?' Throwing her head from side to side between her peers and her lawyer, she assumed an insulted victim posture, which would slot perfectly into a *Little Britain* sketch. 'I ain't done nothin'.'

'Well if you want me to represent you, we need some rapport.'

'Ra-what?' Alison scrunched up her face.

'Rapport, a relationship. Nothing sexual, I assure you.' He rubbed his top lip and straightened up. 'I think we need to get past whatever *this* is. I appear to have your colleagues on board but I think until we get this sorted, I can't represent any of you.'

She looked to Stephen who nodded his head towards the door and whispered *'go on.'* She sighed and rolled her eyes, before following her lawyer out of the meeting room into reception.

'Thomas, why don't you go out and get yourself some lunch,' Mo said to a young receptionist who had a telephone headset. He left the glass reception, which was stamped with Mohammed's firm's logo across the front and a Mac computer on top, and dashed off with his take-out coffee, which his boss had brought back for him after collecting his clients from the train station.

Alison took a pew on a purple couch besides the reception desk and Mo took a chair opposite. He turned his head and looked at his client, trying to determine what caused the anger behind her otherwise gentle looks. She pulled her head back and threw him a look of disgust.

'Why do you hate Muslim people so much, Alison?' he asked with a soft tone.

'Cos you're all perverts who steal jobs.'

Mo's eyes widened and he bit his lip.

'Alison, I know there are some bad eggs out there but there is in *any* religion.' He took a copy of the *Preston Post* and passed it over to her. On the front, a priest, arrested for hurting his young congregation in Bolton, made up the front page. She browsed over the details before turning to her lawyer.

'And?' she said as she shrugged her shoulders.

'Do you know many people who follow the Islamic faith, Alison?'

'No, I keep well away from them.'

'I just wish I could get to the bottom of what started this.'

'Nowt started it.' She rubbed her foot on the ground, before placing it over her other knee as her lawyer spotted her anxious body language.

'I just can't believe anyone would have such distaste for anyone without just cause. Someone who looks like me has upset you at some point. I've met lots of people who don't like Muslims because of something they've read in the papers. But you? You're so angry. It's like Tommy Robinson's stormed my office. And I'm here trying to represent you. I'm trying to help you, Alison.'

'I've met people like you, right? And they ain't good people.'

'Who were these people?' Mohammed tilted his head and squinted his eyes with curiosity.

'I lived on an estate and they'd had a chippy at the end of the road. At first they seemed alright, yeah? But then they took liberties.'

'What kind of liberties?' Mo wanted to move closer and place a platonic hand on his client but caution prevented him.

'They'd give me and my mates vodka but then they'd suddenly want other things back.'

'Were these sexual things?' asked Mo.

She remained silent, clicking her tongue piercing against her teeth.

'Alison, anything you tell me will remain completely confidential. I'm your lawyer, I can't tell anyone without your consent, even if I wanted to.'

She took a deep breath. 'Yeah, they'd be sexual things. They'd pass me around like a bag of crisps.'

'I'm so sorry, Alison.' Mo bowed his head. 'It angers me so much when I hear this. I assure you though, as much as those men might claim they are Muslim, they are not. This is not what the Koran tells us, at least not in my interpretation or the interpretation of anyone I know. What happened to the people who did this to you?'

'The ringleader is dead. My mate stabbed him. She's in prison now for murder. Typical of the system. The others fucked off and they haven't been seen since.'

'I see.' Mo nodded. 'And it hurts you as you didn't get justice.'

'That's why I got into this game. Back then, I told the police and they did nowt to them and my mate got locked up for life. So I take matters into my own hands now. Fuck the authorities.'

'I don't blame you for that. I question the way you go about your vigilante projects, but I can see a good person in there trying to make the world a better place for other people. That's amazing.'

'Look, people have always taken advantage. They pretend to be all nice like you are, but one way or another they always end up doing me over.' Alison continued to chew on her gum and refused to look her lawyer in the eye.

'Well I can't do that, Alison, as I'm your representative. I'd be struck off for a start.' Mo stroked his chin. 'What are you doing tonight?'

'I'm not going out with *you* before you get any ideas,' she replied, pulling a face of disgust.

Mo cracked up laughing and slapped his thigh. 'No I'm not asking you to. Look, just don't rush off when the boys go home. I'll pay for a taxi for you to get home after.'

They returned to the room and the three of them covered the full events of the day Charlie died. They showed him the exchange of messages, their successes with other predators and how they'd even received praise from local MPs and the police for their work.

'Do you have any insurance for this operation you run?' asked Mo.

'Who do you think we are? Richard Branson? Come on, Mo.' Simon chuckled.

'Well we somehow need to pay for the damages if Karen Irvine wins.'

'Well we've got fuck all,' Alison chipped in.

'I have an idea. I think we should counter-sue,' suggested Mo.

'What for?' asked Stephen.

'For the attack. This is assault. If we counter-sue it ends the whole thing. Neither side can benefit from a financial pay-out, but better than that, none of us will lose any money. '

They arranged a plan of direction and departed ways. To the boys' surprise, Alison held back and stayed with her lawyer as they made their way to the train station.

'Go on, guys, it's alright.' She waved her hand to shoo them away.

They looked to their lawyer, who nodded and sided on the air of caution. 'Look, guys, out of the best interests for this case, please can I ask that you don't do anymore vigilante work and keep a low profile for the time being. We really need to keep our noses clean for the next few weeks while we sort all this out. We can't afford to let them have anything on us, or give them more ammunition.'

The boys nodded, embraced Alison and left.

Mo locked up the office and took his client on a walk past the park and into a suburban hub on the outskirts of the centre. The area was made up of takeaways, accountants and small independent shops. Local market traders cleared their stalls as the sun came down. A large green dome took centre stage in the busy commercial district. Alison did a double-take and jerked back as if she'd walked into glass.

'I'm not going in no mosque, Mo.'

'Trust me,' Mo said and she hovered behind him as he walked to the side of the temple towards a red-bricked hall on the back of the building. Beside the front door, a pretty mid-twenties lady welcomed them; she was dressed in a pink and gold sari and a white sheet covered her hair. She held a bag in her hands and she took out a pink headscarf and placed it over Alison's head before retrieving a light blue jacket and putting it around her exposed arms and belly.

'What you got me doin' ere?' Alison stuck up her nose.

'Alison, this is my sister, Asha. She will be with us the whole time.'

They walked into the hall and found dozens of people drinking green tea. Surrounding them were tables lined with copies of the Koran and leaflets on Islam. What came as a surprise to Alison was the number of white people in the room, who looked just like her.

'What's going on?' Alison asked.

'This is a meet and greet with the community,' Asha explained. 'We do this once a month; we welcome people into the community centre to tell them about our faith.'

'Sounds like you're recruiting.'

'Not at all,' Asha replied with a small giggle. 'This is merely a way of building bridges with the wider network of people around Preston. We know with everything which has happened over the past decade or two to make people concerned by people who look like us and are scared by our faith. We're simply here to say that our only agenda is peace.'

'Come over here, Alison.' Mo began walking and held his arm out in his direction of travel. A gentleman in a white shirt, trousers and a white cap above his head hovered in the centre of the room, stirring his tea. The man was of average height, was plump and had a beard. 'Alison this is our Iman, his name is Hussain. He's our leader in the mosque. Shaykh Khan, this is Alison. She has some concerns around some of the abuse which has taken place in some of the communities.'

'Hi, Alison, it's so lovely of you to join us today.' Hussain smiled and nodded towards the petrified girl before him.

'Why do you wear that hat? That's what them terrorists and abusers wear.'

'My Taqiyah? It covers my head. It is believed Prophet Mohammed did the same. It is nothing more than symbolism for my devotion to the religion, rather than any darker motive. Listen, Alison, I am very aware of your prejudices and understand your concerns. Had I been in your position I'd also be worried about people like me. It's not always a nice world out there, but you'll find that in all religions. Please be assured that these people you speak of do not represent my Islam.'

'But doesn't it say in the Koran...?' Alison lifted up her index finger.

'I know the passages you reference to,' Hussain interrupted. 'Interpretation often gets out of hand over time. Literal interpretation and translation never lands well. The Bible is no different, believe me. It was also written thousands of years ago. What was right back then doesn't necessarily mean it's the same today. Despite people's views of us, many of us are progressive and are keen to live peacefully within the communities that we serve. Can I say from the bottom of my heart, and on behalf of my faith, that I am truly sorry if anyone has given you any other impression of us?'

He handed her a leaflet with the key principles of the Islamic faith, shook her hand and walked away.

'I'd like to go now,' Alison groaned.

They departed the community centre and walked out towards a group of black cabs. Mo spoke to the taxi driver and handed him a note, before opening the door.

'Here you go, I'm sorry if we haven't managed to change your mind about us today but thank you for taking the time to come along anyway.'

'I guess you're not all bad.' Alison rolled her eyes and got in the car. 'Some of you are twats though.'

'That's true. Listen, you have my card. Once this is over, if you want to try again at getting the guys who hurt you, you only need to ask. I'd happily help you out.'

'Thanks but I've been there before, I'm not going back again. I don't trust the law, mate.'

Despite her disparaging remarks about his career, he smiled, comforted by her calling him *mate*. He closed the door and waved her off. He pulled out his phone and dialled.

'Thomas, get together everything you can find on Rachel McCann.'

Chapter 11

The high green peaks of Snowdon clashed with the graphite grey of slate. Between, a wooden hut encased the only life within a mile radius. Inside, Karen and Rachel were dressed up in red jumpsuits, suitable for an American prison. White helmets covered their heads and plastic goggles protected their eyes. Harnesses were wrapped around them and chains drooped from their backs. They walked outside of the hut, in line with other adrenaline junkies, mirroring the green mile of a group of IS hostages. In the distance, a train carried passengers to the top of the highest point in the British Isles outside of the Scottish Highlands, while the more determined amongst them walked up beside the tracks; a café at the top was almost a mirage as they sweated their way to the summit.

Their morning drive to North Wales had taken a little over two hours with Rachel remaining schtum over their itinerary. They had lunch in a café beside a waterfall in the nearby village of Betws-y-Coed, before driving over to their final destination in the Snowdonia National Park. The ladies lay on a mattress and they were chained up to a wire above them.

'Why are we doing this again?' Karen called, raising her voice to counter the rush of wind between them.

'We need to build up your confidence. Once we have this case before a judge, I will need you to stand up in court if we even stand a chance at winning it.'

'I know, I'm sorry, Rachel, I just tense up. I don't know why. Why are we going to this extreme though?' she asked, throwing her hands up towards the wires above her.

'Zip lines are a perfect way to boost confidence. You're getting over your fears and if you can do this, you can do anything.'

'Do we have to be so drastic though?' She tugged on the rope above her to see if it was sturdy.

"It's one of the safest things you can do. You've been checked, triple checked, and checked again to ensure you're secure. Just trust me on this, Karen.'

The zip line was advertised as the fastest in the world and, at over two-thousand feet, was also one of the highest. It was certainly a baptism of fire for Karen, who hadn't even boarded a rollercoaster before. The wire itself swooped from the top of a cliff, deep down into the quarry and over a reservoir. The people in front disappeared in seconds into the distance as the end of the line was out of their sight from those who were next in line ready to board the ride.

'Right, we're ready,' an instructor called and the beds beneath them lowered leaving the thrill-seekers hovering in the air. 'We will countdown and then set you off on your flight.'

'Oh God.' Karen quivered.

'You'll be fine, Karen!' Rachel assured her.

'Three, two...'

'Stop!' Karen called. They all turned to the petrified woman dangling beside them. 'I can't do it! Please get me down, get me down. Now!'

'You'll be OK, Karen, I promise!' Rachel reassured her.

'Get me off! Now! Get me off! Get me off! Please let me go!'

The beds were raised and the instructor sat beside a weeping Karen, who appeared relieved to be on safer ground again.

'Are you sure you want to get off?' asked the instructor.

'Yes, get me off now, I can't do it,' Karen screamed.

The instructor, dressed in a red t-shirt with *Velocity* stamped across the front, lifted off the chains and helped Karen get off the bed. As soon as her feet touched the ground she rushed out of the hut, passing the terrified faces of those who stood in line, waiting for their turn.

'I'm going to have to go after her,' Rachel said, tugging at her chains.

As soon as she was taken off the bed, the remaining two adrenaline junkies beside them were flown off into the distance. Rachel ran outside and found Karen crying beside a large piece of slate.

'The crew said they'd take us down in the van in a few minutes.'

'I'm so sorry, Rachel, this must have cost you a fortune. Please just add it to my bill.'

'Don't worry, it's only money. You mean much more. I'm sorry, I should've thought this through sooner. Maybe we should have gone on one of the forest coasters or something first to build you up.'

Rachel sat beside her and wrapped an arm around the weeping creature and rubbed her shoulder.

'I wasn't always like this, you know,' Karen whispered.

'No?'

'No, I used to be so much fun. OK, I wasn't doing things like this, but I was confident.'

'Tell me about the old you.'

'I was a dancer.' Karen smirked and hid her face away in embarrassment.

'Oh, like on the stage?'

'A kind of stage. It was a place called *Coyote*s.'

'Karen Irvine!' Rachel gasped and lightly slapped her client's arm. 'You dark horse!'

'It's how I met Josh. He used to come in the club all the time. I'd be on that bar every night, squirting water at the crowd, downing shots and dancing to country rock.'

'Where did she go?' asked Rachel.

'Who?'

'The old Karen.'

'Well life went a bit crazy. I was drunk most nights on that bar. I only found out later that the other girls weren't swallowing the shots, they were just spitting them out in their empty bottled beers. I ended up hammered. And that's where I met Josh, and we hit it off. But he used to work away a lot and I was left at home alone. My anxiety used to play all sorts of tricks on me and I did silly things. I stupidly slept with my boss one night. It was the most ridiculous thing. I told Josh as soon as he got home, I was so crushed and I couldn't live with the lie. He immediately kicked me out of our home and told me never to call him again.

'A month later I found out I was pregnant.' Karen continued. 'And, despite the dates indicating it was definitely his, Josh didn't believe me and wanted nothing to do with me or

Charlie. When Charlie was born, I sent photographs, I tried to keep him updated with his life, but he didn't want to know. In the end I just sent photographs once a year with a note about how he was doing. He did once try and get in touch but once I'd told him what a handful Charlie could be, he forgot about us. Once again, he was determined Charlie wasn't his. And that was it.'

'I see.' Rachel lowered her head.

'I was a single mum with a child who had autism and I couldn't cope. Nobody was out there to support me besides a few girls from church. Over time, it became too much and I lost everything. And now I have absolutely nothing now Charlie has gone. My confidence left the day Josh did.'

'Look, Karen, you have so much to offer the world. This situation has stripped you of something wonderful but you need to get it back if you're ever to live your life again. You're not living at the moment, you're just plodding along through life, and it's no life, believe me. I was the same after I had Matilda. I was alone trying to face the world, but I was determined to get my life back.'

'You can live again and you can make things right for Charlie,' Rachel continued. 'But I need you to somehow dig deep down into that place which held that belly fire and made you get up on that stage each night. I need you to dig that out and bring it back because I need you to be on your top performance in court, Karen."

'I'm not sure if I can.' Karen shook her head.

'Look, that first night you got on that bar in *Coyotes*, were you nervous?'

'Of course, I was on the loo every five minutes!'

'TMI! Well what got you on stage in the end?'

'The manager said to me that nothing really matters in this world and so it doesn't matter if I screw it up. And if all else fails, picture them all naked.'

'Well listen to those wise words of your old manager and get up and do it, Karen!'

'Yeah maybe I could. Come on then.' Karen stood up and brushed down her jumpsuit and made her way to the cabin.

'The van isn't here to take us down yet. It'll be another ten minutes at least,' Rachel said, pointing to the empty car-park outside.

'I know a quicker way down.' Karen nodded her head towards the hut. They both smiled and queued up once again for their adrenaline-filled ride down the mountain. The instructors counted down once again. Rachel turned to a shivering Karen and they shared a smile before they were let loose. They screamed all the way down, from initial fear to pure elation.

At the bottom, they unhooked themselves from the wire and ran over to each other, grabbing each other into a tight embrace.

Karen stood back and giddily jumped up and down. 'I can do anything.'

Chapter 12

Warren Watkins slouched in his armchair, scrolling through his mobile phone. He finally had the house to himself now his wife was back at work after the Easter holidays. She was a teacher down at the local school, but he wasn't due back for another week; the perks of being a deputy head in a private school.

Their large newly-built four-bedroom detached house sat in the centre of an estate just outside of Chorley. Inside, the house was nearly as fresh as the day they bought it, beside a few touch-ups required here and there where they'd brushed past a wall while shuffling furniture around the place. Shelley kept it spotless, so much so that their family thought it was a show-home whenever they visited, querying if she had a cleaner. Warren didn't help out much; the one time he picked up a duster, he moaned that the cloth was cleaner after dusting and declared it a pointless activity, forgetting that Shelley had given the place a spring clean just the evening before, like she had every night after dinner. All the walls were white apart from a purple feature wall, oak furniture filled the room, and a glass coffee table took centre stage, hanging beneath a crystal chandelier.

Warren himself contrasted with his modern abode. He lounged in a pair of what he called *house-pants*, tarnished by a few holes, and they certainly hadn't seen the inside of a washing machine since his wife last sneaked them in when he was on the golf course with his buddies a week before. His stripy t-shirt barely covered the tyre sitting on his waistline. His greying hair was greasy and his jowls sprouted purple veins after years of drinking too much wine.

After scrolling the internet for hours, he flipped onto a private browsing option and tried to find something a little more entertaining, but he'd viewed the videos hundreds of times before and they just weren't doing it for him anymore. Instead, he opened an application, hidden from view under a password-protected screen from an oblivious Shelley. He typed in his username, *HungryNow1,* and scrolled through the hundreds of profiles which were in his area, swiping left for the twinks and right for anyone who looked older than twenty. He'd uploaded a ten-year-old photograph from a time when he'd been a little slimmer and his hair was a little darker; they couldn't say it wasn't him when he turned up even if he had aged.

The benefit of the swiping feature, rather than the ability to contact just anyone, meant he saved time as those in his remaining list were matches who had swiped favourably for him. He'd tried the other apps and was left disappointed after endless rejection. It was mid-day in the middle of the week so the active users were relatively few, however there were a few people, like him, off on holiday, but it was the students who he was really after. Shirtless males and the odd dick-pic gave him the appetite he craved. The rustling in his house-pants confirmed this.

He hadn't told his wife he was bisexual. Years of bullying at school and the constant use of the word *faggot* in their vocabulary meant he'd kept it to himself from almost everyone. He made the mistake of telling his mother once, who shunned him for years until he met Shelley.

One profile which recognised him as a match had the username of *Edward69.* He looked young. The site was only available to eighteen-year-olds and over, however anyone could lie when building their profile when it came to their date of birth; he'd done it himself but to achieve the opposite, to make himself appear younger. He looked up and noticed the blinds were open and hobbled over, hiding his bulge, to close them before taking a seat firmly back on his armchair, peacefully confident that he was out of view of any nosy neighbours.

'Hello,' he tapped.

'Hi, ASL?' Edward replied. His photograph was limited but he had blond hair, youthful blue eyes and not a glimmer of facial hair. *Oh good*, he thought, the old *Age, Sex, Location* question, something which he recognised as juvenile from the old days on *MSN Messenger.*

'I'm Pete.' Warren replied, hiding his real name. He wasn't going to risk bumping into this twink on the street and him calling his name in front of his wife. 'I'm thirty-five and living in Buckshaw Village. How about you?'

'I'm Edward. Eddie to my friends. I'm just in Chorley, near the big Tesco. I'm not gonna lie I'm a little younger than eighteen though, please don't report me.'

Warren's eyes widened and the line making up his smile crept up. The bulge in his pants grew.

'I won't say anything. How old are you?'

'I'm fourteen. I'm mature for my age though, I'm not like the other kids. I know what I'm doing.'

'Do you?' replied Warren with a winking emoji. He eagerly waited as he spotted the three bubbles floating as Edward furiously replied.

'Well no. I'm a virgin but still I've seen porn, I'm pretty sure I know what I'm doing.'

'Well it would be a great shame for you to have had all those online lessons and not to put all that you've learned to the test. What a waste that would be.'

'Sure would be,' Edward replied. 'Well maybe I could come to yours, I don't have a car though. Can you pick me up?'

Warren looked towards the coffee table which held the keys to his black Mercedes A-Class, sitting on the drive, before responding. 'Sure thing, Edward. Meet you in Tesco's car park?'

'Yes, by the charity bins.'

They agreed a time and Warren quickly ended the chat, running upstairs to shower. He placed some gel in his hair and spiked it up trying to reduce the years on his dishevelled mane. Shelley's moisturiser and concealer rested on the side; he applied a handful as if it would work miracles. When he approached his wardrobe, he found a Jack Jones t-shirt, which was trendy enough for him to appear a little younger, and pulled tightly a leather belt around his jeans, pushing in his gut as far as he could.

Once he was happy that he was somewhat of a shadow of his former self, he walked downstairs and peered over at the photograph of him and his wife on their wedding day, sighing that he was allowing himself to do this once again. He turned it face down onto the ledge so he couldn't have her joyful eyes appearing almost judging him through the picture as he considered his next act.

He drove down the motorway and into the town centre of Chorley. He spotted the Tesco's which they'd agreed to meet at; he knew it well, Shelley forced them to shop there on payday, stating that she was sick of the bargain supermarkets. The argument that the food was no different, that it was just cheaper, fell on deaf ears, but hey, anything to keep her away from Waitrose.

Pulling up in a space beside a large metal case with a cancer charity branding stamped onto the side, he hovered outside his car and lit up a cigarette as he waited. If he smoked, no one would consider it odd that a random man was hovering in the car park alone, especially none of his pupils who were no doubt shopping for new uniforms with their parents while they were in the last week of leave, ready for the new term the following week.

A Ford Fiesta pulled up beside his car and out stepped three, what he considered, thugs. The boys had shaved heads while the girl had pink hair and a lip-ring. They looked at him before turning to each other and nodding. They made their approach. He took out his cigarette as he prepared to speak to them. No doubt they were old pupils; too old for school now. He was used to walking down the high street and being thrown abuse by former students. They could finally get their own back, hurling derogatory names, knowing full well he could no longer punish them. As they got closer, he feared they were ready to beat him up, until he spotted something in one of the guy's hands.

A camera.

'Can I help you?' Warren asked, throwing his cigarette on the floor to free up his hands. The camera went up and began filming the lone man.

'Are you Pete?' asked the girl.

'No I'm Warren.' He coughed and brushed down his t-shirt as if he'd spilt something on it, avoiding eye contact with the film crew, holding his hand up towards his face.

'Well you're Pete online.'

The girl pulled out her phone and brought up a photograph of the image he'd uploaded to the dating app just an hour before.

'That's not me.' Warren gulped and shook his head, his face drained of colour.

'I think it is. You've been contacting young boys on an online app. You were here to meet a fourteen-year-old boy called Edward.'

'No that's not true, I've never even been on *BoysZone.*'

The girl smiled and turned to the camera. 'I didn't even mention the name of the app. Thank you very much, Warren! Or Pete, whichever your real name is.'

131

'Shit.' Warren fell down to his knees and buried his head in his hands. 'Is this my wife who put you up to this? Look whatever she paid you, I can pay you more not to tell her.'

'Warren, I don't think you realise how serious this is. We didn't even know you were married. We're The Predator Hunters. Ever heard of us? We're here to ensure you get charged for soliciting underage boys online.'

'I didn't know he was underage!' Warren pleaded.

'Didn't know? I've got the messages right here. He told you he was a fourteen-year-old virgin. And you must be, what fifty?'

'Forty-five,' Warren replied, his voice quivering.

'You said thirty-five in your message so I don't know what to believe.'

'I need to go.' He stood up and tried to get past the three who blocked his path.

'You can go.' The girl grabbed hold of his sleeve. 'But the police will be here in a minute. So you can either run away or we can make this much easier by standing here with us together and waiting for them.'

In the background, the other man who joined the trio, but wasn't carrying a camera, stepped away and was on the phone. Warren could hear the muffles of him updating the authorities of his crimes.

'Please, don't do this. I've never ever done anything like this before. I promise. It's the first time and I'll never do this again. I'm depressed. I was flattered. I just... I don't...'

'Oh save it, you fuckin' nonce. Save your *depression* and the *first time* bullshit. I've heard it all before. Isn't it funny how we always catch you fuckers on your first opportunity to rape a child? So unlucky for you scumbags.'

'I'm not this person, please have some mercy,' Warren protested. He fell back against the bins and sobbed into his knees.

Pulling into the car-park, a blue and white car with flashing lights silently rolled to a stop beside his Mercedes. The officers inside stepped out and approached them. The girl ran over to the cops and showed the messages which Warren had exchanged with the made-up *Edward.* They nodded and walked up to him.

'Will you come down to the station to answer a few questions?'

Warren gave a resigned nod and stepped back up, shaking as he followed them to their car, his head hanging above his chest.

'And that's a wrap!'

Chapter 13

In the industrial town of Bradford, a small corner shop sat on the end of a row of terrace houses. The convenience store was closed but above, the owners sat in the lounge with their son who had visited for dinner.

'Nice of you to visit for a change,' Aiza, Mohammed's mother, announced as she put down his plate. She wore a black cloak with her hair covered. The only skin visible was her face, exposing her big brown eyes. 'All of our neighbours boast that their sons come home every weekend. You go to the other side of the country. I swear you can't get away quickly enough from us.'

'You know that's not true.' He stood up and kissed his mum's cheek before returning to his seat. He'd dressed casually in jeans and a blue jumper for the family reunion. 'And I only moved to Preston. I'm hardly a million miles away. As for not visiting, I get here when I can, but my work keeps me busy.'

'Ah yes your work.' Asad joined the debate.

'Come on, Dad. You know what it's like. You worked every hour Allah sent us to keep that shop open. Here I am doing the same for my family.'

'I did that to keep you in school,' his father replied. He was dressed in a white shirt and black slacks; tartan slippers covered his feet. 'Your brother now runs the place. That empire could have been yours had you had more interest.'

'Two shops is hardly an empire, Dad, but I have no doubt you worked hard.'

'Show some bloody respect,' Asad replied.

'Sorry.' Mohammed bowed his head.

'So come on then, what are you working on at the moment?' Aiza feigned interest as she picked up some bread in the centre of the table and dunked it into her bowl.

'Well I'm defending a vigilante group called The Predator Hunters who have been accused of kidnapping a suspected paedophile.'

'I've heard of these groups,' Asad jumped in. 'That Stephen... what's his face. He goes round destroying mosques.'

'Well yes he does have some reservations about Muslim people, Dad, but I'm trying to change that mind-set.'

'Always defending those who accuse the Muslims aren't you, Mohammed?' Aiza said with an air of judgement.

'It's not that...' Mo replied.

'Before you were prosecuting those group of Muslim men from Rotherham, now you're representing the people who would rather we not be here.'

'I'd like to think I'm protecting the world against child abuse, Mum, but whatever.' He rolled his eyes and filled his mouth with chicken.

'I get comments at the mosque, you know?'

'Well I'd hope you would defend me,' Mohammed huffed. 'Why don't you tell them about all the good I'm doing in my practice?'

'You know we do, we just wish you made it easier on us. We love you, Mohammed, and we're so proud of what you've achieved. It's every mother's wish to see her son succeed like you have, particularly in such as an important field. I just wish I didn't have to defend you all the time.'

'And of course you're divorced,' Asad chimed in.

'Well that's hardly my fault. She left me for another man.'

'And we never see our grandchild anymore,' Aiza cried.

'I barely get to see her myself.' He folded his arms and grumbled under his breath.

'She jests,' Asad replied and gave his wife a wink. 'We know you work so hard and look after our grandchild when you do get to see her. We just wish we could see you both more.'

'Well I'll make a commitment to come round every two weeks, how about that?'

'Better than nothing I suppose.' Aiza raised her eyebrows before smiling at her son. 'We'll leave you alone now.'

They sat around a circular dining table in the centre of the living room. To their right, a dusty pastel green couch rested on a patterned orange carpet, which served as a time machine to the seventies. There was a red rug with gold patterns shipped over from the souks of Marrakech and the walls were covered in gold. Framed photographs of their children at their graduations filled all the surface space and one hung on the wall of the three of them at his ceremony, welcoming him into the law society. While to an outsider these dinners would appear hostile, Mohammed knew they were anything but. He was loved; his parents just acted up with their apparent misery, when in reality they couldn't be happier.

As he devoured the curry, which his mother had been stewing for hours, his phone pinged. He lifted it up and read over an email from the other partner in his firm. A link embedded in took him to a Facebook page, which he knew all so well.

'See, we can't even keep your attention while you're here,' Aiza groaned.

'It's work. Sorry. Oh bloody hell.'

'What is it, son?' Asad glanced up with a look of concern.

'It's the group I'm representing. I asked them to keep a low profile. They've just released another video of them catfishing another person. I could kill them.'

'Tell me again why you're representing these reprobates?'

'Listen, I'm the best person to represent them. These are people who would usually be thrown under the bus in a court of law because they're poor, have issues and don't help themselves at the best of times, especially when they get caught up with behaviour which can *appear* racist. However at the heart of it, they're good people who have taken a wrong direction in life, and despite the actions they've taken, which I agree might appear like right-wing hooliganism, when they're actually doing something right, we should be looking after them. And by having a person like me, a Muslim, representing them, it takes away the stigma that they're just racist thugs. The court will have to sit up, listen to what is being said and review the subject at hand, rather than any predetermined beliefs.'

'But do they deserve the defence?'

'*Everyone* deserves a defence, Dad. Besides, I think I'm doing more than just defending them. I'm changing their attitudes. They're damaged people who have prejudiced views based on people they've met... people who have done wrong to them. I took one of them to a mosque the other day and she really seemed to be opening up her mind to the fact that there are good Muslims and bad Muslims just like there are good and bad Christians, Jews and atheists.'

'You're a good boy, son.' Aiza rubbed her hand and they smiled at each other.

'We're very proud of you.'

The moment of comfort didn't last long. A moment later a text message came through from his ex. *I'm sorry, we're going away this weekend so we won't be bringing Sunita round anymore.'* He sighed, wondering when he'd next get to see his darling daughter.

Chapter 14

The Bolton Combined Court Centre stood like a castle fortress in a leafy suburb. Outside, Mohammed paced up and down on his phone, his skin turning a furious red. Three elderly ladies stood by the entrance with their picnics at the ready, waiting for the doors to open so they could fill up on their sandwiches and the latest gossip. They shook their heads at the suited-man in a beige long coat and a leather satchel, stropping past them, occasionally swearing.

'I just don't know what the hell you think you were doing,' Mohammed yelled down the phone.

'I'm sorry,' said Stephen on the other end of the line. 'We have to carry on our operation, otherwise kids get hurt.'

'I told you specifically to stay out of the media's eye with this type of attention at the moment while we have this case hanging over our heads. We need to ensure the safeguarding of all the people you are accusing of wrongdoing too, we can't end up in a second trial as, believe me, I won't be standing up for you for a second time.'

'Look, we did everything by the book this time. We called the police.'

'Yes but you also released it online, opening him up to significant risk, which is the exact point of the accuser in the case I'm trying to shut down for you today.'

The line went dead. Mohammed roared with fury and threw his phone into his satchel, slamming it down on the seat beneath a bus stop just steps from the court steps.

'Bad day?' a familiar voice called from behind. He turned around and found Rachel McCann smiling behind him. She stood out in the street in her unlined rust-shaded suit, white shirt and a matching leather bag.

'You shouldn't be listening to my personal conversations with my client.'

'It's hard not to when you're broadcasting it to the whole world.' She turned and nodded towards the ladies shaking their heads at him. 'Don't worry, you didn't reveal anything I didn't already know. I saw the video online this morning. I sure do hope nothing happens to that guy.'

'Well I'm sure you'll be ready to defend the pervert if anything does.'

'Shall we go in?' Rachel said with a forced smile.

The doors opened and they hovered in behind the hobbling ladies, desperately seeking a small gap for them to sneak past. They made their way to room 1B where inside a large mahogany table met them. Dusty white walls which needed a fresh lick of paint surrounded them. In the centre, a large crowned golden lion and a unicorn made up the Royal Coat of Arms. Across the centre, the words *Dieu et mon Droit* rested in the arms of the mythical creatures. To the right of the coat, the Bolton Crest stood proudly; red and black lions faced each other, above them an elephant stood with a castle on its back. Lancashire's famous red roses surrounded the crest.

The lawyers took their seats. A lady in a black cloak walked in. She had silver hair, glasses which hung on the edge of her nose, and a ferocious red lipstick had been applied to thicken up her thinning lips. She looked at the pair up and down and took a seat in a large leather desk chair at the end of the table. Before her, a pack was made up of the case and she browsed through her notes.

'Ms McCann, your client is suing Mr Iqbal's client for an alleged assault and kidnapping on her son which you believe led to his death last year. Have I got this right?'

'That's right, Your Honour. You see the defendants are a vigilante group set up to trap suspected predators. My client's son had autism and was simply trying to find friends...'

'I don't need to know the ins and outs of his potential guilt or innocence, Ms McCann, I just want to know the facts of the day.'

'Apologies, Your Honour.' Rachel cleared her throat and continued. 'However I think his autism is important here as they essentially kidnapped a vulnerable person and locked him in a garage. He was so upset and scared that when he finally escaped, he had no choice but to run into a road where he was mowed down by a driver. I have recently had his death of suicide overturned and the judge stated that there was no doubt that the circumstances he'd been put under led him to run out into the oncoming traffic.'

'OK and you're suing them for...' the magistrate enquired.

'The responsibility of his death. A bereavement award of twelve thousand pounds for the family plus the price of his funeral and any legal costs this case will entail. Mr Irvine, the victim, had no income, however the stress that this has caused to the claimant is by far beyond the value than what we are making a claim for.'

'Mr Iqbal?' She swivelled her seat in his direction.

'Your Honour, this case is a bitter campaign from the claimant who is upset that her son was caught trying to meet young girls online and his downfall was publicised on the internet. They are using this court to simply prove the young man's innocence. It is a vanity project and nothing more. I feel on this

141

basis that there is a better approach for Miss McCann, which is for her client to seek out other publicity for her son's story, such as a newspaper or a self-published book. For these reasons, we are offering half the money for an out-of-court settlement to avoid any further unnecessary hurt for either side of this lawsuit who would rather not relive the tragedy of that day.'

'This is not a vanity project,' Rachel burst in. 'We're ensuring that this does not happen again, and if this stops your client's group altogether then so be it. Innocent people are put in vulnerable positions and then kidnapped. But more than anything, this is to ensure that Karen Irvine can begin to rebuild her life with a small pot of money, which may give her some justice and peace of mind that others will not face the same ordeal.'

'I take it you're not willing to accept the settlement, Ms McCann?' The magistrate swivelled towards her left.

'No way, Your Honour. We're seeing this through to the end.'

'Mr Iqbal, any final words from you?'

'Yes, we'll be counter-suing for Mr Irvine's assault on our client, which we have evidence of on video camera. With the loss of earnings of a month's salary from his second job down at a local call centre, as well as the non-economic damages, the stress caused and the medical records showing long-term damage from the hammer being rammed into his skull, we'll equally be suing for the same amount as Ms McCann is seeking.'

'Very well. I've put in a court date of October 12th. I'll see you two then.'

The magistrate abruptly stood up and left the room without as much as a goodbye, leaving an awkward cloud hovering over the two lawyers who furiously packed their paperwork away back into their bags.

'How are you anyway?' Mohammed asked, lifting his head and smiling. 'It's been a long time.'

'I'm good, how are you?' Rachel smiled back, almost surprised by the welcome. She wasn't used to the friendly chit-chat at the end of a day in court.

'Very well, thank you. Even if my client is driving me mad.'

They laughed and paused, unsure of the boundaries.

'We should've known this would've happened someday. You're only down the road.' Mohammed shrugged.

'I know, I can't believe I haven't faced another Manchester Law Grad from our cohort during the time I've been in practice. I didn't realise it would be so awkward. In any other world, I'd be running over, giving you a huge hug and catching up on all the gossip after all this time.'

'No reason we can't still do that. We just need to avoid talking about the reason we're here today.'

'Very true. There's a café around the corner, why don't we go there and catch up?'

They made their way to a Costa, just a few feet from the court. Inside the scent of cinnamon and coffee beans filled the space, as did the lone writers who furiously typed on their laptops, staring out of the window for inspiration.

'So how is Matilda?' Mohamed began and he sipped his latte.

'My God, you remembered?' Rachel laughed as she stirred her tea.

'Of course, who couldn't remember her? You brought her in to one of your presentation assignments once when you

143

couldn't find someone to look after her. She cried all the way through.'

'And I remember you taking her outside for me so I could focus on my assignment. I got a first for that, so thank you.'

'I had younger siblings, I was used to kids.'

'And how about you now? Do you have a family?'

'In a way.' Mohammed cleared his throat and took out a photograph from his wallet. 'I'm separated. I have a little girl, a bit younger than Matilda. I got married soon after graduating. I was too young and there were family pressures. It didn't work out anyway. Her name is Sunita, but we call her Sunny. I don't see her quite as much as I'd like to, but we talk on the phone every day.'

'She's beautiful,' Rachel said as she looked over the photograph. She followed up with the picture on her phone of Matilda and passed it to him.

'She's a handful. As you probably know full well.'

'Tell me about it, Matilda is so frustrating at the moment. Causing issues at school. At least I have Carl in my life now. He's a massive help, he's a police officer and works nights so he can support me in the day when I'm here doing this.'

Mohammed raised his head and mouthed an *oh,* which Rachel thought she'd spotted a tremor of disappointment within. She tilted her head and moved the conversation on.

'How about you, have you managed to meet anyone else?'

'No, my work keeps me busy. No time for anything else. Maybe one day.'

'I'll keep my fingers crossed for you. Talking of responsibilities, I better go write up my paperwork and let Karen know what's happening. I think you should probably do the same with your reprobates.'

'Careful now, I could sue you for slander.'

'Oh I'm scared.' Rachel winked, embraced her old friend, and left. As she departed, she called Karen and updated her on the case. 'We're on.'

Chapter 15

The cafetière had settled, the brown slush transformed into a silky black liquid. Rachel pushed down on the pump, filtering the granules to the bottom, and poured the fresh coffee into a mug, stamped with '*my daughter's a lawyer but we don't hold that against* her' on the side, a joke gift from her father when he was still around.

She perched on one of the couches and picked up a magazine, which she'd been asked to contribute to a couple of weeks previously. The article focused on successful independent lawyers who'd moved away from *the big four* and now offered a more personalised service to local clients. Rachel perfectly fit the bill having left a corporate giant to set up on her own, but she remained sketchy around the details of her success. Instead the articled focused on the right of every individual to have a defence, regardless of what they had, or hadn't done. She put forward Charlie's story, of an innocent man who had been accused of the worst of crimes and how without lawyers, his legacy would remain tarnished. In the centre of the article a large photograph of her, suited and booted, in front of the building which she now spent her weekdays, and the occasional weekend when she needed some time to herself to fuel her case.

Matilda had returned to school and the feedback from her teachers was that she had settled. A relief for Rachel, who had skipped enough client time to give her daughter another dressing down. At first she considered herself fortunate that she was self-employed. While they were flexible at her previous firm, there was no way she'd have been able to take herself away as much as she had now, especially for her daughter's unruly behaviour. Not when Corporate Casandra across the way was able to turn up every day straight from the children's hospital where little Bella was receiving chemo. That was the corporate world of law, you either gave it all, or you didn't. There was no in-between. However in some ways she longed to be back there. Being self-employed required an element of drive, and her daughter's behaviour gave her excuses to lose focus on her career.

Thankfully Carl had taken a front seat on the parenting wagon. She didn't know what she'd have done without him. He picked her up from school, looked after her on a weekend when Rachel needed to focus on her impending trial, and when Mattie was suspended, he'd stepped up. And her daughter really warmed to him too. He was quickly becoming the father she never had. And his presence appeared to be calming. Since those few days she had at home with him, she acted up less. Maybe this was what she'd needed her whole life; some male dominance. She heckled herself as she considered the latter, the feminist who had to admit she needed a man in her life. *'Oh, Rachel.'*

The phone rang; it was Karen, once again in a panic.

'Someone's here. A man. He's asking for Charlie's computer.'

'That's fine, Karen,' Rachel calmly explained. 'He's been sent by the judge. We need an independent review of Charlie's computer.'

'But why?'

'Well we're making a case that The Predator Hunters kidnapped and attacked an innocent man. They're claiming they performed a citizen's arrest on a paedophile, therefore Charlie's profile is key to this case. They'll be checking his search history and his chat room conversations to build up his character, to show if Charlie's actions that day were the result of his innocence or whether he genuinely wanted to meet underage girls.'

Karen paused before asking the dreaded question. 'What if they find something?'

Rachel took a deep breath, wondering herself how she would react. She hadn't really considered it. She'd focused so much of her time focusing on proving Charlie's innocence, she hadn't even thought about the alternative result. Charlie wasn't here to confirm either way. Nor was he here to hide his computer or attempt to delete any evidence, which would have proven The Predator Hunters right. The entire case had been riding on his mother's word, and what parent didn't believe wholeheartedly that their child was innocent?

'Karen, if you have any doubts, you need to let me know now.'

'No!' Karen shrieked. 'No, it's just, well you just never know. I need to prepare myself for the worst.' She cleared her throat. Rachel could hear the guilt in her voice as she dared consider that her son wasn't entirely innocent.

'If they find anything we will review what it is. We still have the case that Charlie had a disability. He didn't think like others. In his head he was a child. At the end of the day the vigilantes would still be responsible for your son's death. They still kidnapped him and manhandled him. You can't do that to anyone, regardless of what they've done. But it would be up to you, Karen, if you wanted to carry on, as from the beginning this wasn't about suing them, it was about getting Charlie's name cleared.'

'That's still the case. I know he's innocent.'

'Then we don't have anything to worry about.'

The shattering of glass shook the lawyer, who dropped her phone and turned around. A stone rumbled across the ground, wrapped in an elastic band with a note enclosed. Rachel grabbed her chest and screamed. In the distance she could hear the muffled cries of her name. She picked up her phone and a panicked Karen asked if everything was OK.

'I'm alright. I've got to go, Karen, I'll speak to you later.'

She hung up and walked over to the rocky missile which had invaded her office. Through the broken glass, there was no one to be seen. Unwrapping the note, she ironed out the crumpled paper to unveil a message. At first she thought it must have been a mistake, but she soon discovered that she was the intended receiver of this unwanted delivery.

PAEDO DEFENDER.

Dropping the stone on the floor, she hobbled over to the couch, losing her balance en-route. Nausea consumed her as she held her head in her moist hands. A knock on the door gave her a second fright. She hovered over, cautiously, wondering if the sender of her unwanted delivery had returned. Behind it was Graham Watts, the accountant from upstairs. He stood tall in a grey suit with a pocket watch hanging from his breast pocket. A balding man with a spy glass, he leaned over her and peered into her office.

'Is everything alright in here? I heard some commotion.'

'Oh, Graham, thank you for coming. I've just had someone pelt a rock through my window with a less than savoury message strapped to it.' She lifted the paper up to show him and his bushy black eyebrows bounced as he took in the message. 'It's regarding a client I'm representing at the moment. His story isn't very popular with the locals to say the least.'

'How did they know where to find you?'

'Well if it's the people we're suing then they'll have my office details anyway from the exchanges we've had. But if it's anyone else, they may have seen an article I published in a law journal and this has received some significant press.'

'Sometimes I'm glad I'm an accountant. It's the dullest job in the world but no one wants to throw rocks through my window. Shall I call the police?'

The authorities arrived less than an hour later. They took a full statement, looked around to see if there was any CCTV (there wasn't), and gave her a reference number for the insurance company. *There goes the no-claims.* They advised that she worked from home over the following days, giving any vigilantes a wide berth. While they had her office address from numerous sources (they only had to look on Google), her home address remained private.

After she'd cleared up the remaining glass, Carl drove over and nailed in a sheet of chipboard. It wasn't ideal but she had the burglar alarm if anyone managed to break in. Once they were confident that the office was secure, they rode home together. Along the drive, she wept as the shock caught up with her.

'I sometimes have to ask myself if it's really worth it.'

'You're doing a good thing, Rachel, just keep focusing on that. You'll look back one day and see what great work you've done.'

She smiled, leaned over and kissed his cheek. He turned and winked at her before returning his focus to the traffic.

'I know it's not the best time to tell you but when I picked up Matilda from school a teacher called me over. She'd been quite disruptive in class. She stormed out into the corridor after her teacher asked her to read a chapter of *Charlotte's Web* out loud to the class. They were taking it in turns to read a passage apparently and everyone obliged except for Matilda. '

'I can't believe this. She's in more trouble?' She threw her head back onto the rest and closed her eyes, wincing through the catalogue of chaos which her life had thrust upon her.

'She's not been excluded but she has got detention, which is where she is now. The teacher's going to drop her off later when she's finished her lines.'

'I'm going to kill her.'

'Look, just leave her to me. You've got enough going on. Should I have told you?'

'Yes, you should've told me. Discipline isn't your job, Carl. I'll speak to her later when she gets home.'

Matilda arrived home shortly after they did. Rachel apologised to the teacher and waved her off before glaring at her daughter with severe frustration.

'I've got enough going on without you coming along and making it more disruptive. What's wrong with you?'

Matilda stood there in her uniform, looking down at the floor, hanging her head in shame.

'I'm so ashamed of you. You literally have to show up and shut up and you can't even do that. What is wrong with you? I'm trying to build this life for you and you go and do this. You're so ungrateful.'

'A life I don't want,' Matilda screamed back.

'Excuse me? You have a nice house and a nice school. You want for nothing.'

'I want your time, Mum! You're always working. You always leave me here with Carl. While you're out there defending paedos.'

Rachel gasped and did a double-take at her daughter.

'Where did you hear that?'

'At school. All the kids are saying it. Emma's mum said you were and now they all think my mum's a paedo.'

'Do you even know what that means?''

'It's a child-catcher like off *Chitty Chitty Bang Bang.*'

Rachel nodded her head; she couldn't disagree with that.

'What Mummy does is very complex....'

'Oh just fuck off.'

Matilda flew through the air and landed on the ground. Her head bounced off the concrete floor. It all happened in slow motion. Rachel stood beside her, aghast at what had just happened to her daughter. She looked up and found Carl standing at the entrance of the house, appearing equally horrified. All sound appeared to drown out for just a few seconds, before Matilda's cries burst the rhythm of her heart.

A warm stinging radiated from Rachel's palm. She looked down and it was red. To the right of Matilda's face, her chin was red, in the shape of a hand mark.

'Oh God, what have I done?' Rachel whispered, her bottom lip trembling.

Carl rushed over and picked Matilda off the floor. 'Are you alright, Mattie?'

She sobbed and he held her in his arms, throwing a piercing disapproving look towards her mother.

'I'm so sorry.' Rachel moved towards her little girl, but Carl shook his head and held out his palm.

'Stay there,' he whispered.

He carried Matilda inside, while Rachel leaned on the bonnet of her car, shaking and crying. She tried to calculate everything that had happened but it was all over so quickly. Taking a deep breath, she neatened up her hair and returned to the kitchen.

'Where is she?' She glanced around but only Carl was in the lounge.

'She's gone to her room to lie down. I should really report this, you know?'

She shot a look at his police uniform hanging off a chair in the kitchen, and sighed. Terror spread across her face and her eyes welled up. 'Please, Carl, I know you have certain obligations with your job. But I just can't face this right now, I'm so sorry. I've just had so much on.'

'I won't. But seriously, that's not on.'

'I won't ever do it again. She just… I just…'

'Hey, I understand.' He wrapped his arms around her and kissed her on her forehead. 'You've had a stressful day, you won't be the first or last parent to have done this. You lost your shit. We all do it. My parents used to hit me all the time.'

'Yes but we've moved on and I've never raised her like this. What sort of message is this if I can't even teach my daughter that violence doesn't sort anything? No wonder she's been hitting other kids when her mother acts in the same way.'

'You've got so much on. Why don't you have a night to yourself? There's a bottle of wine in the fridge. I could take Matilda to mine. She has her own room and I have the games console, which she can play on… it might give you both a break from each other.'

'She said before that she doesn't see me enough, surely I should be with her?'

'Do you think she wants to be near you right now? I'll take her home, give you two some space. By tomorrow it'll all be forgotten.'

'Maybe you have a point...' Rachel reluctantly admitted.

Half an hour later, Matilda came down with her bag packed. She looked accusingly at her mother, sitting in an armchair beside her grandma, with Peppa on her lap. Rachel was half way through a bottle of Pinot.

'I am sorry, Mattie. I love you.'

Mattie didn't reply. Instead she nodded at Carl, who opened the door. And she left. Carl turned around and forced a half-smile towards his girlfriend. 'She'll be OK.'

The bottle of wine didn't last long. It was getting late and Rachel's head was pounding. She considered everything that had happened over the past few hours and wondered what was in store for her before the end of the trial. She threw the empty bottle in the recycling bin and helped her mum up to her bed, before falling on her own shortly after. She placed a pillow over her eyes and wept, rolling from side to side. In the corner of the room, Peppa whimpered with concern for her owner's welfare. She wrapped her arms around her puppy and had to admit, she was glad of her company.

She must have cried herself to sleep as it was nearly three in the morning when the smell of smoke woke her up. The landing light had been left on and she squinted to see through the smoke that had consumed her house. An alarm rang and she jumped out of bed, running downstairs towards to the front door where the trail of smoke had led her. The mat lying beneath the

155

letterbox had a rag on it. The smell of petrol was nauseating. The flames blocked the entrance.

She looked around for Peppa. In the corner a white, brown and black lump was curled up in the corner. Rachel ran over and shook her fur but she didn't move.

Peppa was dead.

Chapter 16

Rachel's first suspect was her mother. It wouldn't be the first time she'd nearly burnt the house down. But as she distinguished the flames, the hefty whiff of petrol radiated from a rag she didn't recognise. This couldn't be her mother. Upstairs, Dorothy was soundly asleep, while Rachel was wafting the smoke from the lounge, opening the door to release the fumes.

The moon poured light down onto the bleak night, illuminating a message spray-painted onto her door in thick red letters. **PAEDO.** She gasped and stood back. It definitely wasn't her mother. This was a targeted attack on her for the work she was doing. First the office, now her home. It was becoming personal. But how did they get her address? She could have been followed. But this was terrifying. *Thank God Matilda is at Carl's,* she mused.

She called Carl, and despite her protests, he sped round to the house with Matilda in tow. Despite their bust-up a day earlier, Mattie, dressed in her pink *Disney's Frozen* pyjamas, ran to her mother and wrapped her arms around her, with tears in her eyes.

'Mummy, why did this happen?'

'I don't know,' Rachel replied. She tried to block the message, stamped on her door, from view of her only daughter. She didn't want to have to begin to explain what that message meant, or why it was directed at their house. Carl placed his arms around them both and locked into a group hug, kissing his girlfriend's forehead.

'I need to tell you something, my love.' Rachel grabbed her daughter and held her close. 'I'm so sorry but Peppa died.'

Matilda sobbed into her mother's arms. Carl walked in with a glass of sherry to calm Rachel's nerves. He took Matilda in his arms and walked away, leaving Rachel alone wrapped in a thin mustard blanket.

The police tried to support her but they had little to go on. They couldn't find any tire tracks or markings from the soles of shoes. As for the red rag, it was one of many stacked high at a local discount supermarket and would've had hundreds of customers picking up the item in bulk, especially as it had been on sale that weekend for less than fifty pence for a pack of five. They said they'd enquire around some local garages to determine if anyone had bought petrol in a jerry can, but they didn't hold out much hope in their investigations.

'I don't understand why Peppa didn't call. She barks at the subtlest of noises,' Rachel asked the policeman who furiously wrote down notes in their lounge.

'We found remnants of mincemeat by the door. It is possible that if the arsonists knew you had a dog, they would have poisoned it to ensure it didn't wake you with its barking. We see it frequently with burglaries unfortunately.'

'How do I stop this from happening again?'

'Invest in CCTV is my advice,' said the constable.

'I'll be on it tomorrow,' Carl assured.

They spent the night in the safety of Carl's house, which for the second time had been their saviour from smoke inhalation. The following morning, Rachel returned to the house early to begin scrubbing the vile message off her front door. By lunchtime, she'd at least managed to hide the original message with some gloss which she found in the garage; no doubt left there by her father before he passed away. He was always handy with that sort of thing. She couldn't comprehend what half of the concoctions were in the workshop at the back of the room. Old coffee jars, emptied and filled with multi-coloured spirits and oils, lined the walls on his makeshift shelving. Paintbrushes dried with old paint scattered across the worktops. She rarely came in, but if there something she was looking for, whether it be paint to touch up where Matilda had scuffed the walls, or a nail to hang a picture on the wall, it was there.

Returning to her office in Horwich was another reminder of the public's reception. A team of window-fitters arrived to replace the glass which her enemy had smashed. She let the workmen in and left them to fit it while she examined the review of Charlie Irvine's computer. The Digital Forensic Investigator had determined that Charlie had not demonstrated the behaviours typical of a paedophile. There was no evidence of any access to the dark web, which would require special configurations to his devices to access. The dark net would allow anyone searching to gain access to more sinister graphics, which would usually be inaccessible through standard search engines, allowing the user to source and share illegal materials, whilst keeping their anonymity.

Charlie had used the computer to access porn, but from what the investigator could see it was legal with the usual interests that he'd expect from a nineteen-year-old man. There was one image where the investigator couldn't determine the age of the people within it; they appeared younger than the other models. However he was happy that the rest of his search history carried a common adult theme, typical of a teenager who had a healthy interest in activities which were safe and legal.

The investigator found that Charlie had predominantly spent his time on chat rooms, in which he'd only been able to establish his username; *CharlieIRV2001*. He'd made an access to information request to the host of the chat rooms for Charlie's chat history on *TeenTalk*, to which they had up to forty days to respond. But having completed an initial profile of Charlie's online activity, he was happy to advise that Charlie was a responsible adult without any unhealthy interests in children.

Rachel wiped her forehead. She'd forgotten all about the report as the rest of her world took over. But seeing the brown envelope stamped with the investigator-s logo on the top right-hand corner, her stomach grumbled as she considered the *what-ifs* and the doubt that even his own mother had shown a shimmer of. Now she could relax. Karen had asked for the report to be sent to her, but Rachel instead sent her a text message to tell her everything was fine. Charlie, if nothing else, deserved a little dignity in his death without his mother reviewing his internet search history in such detail, listed in Appendix B at the back of the report.

The window-fitter nodded his head to confirm his work was done and left her with a hefty invoice, which she hoped the insurance would cover. She would put that on hold for another day. Instead she returned home to find Carl with a team of electricians in her house.

'What's going on?' Rachel asked Carl as she walked through the door. Her shoulders sank as she realised her hope of a quiet couple of hours alone had gone out of the window. The people surrounding her, dressed in blue overalls, white hard-hats and protective glasses, were halfway up ladders and drilling into her walls.

'We're installing CCTV. This is the best in the business. I got a recommendation through a contact at work. With these bad boys nobody will mess with us again.' He smiled and kissed her cheek. Rachel glanced around with a look of discomfort as she considered the privacy she'd given up for the sake of her safety.

'And this is inside the house?' asked Rachel.

'As well as out. Nobody will be able to make a move in here without us knowing about it.'

160

One of the electricians came downstairs and took a sip of his cuppa before returning to her bedroom.

'And upstairs too?' Her jaw dropped and she wiped the perspiration from her forehead.

'Yes absolutely. In all the bedrooms and living spaces. It'll be a lifesaver for your mum too. You can be out and about and check she's OK on her own at home. Or you can check up on Matilda and make sure she's doing her homework.'

'I don't know how I feel about this, Carl.'

'Look trust me, love,' he said, interrupting her hesitation. 'I'm a policeman, believe me, I see this equipment in motion all the time. It's going to keep you safe. Nobody will dare come near us with all this equipment and if they do, you'll have them bang to rights.'

'But who will have access to this footage?'

'Just you,' Carl assured her. He asked for her phone and she obliged. He downloaded an app and put in the password, printed on a document enclosed with the information booklet. 'You can see everything right from your mobile phone and the footage will only be available to people who you decide to share it with. You can email footage to the police if you needed to. But if you don't, you'll be comforted in knowing everything that happens under your roof.'

On her screen she could see the hallway, which she now stood within, and the back of her own head. Carl turned her around and waved towards the camera, grinning as he watched himself on the phone.

'And then if you click this…' he said as he tapped on her screen.

The image changed to Matilda's room, where she was sitting on her bed playing with her phone.

'Hey! Matilda!' Rachel shouted up the stairs. 'Homework! Now!' On the screen, she jumped off the bed and returned to her desk. Rachel and Carl turned to each other and laughed.

'You see this is a great piece of technology!'

'You're right. Thank you.' She kissed him on the lips and made her way to the kitchen, where she sat down at the dining table and sighed, considering all that had happened in the last couple of days. 'How is Matilda?'

'She's fine. Kids are resilient to these things. She's a strong girl.'

'I just can't believe I messed everything up last night.'

'You didn't.' Carl sat next to her and rubbed her arm. 'You're stressed. We all are. There's so much going on. You couldn't help it.'

'But I should be able to. My little girl needs me more than ever. I just wish she would settle down at school. Although I'm sure everything I've put her through isn't helping.'

'I've been thinking about that,' Carl replied and Rachel peered up at him with interest. 'I was reading online about parenting. Not that you need any advice, you could write the textbook, I'm sure…'

'Go on.' Rachel rolled her eyes.

'Well it was talking about kids who are being difficult and it did mention disruption at home, which I suppose she's had plenty of recently.'

'Don't remind me. *Bad Mother Award* goes to me!'

'Don't say that. Well it was saying that we should incentivise good behaviour. So we should meet up with the school every couple of weeks and if she gets a glowing report, we give her a treat. In one-parent families where a new partner has entered the family, this should come from the new entity to establish trust and a positive connection to the new partner.'

'What are you thinking?'

'Well, why don't we, say, on her next parents' evening which is in a few weeks, if she's behaving, we take her to Alton Towers for the weekend. The full shebang, the themed hotel, *Splashland* and *Nemesis*.'

'I don't know about *Nemesis* but I like your thinking.'

'OK, OK, then *The Smiler*?'

Rachel laughed and shoved him away.

'I'm going to be so busy though around then. I'll have the court case. I don't want to promise something I can't deliver.'

Carl sighed, his face screaming disappointment.

'Well, you could take her,' she proposed. 'She really likes you and you're good with her. If you don't mind that is…'

'I'd love to, but you should really be there.'

'I'm the last person she wants there, it's not cool to hang out with your mum. She should go and you should be the one to take her. It was your brilliant idea and as you say, the research even suggests it. It should come from the *'new entity.'* I'll happily cover the costs.'

'Don't be silly.' Carl waved his hand. 'It's nothing and I love theme parks.'

'Then it's sorted then,' Rachel said. 'Are you going to tell her about our plan or should I?'

163

'Given you deserve the opportunity to earn some brownie points from her, maybe you go.'

Chapter 17

'All rise.'

The delegates rose and stared towards a wooden door, which opened. Out walked a fifty-something man, slim with white eyebrows. On his head he wore a white long wig and he was wrapped in a red gown.

'Will the defendant stand?'

Warren Watkins stood up and glanced over those who had taken the opportunity to peek into the fate of his future. He was dressed in one of his finer suits, ill-fitting now he'd lost some weight after the tremendous stress he'd endured in the previous months. Most of the faces were strangers; pensioners who filled their days attending funerals and court cases of those they never knew, a representative from a children's charity, and of course the press, who would no doubt ensure he was plastered all over social media before he'd have the chance to leave the building, whether that be in a taxi or a prison van.

There were a couple of faces he did know. His mother of course, dressed all in black as if she was attending a funeral; she appeared frailer by the day. This had really damaged her. The wife, or ex-wife as she would soon be once the divorce was sorted. He didn't blame Shelley, he'd put her through hell, but he questioned the vow of *'for better or worse'* as he stood alone on the worst day of his life. She had dark black hair and wore a white shirt and black skirt like she was Wednesday Adams. He understood her humiliation. Not only was she was married to a man who apparently liked children, but he was now publicised as gay too. He wondered which of those headlines frustrated her more. There were a few other dotted faces he recognised from his neighbourhood too; *nosey bastards.* They were taking neighbourhood watch to the next level.

And then he spotted Alison. The girl he was actually talking to online when he thought he was talking to a young teenage boy named Edward. She turned up in the Tesco car-park, camera crew in tow, exposed his intensions and rang the police. It was so humiliating. He didn't run. He sat by and waited for the police. But he knew his life was over the minute she revealed who she was. In the station, he replied to all questions with a '*no comment*' and hired the best lawyer he could afford; a dwindling amount as his wife continued to freeze his assets until the paperwork was complete. Regardless of the outcome, he'd never have the life he had; the house would have to be sold and his car would be taken away. And his remaining working years, if he could indeed get a job, would be paying off Shelley for whatever she was entitled to. Half of his wage and his pension.

The station had initially released him on bail, with the condition that he'd stay away from children. He'd broken that condition at a family birthday party for his cousin's daughter's thirteenth. They didn't know and he didn't plan to tell them. But everyone would know now.

When he got home from the station on that dreadful day, his wife was already waiting for him. She'd seen the footage online. She was horribly embarrassed. She threw him out and he moved in with his mother. Even she'd heard about the video and she didn't even have Wi-Fi. His brother had told her. He blew a raspberry as he considered his rich, perfect, could-do-no-wrong brother. Oh the shame of a deputy head who had all-year-round access to children, now caught up in a child abuse scandal. Everyone had lapped it up.

His employer wasn't showing any sympathy. They couldn't afford to have the case hanging over them, so they made a mutual agreement to part ways, with a brown envelope in hand.

The cheque inside barely covered the first consultation with his solicitor.

And since then it had all just been a waiting game, interrupted by investigators and digital forensics. He took to online shopping as he became entrapped within the house. The neighbours made sure he wasn't welcome. They had to board up the letter box after a burning rag was posted through the door. Now they waited by the window for the postman and took it off him personally, closing the door quickly enough so that the neighbourhood kids on their bikes couldn't shout *'paedo'* across the street.

He looked towards Alison and glared. She'd set him up. *Bitch.* She'd been a witness in the trial and stayed to watch the rest of it. She'd stood up and talked about how The Predator Hunters operation worked, discussed the conversations they'd had online, how Warren had pretended to be called Pete online and sent younger photographs of himself to entice a young boy to his lair. Even she'd made the effort today; dressed in a hand-me-down shirt and trousers. A far cry from the tracksuit he'd previously seen her in, but her pink hair continued to show her true colours.

His bitter ex-wife stood up and talked about how she'd had her suspicions. She hadn't, but she'd do anything to destroy him. Ridiculous really, as she'd get a lot more money from him if he walked free, but what's money worth when you can seriously hammer a nail in the coffin?

For the defence, his solicitor had argued that this was a case of entrapment. That no illegal images had been found on any of his devices. That he hadn't actually broken the law as there was no evidence that he'd inappropriately touched a child, and the person he was talking to that day was in fact an adult. As for his intentions, he'd been through some serious stress, having realised that his marriage was on the rocks and how he'd had a difficult time trying to accept his sexuality. He had come to the realisation that he was gay and he had acted inappropriately, yes, but not illegally. He was desperate, and this was the one person who had shown him any attention on the dating app.

'Warren would do anything to be loved, to be touched, by practically anyone, having had the frosty distance of his wife in the bedroom for years. Even his annual birthday bash had been replaced by a wrapped pair of socks. It was a moment of weakness in a bleak time of his life. And had he seen a young boy appear at that Tesco car park, instead of Alison, he was sure to have seen sense and gone home.'

There were no character witnesses on his side. His friends and family members distanced themselves from him. His only support was his mother, which his lawyer agreed wouldn't be a valuable statement as what mother doesn't stand by her son?

'Will the jury please stand,' the judge ordered.

Twelve people stood up and turned towards to the judge.

'Have you reached a verdict on which you all agree?'

'We have, Your Honour,' responded the head juror, a young man dressed in a shirt and jeans, who looked barely out of college. Warren considered that he didn't look fit to judge a talent contest, never mind his future. But that was democracy, he supposed.

'And do you find the defendant guilty, or not guilty?'

There was a gap. A moment of silence. The spectators sat on the edge of their seats, some holding hands with their loved ones. Warren's mother was shaking. His ex-wife was praying. Alison bit her thumb. Warren's bottom lip trembled. He grew a pale white and his heart thudded.

'Not guilty.'

A gasp echoed across the court. Warren fell back onto his seat and held his head in his hands, panting as he took in the verdict. His mother cried. The ex-wife shook her head and stormed out of the room, her designer heels stomping across the wooden floor. And Alison? She shook, her face grew red and she stood up, pointing at the man in the defendant's box.

'He's a fuckin' paedophile!'

'Silence!' shouted the judge.

'He's a nonce! You can't let him free! How could you?'

'If you don't be quiet, I'll hold you in contempt.'

Alison gulped and returned to her seat, shooting a glare at the soon-to-be-free man. She held two fingers together and glided them across her neck as she intently stared at him. He swallowed and turned away.

'Mr Watkins.' The judge turned to the defendant. 'You have been found not guilty of the accusations before you. It is quite clear that this court has seen a weak and vulnerable man be entrapped by a vigilante group. There is a reason we leave these matters to the police and I believe this is one of them. I don't condone your intentions of that day, but we can clearly see that this was not in your nature and that you acted completely out of character. I believe the loss of your marriage, your job and your reputation is punishment enough for this silly behaviour which you've undertaken online. However we've ruled you an innocent man, so you're free to go.'

Warren walked over to his lawyer and shook his hand, before turning to his mother and embracing her. As he walked out of court, he turned to the cameras who were eagerly waiting for a statement.

'The jury have found me not guilty today. This has been the worst few months of my life. The Predator Hunters group
170

have destroyed innocent lives time and time again. This has been made more apparent by another concurrent court case whereby another innocent life has been destroyed by their actions. I want to call an end to these harmful groups and ask the government to invest more in our police instead to ensure the safety of our families and our children. Thank you.'

Alison watched from across the road. Tears streamed out of her eyes as she witnessed another vile predator get away with his crimes. She'd done all the right things. She took her lawyer's advice and got the police involved. Instead, she wished she'd allowed the public to do its worst. Warren took a last look at her as he climbed into his taxi. He squinted as he tried to make out her whispered words. 'This isn't over.'

Chapter 18

As a man of Pakistani descent living in the UK, Mo had felt like he didn't belong plenty of times in his life. When he attended a Christian primary school, he was the only person of colour in a class of twenty. Things improved in high school when there were two others in his year and they naturally formed a friendship, even though he didn't particularly like either of them. And when he studied law, he again felt like an outsider, struggling to fit in amongst the white middle-class men who made up his class. The only person within that class who made him feel included was Rachel McCann.

'You should have run the bloody shop,' his father once groaned. 'You're not a minority in there.'

But now as he climbed the stairs of a tower block in Chorley, he felt like an outcast once again. This time though, it wasn't for the colour of his skin. There were plenty of people who looked like him on each passing floor. Poverty certainly did not discriminate. He was, however, the only one in a suit.

The double glances as he passed the gangs of pot-smoking teenagers in the corridors did not put him at ease. He hid his iPhone and was grateful he'd left his laptop at home. The three-hundred-pound brown leather pouch he now carried was the most expensive thing they could take, not that they'd have much use for it, or consider it of any value.

He knocked on the door of his client and Simon answered. He stood aside to allow the lawyer to enter. Behind, Stephen was smoking a spliff and playing on his game console.

'The governor!' Stephen jested and patted a dusty deck-chair, which Mo took as a seat upon.

'No Alison with you today?' He glanced around and noticed her absence.

'Nah, she's taking a break. I think it's all got a bit much for her. We haven't heard from her since the Warren Watkins case.'

'Ah yes, I did read about that. It was the last thing we needed.'

'He was a nonce though,' Simon interrupted.

'I'm sure he was.' Mo feigned interest.

'So what brings you here?' Stephen put down his control and stubbed out his cigarette.

'Well the forensic investigator who reviewed Charlie's computer has now completed his report. As we know he didn't find anything conclusive or state that there were any trends to suggest Charlie had an unhealthy interest in children. However there is this one image in question in which he said he couldn't categorically determine the age of the models. I'm going to ensure we get our hands on the image and use it.'

'Alrighty, what else have we got?' Stephen replied with an air of disappointment.

'We've got the conversations from the chat room you approached Charlie on. For the most part, he was having innocent conversations. And for nearly all of them, he was listing his favourite films, foods and television shows. Quite typical with his condition, if I'm being honest. And there was no discrimination by age or gender. He'd talk to anyone. Most teenage girls gave him a wide berth or blocked him quite quickly as they thought he was even younger than they were, because of the way his brain worked.'

'So we've got fuck all then,' Simon grunted.

'Well there's one person who we are sure he met. Multiple times in fact. She's a thirteen-year-old girl called Becky. She's based in Westhoughton, just a short ride away from Charlie's home. I've managed to track down her details and I think if we get her, we've got him. And this all goes away.'

'The Irvines could still sue us though?'

'Yes, technically, but would you want to fight in court knowing we're about to reveal your son's a sexual deviant? That's the whole point of this case. More so than the money.'

'I trust in you,' Stephen nodded. Simon, bored with the lack of development, returned to his desktop computer in the corner.

'I better go, I just wanted to give you an update. Keep out of trouble, you two, won't you.' He nodded towards the computer. 'Especially on that thing. I don't want to see you both back on social media, or having us destroyed in court again without me being there!'

'You're the boss.'

Mo left and Stephen returned to his console. He heard the tapping of his colleague's keyboard in the corner.

'What did he just tell you?' Stephen lectured him like a disapproving parent.

'Yeah, yeah. Meanwhile kids are out there being attacked because the police are too damn skint to do owt.'

'Well just be careful. He's a good guy, this Mo. We just need to stand by what he says.'

'I know, I know. First time I've heard you defending a Paki, Steve. That better stop when this is all over. Besides I think you wanna see this.'

174

'What's this?' Stephen threw down his controller and walked over to the computer. He glanced over the chat conversation. 'So what? Another nonce. I told you, we gotta be careful. Keep him warm until after the trial.'

'No, wait,' Simon replied. He opened up an image file, sent through the chat room from the correspondent. 'Look who it is.'

'No fuckin' way.'

Chapter 19

Butterflies danced in Rachel's belly. She was in court for the first time on her own, preparing to win a case for her client. She'd been in court plenty of times before, but she'd always had a team around her. It was never *her* client. It was the company's client. And that client had seen multiple lawyers represent them throughout a single case. Now she was on her own, ready to show the world that she was worth her fee. She stood within a small claims court. The room was modern and white. A desk lined the front of the room where the judge sat. Beside her was a young man transcribing every word uttered within the court. Before the judge, two tables sat parallel, Rachel on one with her client, the defendant on the other with her lawyer.

'Final statements from the claimant please.'

She took a deep breath and turned to the judge. She dressed in a black trouser suit and a black cloak around her shoulders. Her hair was tied back and she wore glasses; she was on the fence about whether she needed them with the optician, however having looked in a mirror she acknowledged how professional and intelligent they made her appear.

Behind her sat her client, Mr Romano, an Italian man with olive skin and white hair, dressed in a white pinstriped shirt and grey trousers. He was short and had a thick European accent as he addressed the court earlier in the case. Now he'd done everything he could and it was his lawyer's opportunity to make one final argument on his behalf.

'Your Honour, throughout this case we've demonstrated to you that Mr Romano is a good, hardworking man who came to this country with nothing and worked tirelessly to build up a small, but by no means insignificant, empire. It was his life's work. Every penny he earned from that business was either spent ensuring that his wife and children had food on the table, or was reinvested into the restaurant. He poured his life and soul into what became a very popular Italian eatery.

'Fabiana Towers...' Rachel continued '...was opened in 2011, named after his daughter, the apple of his eye. It had humble beginnings but, until last year, stood proudly at the foot of the Rivington gateway in a grand converted tower. Mr Romano had a fantastic hygiene rating, was voted *Best Restaurant* in *The Rivington Restaurants Guide*. And then TripAdvisor came along. It was clear he treated his customers well. He regularly received five-star average ratings; one customer even said *"Mr Romano's clean and friendly restaurant is the perfect place to eat".'*

Rachel paused, allowing the judge to take in the positive history of Fabiana Towers. She sipped her water before composing herself.

'And then Emma Cook came to visit. Emma has a history of giving poor reviews on TripAdvisor. Her average rating is two stars. Out of three hundred reviews, I could only find three reviews which were rated higher than three stars. Each one brutally attacking the restaurant. And why? For free stuff! Multiple managers have got in touch with her offering her free meals if she comes back. Free drinks. Free hotel nights. You name it, she's received it.

'But Mr Romano thought, *no, I'm not going to give in to this,'* she continued. 'He was smart enough to read her other reviews and realised exactly what she was up to. She said in her review that the food was terrible, the service was rubbish and she was left with food poisoning. Following this review, Mr Romano had people cancel their bookings, the number of diners dwindled, and then he had to close his doors last year following his inability to keep up his rent. Your Honour, Emma Cook's selfish and greedy behaviour has forced Mr Romano's business to close.

We're here today to clear his name and to reclaim some of the financial damage which she has caused him.'

Rachel nodded to the judge and returned to her seat. Her client whispered a thank-you in her ear. She looked towards Emma, the girl who destroyed her client's business. She was in her twenties, caked in make-up and her hair was bleach blonde. She wore a pink puffy jacket over a white top and a flowery skirt. She'd chewed gum for the last hour, occasionally lifting the stringy substance out and twiddling it around her finger. Her lawyer had encouraged her not to take the stand, no doubt due to the fact that she didn't represent herself well. Rachel had heard her talk in the corridors; she was mouthy, arrogant and rude. Instead, her lawyer brought the person who was with her that night, her boyfriend Liam, who confirmed that they'd both been ill and reiterated the quality of the service they'd received.

Her lawyer, Jonathan Khon, stood up and faced the judge. He dressed in a grey suit, and his black hair was thick and curly to the sides, with a Kippah covering up his bald patch. He took his notes and addressed the court.

'Your Honour, I'd like to thank my learned friend here for her insight into my client, Emma Cook. Yes her TripAdvisor account does have some scathing reviews, we can't deny that. However this is due to her high standards rather than some opportunist looking for a freebie. Why would she want to return to a restaurant or a hotel where she'd had such a terrible experience? She hasn't. Miss Cook's attitude is quite welcome in a day whereby restaurants are having to become more competitive and our health is paramount. She uses TripAdvisor herself when planning her social outings to determine the best places to eat. And then she returns the favour by giving her honest opinion to her followers. And to prove it, her boyfriend has also testified how terrible the experience she has received as he joined her on that night.'

'As for Fabiana Towers...' he continued. 'It sounds more like Fawlty Towers. My client's review isn't the only negative feedback received for this dwindling restaurant. *"Poor service, inedible food and dodgy tummies"* are some of the many quotes which come up on this particular site about Mr Romano's establishment. It was a catalogue of errors which led to his failings, not my client's scathing review. Did she have a hand in the closure? If she did, then she was one of many people who should be sitting here today, who also gave honest reviews of their experience.

'Having reviewed the feedback, I can very much see that Mr Romano once had a successful restaurant. He had excellent reviews, five stars. However the pattern declines as you get to the last twelve months before its closure. I believe Mr Romano became complacent as those around him grew. He's also running a restaurant in a very turbulent time. Over fourteen hundred restaurants closed last year in the UK. Rates are going up and people are eating out less. Mr Romano failed to remain competitive in a busy and turbulent market. That's why his restaurant closed and I ask you today, Your Honour, that you exonerate my client from these horrendous accusations.'

The judge, an older lady with dyed brown hair, wrinkled skin and thick round glasses, read over her notes. She took a deep breath, took off her glasses and bit on the end of one of the arms as she considered her verdict. Returning her glasses, she turned to the four people before her.

'I've made my decision. Mr Romano, I have no doubt there are lots of people, including Miss Cook here, who like to take advantage of the kind nature of a restaurant manager. However I cannot believe that this one review forced you to shut down your business. I've read over the feedback on TripAdvisor, your books and the local market and I've found that a number of factors hurt you. Did Miss Cook help shut your business down?

179

Possibly, however she was the final nail in a coffin, which was already halfway in the ground. Miss Cook, you're free to leave this court, I award Mr Romano nothing.'

Emma cheered as the judge departed the room. Rachel glared at the defence's unprofessionalism, before turning to her client and embracing him. He had tears in his eyes, which he wiped away with a cotton hanky.

'I'm so sorry, Mr Romano.'

'It's OK, my dear. I will try again.'

They parted ways. As she left court, she glanced at her phone, which she'd been forced to keep switched off during the proceedings. There were no messages, but she opened up her security app and reviewed the activity occurring in her home. Matilda and Carl were sitting at the table; he was helping her with her maths homework. She smiled, content that she'd found someone so intelligent and caring enough to help someone else's child pass their tests.

The phone bleeped and it was the man she was staring at on her screen sending a message.

'How did it go?'

'We lost. It was my first case and I've lost!'

'You'll get there.'

It would be a lie if she said she wasn't gutted. She really cared about the client, whom she'd found ample time to invest in as her first customer. He was a lovely guy and that Emma, well, wasn't. It was also a personal low. When she's travelled to America, she saw billboards of top lawyers advertising their ninety percent success rates. It would be a while before she could say that about herself. At best, she was now on track for a fifty percent success rate and she wasn't too confident about the Irvine

180

case either. It wasn't the best advertisement to anyone seeking representation.

There wasn't time to fester in her misery, she drove to her daughter's school where a poster advertising a parents' evening welcomed her into the car park. She parked up and followed the crowd of parents into the school hall. A stage formed the front of the room, while tables and chairs lined the walls with a teacher behind each desk talking to parents as they poured into the room. In the centre, prospective high schools from the area advertised their facilities to parents whose children were approaching the next step in their education. She took a leaflet of a local private school, advertising their eleven-plus scholarship programme, and placed it in her handbag.

After rooting around the cards, keys and mounds of paper in her bag, she lifted out the invitation she'd received to attend the event. She glanced at her watch and saw she was just on time and made her way to table three where Matilda's teacher, Mrs Selby, sat. She was round, had grey long hair, and was dressed in various shades of beige. Loose skin hung from her arms and she wore orange-shaded glasses. As she smiled her crooked yellow teeth shone through her purple lips. Varicose veins sprouted across her meaty legs.

'Miss McCann, how lovely of you to join us.'

'Thank you for your time tonight. How is Matilda doing?'

'Well she's vastly improved. Her behaviour is much better. She's much less disruptive. And she seems much more positive, despite some of the disruptions she's received at home. I have to say she's really taken to your partner, Carl, is it?'

Rachel nodded and smiled.

'Yes, he's having a positive impact on her, she talks about him a lot. Obviously your career has had an impact on her school life, the other kids know what you do and who you're representing. But kids are kids and can be cruel and don't worry, we'll manage that. But she's a bright resilient girl and I have high hopes. Also she was given a trophy for her achievements in netball today, you should be very proud.'

'That's wonderful,' Rachel replied. 'We said if she behaved, we'd take her to Alton Towers. It feels like a fitting time to honour that promise.'

'I think that would be a nice treat, and suitable to ensure she knows she will be rewarded for good behaviour. Just remember to remain firm with her if she demonstrates bad behaviour too. Just not too firm, hey?'

Rachel looked up and caught the judging eye of Mrs Selby. She gulped, guessing Matilda had told her teacher that she'd been slapped by her mother. *Thank God she didn't ring social services.* Instead of responding, she nodded, forced a smile and left the parents' evening. She stopped by the local chippy and picked up her daughter's favourite takeaway, sausage and chips, with some battered fish for her and Carl. Gleefully driving up the driveway, she felt her optimism sour as the car-lights drew in on her front door.

PAEDO had been spray painted across the front of her house again.

She jumped out of the car and ran in.

'Have you seen the front door?'

Dorothy, Carl and Matilda were sitting in front of the television watching *Hollyoaks*. On the screen, Sally St. Claire was hosting a parents' evening not too dissimilar to the one Rachel had just left. Rachel's family looked up in terror, shaking their heads. Above the fireplace, she spied the glass trophy, which Mrs

Selby had made reference to earlier at the parents' event, honouring her daughter for her netball skills.

'Someone has vandalised the house again. Did you see anything?' Rachel said in a panic.

'No?' Carl stood up and kissed his girlfriend, before running to the front door. 'Not again! I can't believe it!'

'Who could do this?' Dorothy chimed in, before returning to the television as if nothing had happened.

'Check your app!' Carl called from outside, before stopping an excited Matilda from running to see what message had been left for the family. 'Back to your seat, young lady. Your mam's got your tea, get yourself a plate and eat up before it goes cold.'

Rachel took off her coat and sat on the couch, rewinding the footage from the front door. At approximately six PM, a hooded figure sneaked up to the door and painted across the front. Before the vandal walked away, they looked up into the camera, offering a clear shot of their face.

'Oh my God!' Rachel gasped.

'What? Who is it? Do you know them?'

'It's my sister… Lisa.'

Chapter 20

The house was a new-build detached property in a quiet estate on the outskirts of Westhoughton. The cul-de-sac was made up of ten Giallo-brick houses, all with a built-in garage and a large rectangular garden out the back. Despite the garage facilities, each house proudly showcased their white Range Rovers on the drives, while gym equipment sat inside the concrete spaces.

The middle house was owned by the Grahams, who were the perfect nuclear family. Father, Benjamin, was an accountant. Wife, Deborah, worked part time at a school. They had two children; the eldest was George, who was fifteen and played for the local under-sixteen football club and had already been poached by Bolton Wanderers as someone who was deemed promising. And the youngest was Becky, who was thirteen, liked Justin Bieber and spent far too much time on the internet.

Mo had retrieved Becky's details from the digital forensic report. An IP address had identified the location of the computer and the details contained within the chat history showcased that it was she who was the correspondent with Charlie Irvine. A private investigator report gave Mo all he needed on this seemingly happy family, but he wondered what dark secrets festered behind these visibly pleasant walls.

He knocked on the door. A few minutes later, Benjamin answered. He was an attractive man. His friends would call a 'DILF'. He had blond hair, few lines for (what his detective informed him was) a man approaching forty-three. He clearly worked out, both from his trim physique and the fact that he was wearing blue running gear.

'Sorry, are you just about to go out?' Mo asked, feeling agitated.

'Well I was, but how I can help you?' Benjamin replied, spotting the man dressed formally in front of him. It must be important.

'I'm Mohammed Iqbal. I'm representing a group called The Predator Hunters. Have you heard of them?'

'I've seen their work online.' Benjamin looked uncomfortable, scratching his neck as he spoke. 'What's this got to do with me?'

'Don't worry, you're not in trouble, Mr Graham. However one of the people who they claimed was a predator, was a man named Charles Irvine. Do you know that name, Mr Graham?'

He shook his head. 'It doesn't ring a bell.'

'Mr Graham, we did some research on Mr Irvine's computer and we found that he had been talking to your daughter, Becky.'

Benjamin's eyes widened. 'You better come in.'

Inside the house was filled with white walls and cream carpets. In the kitchen, an island broke up the open space between the dining and cooking areas. The benchtops were brown wood, covering cream cupboards. The floor was of white marble. Benjamin offered Mo a seat on a high stool at the central island, while he made them a latte with his coffee machine. The house appeared to be empty. Benjamin explained that his family were at the Trafford Centre as they were due at a wedding the following month and they needed suitable attire for the big day.

'Do you think anything happened to my daughter?' Benjamin asked, a lump lodged in his throat.

'That's what I'm here to find out. We know they talked to each other online and there's evidence to suggest they met up.'

Mo retrieved papers from his satchel and passed them across to Benjamin. Pages of the chat history between the pair dating back over several months sent Becky's father pale.

'His name was Charlie?' Benjamin spoke after several minutes and looked up at Mo.

'That's what he was known as to his friends and family. Do you know that name?'

'She was meeting up with a Charlie. We thought it was just some boy from school.'

'I see.'

'There were lots of names around that time. It was just kids. We've never been overly protective about boys as we knew she'd meet them anyway. We'd rather know about it, if you get me.'

'We were all young once.' Mo smiled and sipped his coffee.

'She never hid Charlie from us and she was always talking about him, but we assumed he was the same age as her. We always knew where she was as we had a tracker on her phone. We could see she was at the park. We had nothing to be worried about. Then one day, her Nana fell ill and we needed to collect Becky quickly so we could go and visit Debbie's mum at the hospital. We pulled up near the park. I walked over and I found her on the swings sat beside some grown man.'

Benjamin took a seat on a stool and placed his head in his hands. 'I ran up to her and asked who he was. She said he was Charlie.'

'What did you do?'

'What any father would do. I grabbed him by his collar, threw him on the floor and told him to keep away from my

186

daughter. He ran off, petrified. I grabbed Becky, threw her in the car and once I had dropped Debbie at the hospital, I said I needed to take Becky home. I made some excuse that she found hospitals unsettling and left George there to support his mum.'

'What did Becky say?'

'I questioned her, endlessly. *Did he touch you? Did he ever do anything inappropriate?* But she kept saying that they just met at the park and played on the swings.'

'Did you ever tell Debbie?' asked Mohammed.

'No. She had so much going on with her mum and then, when that was all over, it was too late to start bringing it up. Instead I banned Becky from these chat rooms and said she could only play out with girls after that. Debbie naturally wondered why I was suddenly being so strict, but I said our little girl was blooming and we had to take extra care, especially as I knew what lads their age were like.'

'And how is Becky now?' Mo tilted his head and softened his eyes.

'She's perfectly fine. I honestly don't think anything happened. As I say I always kept an eye on her location. It's a small but open park by the side of the road, somebody would've seen if anything inappropriate happened. I'm surprised no one approached him sooner. Maybe they thought he was her older brother. So where is this Charlie now?'

'He's dead.'

'Oh.' Benjamin swallowed and glanced down at the bench.

'He died after being exposed by The Predator Hunters. They're being sued for his death.'

'Well I'm glad he's dead. One less creep on the streets.'

187

'Exactly, this group keep creeps like Charlie Irvine off our streets and our children safe. I'm a father too and I completely empathise with your need to keep your daughter secure. But I need people to help testify in favour of The Predator Hunters group. I need your help. Mr Graham, with your authority, I'd like to ensure Becky sees a psychologist. We'll pay for it all naturally.'

'No. No way.' Benjamin folded his arms and grabbed the half-empty cup from Mo's grip. 'She's been through enough. I'm not allowing her to go through that again.'

'But if something did happen…'

'We don't know if anything *did* happen,' Benjamin intervened. 'She's absolutely fine.'

'Listen, Mr Graham, believe me, childhood abuse often leaves repressed memories which children take into adult life and they often relive what happened to them when they're much older. They're scarred for life. It would be much kinder for a professional to determine if she had been put at risk now and work with her to recover from that trauma while she's still young.'

'Absolutely not, and right now I'd like you to leave.' Benjamin walked over to the front door and held it open for his suddenly unwelcome guest. Mo stood up and walked to the door. Pulling out his wallet, he selected a business card and handed it to the patriarch of the Graham family.

'If you ever change your mind, you can call me. Nobody will ever think you're a bad father. I know it might not be want you to hear, but if it did happen, you'll want professional support, and you'll want justice. I can make that happen. The vigilante group I'm representing stops people like Charlie coming near your daughter. They protect your children. We want to ensure that the lawyer representing Charlie's family does not get their way in preventing these groups from existing. And who knows, you might be able to claim some money from the family yourself for what may have happened to your daughter.'

'How dare you!' Benjamin barked. 'I don't need money. And I'm not using her to extort money from people.'

'I didn't say you were, Mr Graham. But one day your daughter might really value some therapy, some support, or maybe even a bit of money to enjoy university. Think about it.'

Mohammed left the house, leaving Benjamin at the door reading over his business card.

Chapter 21

A herd of alpacas greeted her at the metal gate. Acres of land surrounded her and a muddy track trailed up to a converted barn. Rachel opened the gate and drove up to the house. Outside, an old green Land Rover slept beside a tractor. The front door of the house opened before she'd even left the car. Out of it came a short dumpy lady with short brown hair. She wore a green gilet, a tartan red shirt and jeans which wrapped tightly around her thighs. Wellingtons covered in dirt rose up to her knees.

'Well, well, well! Rachel, it is a surprise to see you.'

'Lisa.' Rachel nodded and gave her sister a light embrace.

'What brings you up here?'

'I think you know.'

Lisa squinted her eyes and looked her sibling up and down before nodding towards her house. Rachel followed her in. The kitchen was the entrance to the house. It had a country-cottage vibe with cream cupboards surrounding a cast iron stove, stone flooring and wooden beams along the ceiling. An oak table rested in the corner and Rachel was invited to take a seat while her sister boiled the kettle. A tabby cat slept by the windowsill.

'It's been a long time since you've visited.'

'I've been busy with Mum. She's a handful. You really should visit her sometime.'

'You know I can't do that. I don't want to see her.'

'She's old and frail now, she won't be for this world much longer, Lisa. You should really forgive her. She's not done anything wrong, not really.'

'She allowed it to happen.'

Lisa slid the cup of instant coffee towards Rachel; hot brown liquid poured out along its journey. Rachel picked up a tissue from a box off the windowsill and wiped the spillage away.

'So come on then, why did you do it?'

'Do what?' Lisa shrugged her shoulders. Rachel sighed and lifted out her mobile phone and handed her the device. On the screen was a photograph of Lisa spray-painting her front door.

'Why did you vandalise my house?'

Lisa sighed and looked down, staring into her coffee while she considered the right words. As she sat silently, Rachel looked over her sister and noticed how much she'd aged. Lisa was fifteen years older than her. Rachel was, let's just say, a little bit of a surprise to her parents. There was always a distance between the pair; for a long time Rachel put it down to the difference in age and the fact that she'd taken away Lisa's parents' attention at the critical age of fifteen. But she later discovered the real reason.

'You know why.'

'I'm sorry? I'm supposed to know why you'd vandalise your sister's house? Putting your niece at risk? I'm scratching my head for answers here.'

'I wanted to scare you, not harm you!'

'Oh how lovely. So thoughtful. What the hell is wrong with you?' Rachel barked.

'I can't believe you'd represent a kiddie fiddler and then sue the organisation trying to prevent these perverts from doing harm to children!' Lisa replied.

Rachel sat silently as she soaked in the reality behind her sister's vengeance.

'You know what happened to me,' Lisa continued. 'Uncle Harry for years treated me like I was some sex slave. All under Mum's nose. And nobody did anything. Do you know what that did to me? How damaged I am today? All those years of counselling and I'm still no better.'

Lisa sobbed into the arm of her shirt. Rachel grabbed her sister's hand, but she yanked it away.

'You never said anything,' Rachel replied, instantly regretting her words.

'It was right under their noses. But they were too busy with *you* to notice!'

Rachel winced as she considered her part in her sister's abuse. She was a helpless baby at the time, but it didn't hurt any less. If she hadn't been around, Lisa would have had her parents' entire attention and visits to Uncle Harry would have been very different.

'It was a different time, it didn't make it right. But people just either were blind to it. Or… I don't know what to say, Lisa. But it still hurts Mum to this day. Sadly it's one of the few things she *does* remember. You *have* to forgive her. You only told us when Harry died. We couldn't do anything about it before.'

'He threatened to kill us *all* if I said anything. I wasn't going to bother rocking the boat when he died. What would be the point? But I couldn't stand everyone gathering around his grave talking about what a great man he was, when he wasn't!'

'Well you sure did make it an interesting wake.' Rachel sniggered, but her sister shook her head in disbelief.

'And then that old miserable cow defended him. "*Well he was grieving, he was never the same after Sheila died.*" No! He was a predator! Stop defending him!'

192

'Mum isn't as *woke* as we are,' Rachel pleaded. 'You can't hold her accountable for that.'

'No, but *you* are. And here you are defending those perverts! Destroying people who are trying to keep our world safe! If you're successful, someone out there, like me, will be abused again and again because you'd rather see them free. Typical bloody millennial!'

'Lisa, you won't ever find me defending Uncle Harry. What he did was disgusting. And Mum knows that, regardless of what she says. She lives with that guilt every day. We all do. But Charlie Irvine is very different. He was not of sound mind. He didn't think like us. He was a child at heart. And all he wanted was a friend. In any normal circumstance, the police would have intervened and they'd have seen the person he was and ensured both his and the child's safety. But they weren't involved. Instead he was set up by a vigilante group and exposed on the internet, leading to his death. Charlie would be here today with proper support if it wasn't for that group.'

'And what about the others?' Lisa protested.

'Just the other week this vigilante group set up a real predator. He was let off because it was entrapment. Had the police caught him, he'd likely have been sent down.'

'That may be so but he won't be doing it again, will he? I bet his life will be in tatters now.'

'Yes it probably is. And so is mine, Lisa.' Rachel spoke through gritted teeth. She stood up and opened the door, grabbing her coat from behind her chair. 'So I'll tell you this. You leave me and my family alone. Forget the spray paint, the dead dog and the burning rags, if you even step on my driveway again, I'll report you to the police. I don't care if you're my sister. Nobody puts my daughter's life at risk.'

'Burning rags? Dead dogs?' Lisa stood up and chased after her sister. 'I don't know what you mean! I only spray painted your front door! I wouldn't have done anything like that.'

'Whatever, Lisa. You couldn't be arsed being in our lives for all of this time, why start now, eh?'

'But wait!' Lisa called.

Rachel got in her car and sped off down the road, leaving a sobbing Lisa on her knees in the mud by the entrance of her house. Dirt gushed from Rachel's tires as she sped down the drive. The car was a four-by-four in looks but it certainly wasn't ready for off-road.

She drove out of the gate and returned home. Walking into the lounge, she found her mother on the couch, blissfully ignorant to the world around her. Rachel sat beside her and placed her arm around her, kissing her hair while she caught up on the latest episode of *Neighbours*.

'Oh, Mum. You've been a great parent, you know?'

'Shhhh. Karl Kennedy's arguing with Susan. They might break up again.'

'You can't remember to switch off the stove, but Karl and Susan Kennedy you know.' Rachel rolled her eyes and walked into the kitchen. She threw her handbag onto the table and her phone rolled out, which she noticed had a message on it.

The text message was from an unknown number but its contents held the details of its sender. It had a request to call and so she obliged. It rang three times before a male voice answered.

'Stephen Fletcher, this is a surprise. I should really be talking to you through your lawyer. This is highly unusual.'

'Then hang up and call Mohammed.'

'You've caught my interest. What is it you want?' Rachel stroked her chin.

'How would you like to see the inner workings of The Predator Hunters?' Stephen asked.

'It would be interesting but bizarre that you'd show your hand when we have an impending court case.'

'I'm willing to take a risk.'

'Does Mo know you're talking to me?'

'No and I'd rather he didn't. Look, what do you have to lose? You might pick up something for your side of the case,' said Stephen.

'I just don't understand what's in it for you,' Rachel replied curiously.

'I reckon I could change your mind about representing Charlie Irvine.'

Rachel sat down and considered his invitation. What did he know about Charlie that she hadn't found out? On one hand, it felt completely unethical to meet the defence team without their lawyer present. On the other, even if they showed her something she didn't like about Charlie, at least she was prepared for it and could advise Karen appropriately. There's nothing worse than a surprise in court.

'OK, send me the address. I'll be right over.'

Stephen hung up without a goodbye and a minute later an address in Chorley was sent to her phone. As she returned to the lounge, she looked over at her mother and wondered if she'd be alright on her own for another couple of hours.

'I'm going out, Mum, I won't be long. I'll be back to make you dinner.'

'Shhhh... Karl Kennedy!' her mother said, pointing at the television. Rachel rolled her eyes again. As she made her way for the door, the other *'Carl'* in her life, stumbled down the stairs with an overnight bag in tow.

'I'd have thought you'd have already left,' Rachel said with an air of surprise. She embraced him and kissed his cheek.

'Well Little Miss Princess took her sweet time packing her bag. She couldn't decide which dress to wear.' Behind, Matilda followed with a small pint-sized carry-case.

'I hope you two have a fabulous time at Alton Towers!'

'We will! You should come, Mummy!' Matilda pleaded with her puppy-eyes.

'I wish I could but I have so much on with the case. But why don't the three of us go to Disneyland in the summer?'

'Yay!' Matilda called. 'I love you, Mummy!'

'I love you too. Have a brilliant time!'

She waved them off and jumped in her car. She drove down the bypass towards Chorley and found the tower block listed in the text message. An Out Of Order sign on the lift meant she had to walk up fifteen flights of stairs and she was exhausted as she approached her required floor. The gangs of kids, the obvious drug dealers and the occasional sex worker made her wonder whether she should have insisted someone had joined her. But it was too late now. Curiosity killed the cat. She just hoped she had enough lives to survive this adventure.

Three knocks in and the door opened. Simon, Stephen's colleague, was behind it and welcomed her into the apartment. The stench of weed hit her as she stepped in. The grungy apartment was more like a bedsit than the head office of a slick operation. How she had fallen from fighting large corporate giants with high-rise offices on Canary Wharf.

'Well this is a first for me, I can tell you,' Rachel said light-heartedly to break the tension.

'So good of you to come.' Stephen stood up and shook her hand. His fingernails were black and she slyly wiped her hand when he was out of sight. 'Simon will talk you through it.'

Simon showed her around the cameras. She was surprised at the size of the equipment. She expected most of it to be done on camera phones, so easily editable online and posted quickly to the sites. But this group acted like they were preparing a production for an ITV drama.

'And here is the computer. Take a seat.' She pulled up a stool beside him and watched him log into the chat room. He logged in with a username, *Grace2009,* to fool the other users that this was someone who was far beneath the eighteen-plus guidance. A photograph was added to the profile, which she vaguely recognised.

'We used one of those Face-Apps which you can see what you look like when you're old or when you're a baby. We brought Alison down to a teenager. Clever, isn't it?'

'It is. Does Alison not have any photographs of her when she's younger?'

'Not really.' Simon shrugged. 'She's very cagey about her past. Besides they'd all look a bit dated now, with kids today have their iPhones and taking selfies.'

'Very true.'

Rachel jotted notes down on her pad as she watched him engage with several men who all appeared interested in this young girl. She felt a bit sick as she considered what they were

197

probably doing behind those screens and who they were thinking of. As she read over the exchange in messages, she considered the conversation between Charlie and Anna, the girl he believed he was talking to on *TeenTalk*. His replies were innocent, with an interest in her favourite ice cream appearing to be their main debate. It was nothing compared to these men who were asking what these supposed young girls were wearing.

The chat ended with an agreement to speak again the following day. She was surprised it was so short with no agreement to meet up in person. When she considered Charlie, they were agreeing to meet very quickly, but some of that may have been down to Charlie's innocence. These men online knew how to play the game.

'So what has this got to do with Charlie?'

'Charlie?' Simon scratched his head.

'You said whatever I saw today would probably change my mind about representing him.'

'Show her the file, Si.' Stephen called from his couch as he continued to play on his console. Simon closed the webpage down and shut off the monitor. To the side of the computer was a chest of drawers; he opened the top drawer and lifted out an A4 yellow file and handed it to the lawyer. Rachel glanced over the papers. Pages of conversations between *Grace2009* and a user known as *LostockCallum* were presented to her. She browsed through the messages, which made Christian Grey look bashful.

'What is this?' Rachel shrugged. She looked at the date of the conversation; the exchange took place the previous day. Too late to be Charlie.

'Look at the photographs he sent us.'

She sifted through to the back of the file where she found a photograph of someone she knew all too well. It was the same photograph which he'd used as his profile picture on Facebook. It was taken a few years before in Benidorm on a lads' holiday. He had bleached blond hair back then; he still had a smooth and toned tanned body, and his designer shades made him look like he should be in a boy band. She'd even mocked him for not updating the photograph over the years.

'Is this a joke?' She turned to Simon.

'Nope.'

'Anyone could get this photograph. It's in the public domain. I know what you're trying to do and it's not going to work.'

'Look at the picture behind.'

She lifted the page and found another photograph. It was the same man but completely nude. More up to date than his first picture. She recognised the birthmarks, which only she knew about, around his inner thigh.

'Oh my God.' She dropped the package and lifted her shaky hands to her open mouth.

'I'm sorry to tell you this.'

She threw the photographs towards him and stood up, turning to Stephen, who had paused the game to gauge her reaction.

'Why didn't you tell me about this immediately? He's currently on his way to Alton Towers with my daughter!'

'Oh shit...' Stephen replied. 'You better call the police.'

'I can't believe it's Carl.'

Chapter 22

They'd just finished dinner and had settled in the bar. Matilda wrapped her tiny hands around a large milkshake while she glanced over the map of the theme park, which she was due to visit in the morning. There were so many rides and experiences, she didn't know where to start first. The room was white with a talking tree in the centre. The floor was chequered black and white, and they sat on grey seats around circular wooden tables. Occasionally a talking tree broke into song whenever a child walked within its path.

'Do you think I'll be allowed on *Nemesis* this time? I was too small last time.'

'You'll have to stand by the height-guidance and see. I looked online before we booked it and I think you'll be OK.' Carl smiled and grabbed her hand.

'*The Smiler* looks a little too scary for me.'

'And me.'

'You can't be scared, you're a grown-up.' Matilda laughed.

'Grown-ups can be scared too!' Carl replied.

'Of what?' She looked confused, but he couldn't tell if her eyes were squinting because she was tired or trying to work him out.

'Well the dark for one.'

'I can't believe you're scared of the dark, Carl.'

'I told you, call me Dad around here,' Carl whispered. 'They'll only ask questions and they'll take you away if I'm not your guardian.'

'Sorry, *Dad*,' she said with inverted commas and giggled. 'Good job they only had a double bed then if you're scared of the dark. I can look after you.'

'Well don't tell your mam that. Let's tell her the hotel got the booking right and got us a twin, yeah? She'll only worry and she really doesn't need more stress right now.'

'Yeah, OK. I'm feeling a little woozy. This milkshake tastes funny too.' Her eyes skittered from side to side like they were dribbling a ball. She pushed the milkshake away but Carl put it back in front of her.

'Drink it up, it's good for you. We'll take you to bed in a second.'

She consumed the rest of the shake through her large purple straw until the glass gurgled. She leaned back and rested her eyes.

'Right come on, you, bed time.' She gathered up just enough strength to follow him into the reception. As they approached the elevators, two police officers dressed in luminous yellow jackets and caps walked in and talked to reception. The front desk was like a beach hut, with palm trees lining the walls. The hall was decked out with marble floors and in the centre a black plastic elephant carried a statue of man playing the horn. A lady behind reception pointed towards the seemingly happy but tired family waiting for their lift up to bed.

'Carl Packer?'

He turned around and his eyes widened as he acknowledged his surprise visitor.

'Yes, can I help you?'

'I'd like you to come down to the station to answer some questions.'

Carl placed his hand around Matilda's arm.

'We'll take care of Matilda at this point I think, Mr Packer.'

Despite her protest, Matilda was pulled away from the man she'd seen as her dad for the previous months and followed the police lady to her car. It was pouring with rain outside and it lashed down on the car window. In the dark night, she could just about make out through the distorted glass her mother's boyfriend being handcuffed and put in the back of another car. The Georgian style house, which offered a magical entrance on their arrival, was now a place of nightmares. A cackled laugh roared out of the speakers hidden in the bushes. Matilda hid beneath a small pink blanket which they'd given to her upon entering the car; her tummy ached, her body ached and all went black.

*

Rachel sat in the corridor on a plastic chair. The hallways were white and the stench of chlorine followed her. She watched people come and go. Some were carried in wheelchairs, others on trolleys with their faces covered. With her head in her hands, she sobbed. How could she have let this happen? How long had this gone on for? *Had* anything happened? She considered every time she'd left them alone, her words of encouragement for them to bond. Oh God, and that CCTV in the bedrooms.

Matilda was only ten metres away from her. She was in bed being fed fluids to return her from the anaesthesia which they'd found in her blood after she passed out in the police car. GHB, they'd confirmed. And now they waited for her to wake up. Rachel wasn't allowed near her daughter. A police officer and a social worker stood guard beside her bed whilst they assessed the situation.

'It's my little girl,' she begged as they blocked her path. 'She needs me.'

But now she waited. Her mother, Dorothy, had already called; some strangers had come in and ransacked the house, asking when she'd be home. Rachel assured her mother that it was the police and she just had to sit tight. And no, she wouldn't be home for dinner. At times like this she wished she could rely on Lisa to step up. She really had nobody.

The only person she could think of was Karen Irvine. Her client. Was this acceptable? Weren't they kind of friends now? She was the only person she knew. After a brief phone call, Karen kindly jumped straight in the car; there was a key under the mat for emergencies, which Rachel briefed her on so she could let herself in and take care of her mother.

The social worker stepped out of the ward and sat beside Rachel. She was a pale girl with ginger hair. Tall, thin and pretty, she wore a purple cardigan over a white blouse and had jeans on. Relaxed for a social worker, Rachel thought, but maybe that was the vibe they went for these days. There's nothing more intimidating than a suit.

'She's woken up,' Lesley said; she carried a notepad with her and had a page of jottings.

'Can I see her?' Rachel asked with a frog in her throat.

'Not yet, we need to assess both of you and ensure that she is in a safe environment. I know it's hard but please believe me we're doing this to ensure she's protected. We can't take any chances.'

'I understand.'

'You're a lawyer?' Lesley asked, reading her notes.

'That's right. Funnily enough, suing the group who exposed that prick.'

'And Carl's your partner?'

'*Was*,' Rachel stressed, feeling sick as she considered him once a boyfriend. It was certainly over now.

'How long has he been in your life?' Lesley enquired.

'For a few months. He was great. He looked after all of us. He was so good with her. I never could imagine...'

'Few do.' Lesley rubbed Rachel's arm before jotting more notes.

'I'm such a terrible mother.'

'I don't think you are, Miss McCann.'

'You're not letting me near my daughter,' Rachel replied before giving her a tilted glance. 'I think that speaks volumes.'

'That's a precaution, Miss McCann. She's been through a lot. We just need to establish what has happened and I assure you once we have it cleared up and we're certain she's safe, she'll be allowed home with you. Is there anyone else we can call to come in? Maybe another family member? A family friend?'

'No,' Rachel sobbed. 'My mum has dementia. I have no real family or friends. Carl was really the only person in my life. And now he's gone...'

'It won't be long, I promise you.'

'Have you spoken to her?' Rachel grabbed a tissue offered to her by the social worker.

'Yes. She's a little groggy but so far she's saying nothing has happened between her and Carl. She said he was like a father. She remembers travelling to the hotel and seeing him being arrested but she felt ill after drinking a milkshake. I think we've been very lucky, Rachel. I think we caught him just in time.'

'Lucky? I've allowed a monster into my home and I sent them on holiday together alone.'

'It could've been so much worse. You did the right thing.'

The social worker returned to the room where Matilda lay. Rachel wiped her snotty nose and looked around the ward. There were children battling cancer, parents running out of rooms screaming and a trolley brought in with someone covered in so much blood she couldn't determine their features. It *could* be so much worse, she considered. Then she thought of her sister, Lisa, and wondered how much damage this would cause Matilda in the future.

A police officer approached her, stepping out of her daughter's room. Her afro-hair was tied back, she had dark freckles covering her cheeks and white pearly teeth, which Rachel would've killed for. She was dressed in a black suit jacket and a knee-length skirt. Only her badge gave away her authority.

'Miss McCann, I'm confident that nothing happened to your daughter. We recommend you follow-up with psychotherapy sessions just to ensure there's no delayed memories, and to be honest the experience tonight could have been traumatising enough for her. We have evidence to suggest that your daughter was drugged. And on Mr Packer's phone there are images which are more than incriminating. But none of them are of your daughter, Miss McCann. I hope that at the very least should be a blessing. Although he had access to cameras around your house. I'm sure you'll find that rather unsettling.'

'He set them up, for our safety supposedly.'

'Were you aware he's been accused of this before?'

'No?' Rachel gasped. 'No, never. I wouldn't have...'

'We've found some reports of accusations against him when he used to work down south. It made some local press but he was never charged. Apparently it's the reason he moved up to Lostock Hall. I know he had some family there once but...'

'Oh my God! How was I not informed of this?'

'He was never charged, Miss McCann, therefore he is not considered a danger to the public. But we'll of course review everything that happened and pass it all on to the police commissioner.'

Rachel nodded her head, wiping a tear from her eye.

'We've arrested Mr Packer. He isn't being very forthcoming but I'm sure they will charge him. Even if he's allowed out on bail, he will *not* be allowed near you or your family, do you understand?'

'Yes, thank you. I hope to God they don't let him go.'

'Me too. You should be very grateful to The Predator Hunters. Without them, who knows what would've happened tonight. I don't always condone what they do, but I guess it's lucked out for us tonight, huh?'

'I can't deny that.' Rachel smiled and nodded. 'When can we go home?'

'I think the doctor will keep her in overnight, I recommend you go home tonight, Miss McCann. You have an elderly mother at home who needs looking after and you're not much use here. We'll be on overnight guard by your daughter and by the morning we should have clearance for her to be back under your supervision. We'll bring her home to you tomorrow.'

'I want to be here,' Rachel pleaded.

'Here's my advice. Go home and get some rest. Take care of your mother. Be sprightly for when she returns home tomorrow as she's going to need her mum.'

Rachel nodded and grabbed her belongings. She looked into her bag and lifted out a teddy-bear, her daughter's favourite. 'Please can you give her this?' The officer took the teddy and nodded, returning to her room.

The drive back to Horwich was a painful one. She struggled to see the road between the rain and her tears. She relived every moment with Carl, assessing every conversation, cringing as she considered the times she let him tell her how to parent, or the times she allowed him to spend with her daughter. She was so wrapped up in her own work, she'd forgotten to look out for the most important person in her life. Had she been like her own mother? Blind to what her daughter had gone through? Would Matilda grow up to be like Lisa? Bitter, angry and refusing to speak to the woman who should have protected her?

Arriving home was a relief. She walked in and found Karen asleep on the couch. The closing of the door woke her up and it took her a second to get her bearings. She shook her head and then glanced up at Rachel in the doorway, drenched and upset.

'Oh, Rachel.' She ran over and embraced her. 'I can't believe this has happened.'

'I just don't know what to do with myself.'

'You just get yourself dry and off to bed. It must have been an exhausting day. Do you want a cup of tea first though?' Karen pointed towards the kettle.

'No, you get home, you've done enough today. I can't thank you enough.'

'No need.' Karen smiled and rubbed her arm. 'Your mum is in bed sound asleep. She was a little disturbed by the police but we've tidied up and she's forgotten all about it now.'

'The good side of dementia, I suppose,' Rachel said.

'I'll be off then, call me if you need me.'

'Thank you, Karen. I mean it.' As her client walked towards the door, Rachel was reminded of what the officer had said to her before she left the hospital. 'Karen!' She turned around. 'I'm so sorry to do this to you but I can't represent you anymore. Not after this.'

'But…' Karen gasped.

'I'm sorry, I know this is horrific to do this to you at this stage in the proceedings. And I'll refund any money you've paid to me so far, of course. I'll even put you in touch with a good lawyer, but I can't sue an organisation which saved my daughter.'

'You can't do this to me, please, Rachel.'

'Karen, please understand. It's over. As much as we hate what it's done to Charlie, we need The Predator Hunters to ensure that predators like Carl are kept well away from children.'

'So what does this make my Charlie?' Karen broadened her shoulders as if she was ready for a fight.

'Collateral damage,' Rachel replied. Karen's eyes widened. She shook her head, turned around and slammed the door.

Chapter 23

The heavy banging at the door forced Stephen Fletcher to jump. He pushed Simon off the couch and instructed him to hide his marijuana before grabbing an air freshener to extinguish the stench of his herb. Stephen could identify the knock of a police officer any day; he'd had enough visits.

Once they were confident that the flat was as decriminalised as possible within a five-minute clean-up, he opened the door to find Mo, his lawyer, standing behind it. He sighed, nodded his head towards the lounge and waved his hand in front of his neck, informing Simon that he could relax.

'What the hell have you two done?' Mo yelled as he walked into the lounge. He kicked aside a beer can to create a small path to Stephen's armchair, which was grey and covered in burn holes from the end of his spliffs. The lawyer lifted a local newspaper out of his satchel; on the cover, Rachel McCann's photo took centre stage, taken from her corporate profile off her website. In the corner a picture of Stephen with his arms folded and appearing particularly smug after multiple successes.

The headline read *'LOCAL LAWYER STUNG BY ANTI-GROOMING GANG.'* Underneath, a sub-heading: *'Vigilante Group She Was Suing Discovered Lawyer's Cop Boyfriend Abused Kids.'* Stephen picked up the newspaper and smiled as he read the grim details. The story blamed the lawyer for leaving her only daughter alone with Carl, her downfall having attempted to undermine the gang, and questioned whether the public could truly trust the police anymore.

'We did our job, Mohammed,' Stephen replied.

'I told you to pause on these searches until we finished the court case. You continue to go against everything I say. I can't represent you if you continue to ignore my instruction.'

'Mo, Mo!' Simon chirped in. 'We didn't put this online. We invited her over...'

'You invited her over?' Mo gasped. 'And she accepted?'

'She sure did.' Stephen smiled smugly.

'Well that was highly unprofessional of her. You two should've spoken through me. And then what happened?'

'We showed her the images of her fella messaging girls and sending nudes.'

'So this wasn't an online sting?' Mo appeared relieved, his shoulders relaxed.

'Nah. We just wanted to freak her out. Show her why we're here. He'd have had her kid had we not done owt.'

Mo placed his head in his hands as he considered his poor friend and the humiliation she'd have felt. Yes, they were in competition, but they were professionals and he had a deep respect for her. As a parent, he completely felt her pain too. In one respect he was grateful they'd prevented any harm to Matilda, on the other he thought about her career and what this meant for her now.

'Sorry, boss.' Simon said, patting Mo on the back. 'We thought she might back off if we showed her how close this problem was to home, like.'

'Well it worked,' Mo replied. 'As of this morning, she is no longer representing Miss Irvine. I've caught up with Karen this morning and right now she's too exhausted to continue. Therefore it looks like you boys are off the hook.'

'There you go.' The boys high fived each other before turning to their less than celebratory lawyer.

'I want you to know, Mr Fletcher, that this is not a win for us. This is not how I like to do things, and I recommend if you ever require my services or anyone else's again, you consult advice before you act. You could have really damaged the case yesterday and put yourself in some serious danger. You got lucky this time but in any other circumstances I'd have had every right to stop representing you and then you'd have been on your own scrambling around for a crap lawyer, no doubt.'

'Noted, appreciate it anyway.' Stephen nodded his head and bowed his head in what could have almost passed off as shame. 'What happens now then?'

'Well it's over, for now at least. I'll be in touch if Karen Irvine instructs another lawyer but I highly doubt she will at this point. Anyway, good luck, guys. And stay out of trouble.'

Mo lifted out his hand and shook Stephen's. Simon nodded from a distance before making his way to his computer.

'Where's Alison, by the way? I haven't seen her in a while.'

'She's been a bit distant to be honest, mate,' Stephen replied.

'Have you got an address I can reach her at, I'd like to inform her myself that it's all over. No doubt it'd have been hanging over her.'

'Yeah.' Simon stood up and walked towards the window and pointed. 'She's just in that estate across the way, in that cul-de-sac. Number ten.'

'Thanks, Stephen. Good luck anyway, no doubt I'll see you guys online soon.'

212

'We'll try to keep it legal this time, boss.'

They shook hands and Mo left. The apartments were accessible via an outside corridor and he held back for a second while he stared down over the house which Stephen claimed Alison lived within. Squinting, he tried to adjust his eyes, as if it would give him supersonic vision, allowing him in some way to spot Alison in the lounge watching television. But it didn't, it was too far down.

Having descended the stairs he stepped into his black Jaguar, which raised a few eyebrows with the local residents, and drove around the corner to the house which he recognised from the video in which Charlie Irvine was held hostage. Pulling up outside, he stepped out and knocked on the door. The man who answered intimidated Mo with his huge physique, shaved head and snake tattoos running from the back of his head round to the front of his neck. While his exposed arms were muscly, bursting out of his white tank-top, a large spare tyre was wrapped around his midriff.

'Yes?' he answered, appearing confused by the smart Asian man at his door.

'I'm looking for Alison,' Mo timidly replied.

'What do you want her for?'

'I'm representing her on a case, I'm her lawyer. Please tell her it's Mohammed.'

'Alison.' The man shouted up the stairs. Glancing the lawyer up and down one final time, he sniffed and walked away from the door. 'Man here to see you,' he said to the figure stumbling down the stairs.

Behind, Alison widened the door and appeared surprised to see Mohammed at her house. She squinted with confusion before greeting him. She was a skinny thing but dressed in an

213

oversized blue shirt which hung down to her thighs, which was big enough to fit the man she was cohabiting with. Beneath her bare legs and feet were white as snow. 'What are you doing here?'

'Can I come in?'

She moved out of the doorway and Mo walked in. He followed her into the kitchen, closing the lounge door with frosted glass to her right to avoid disturbing the man of the house. The carpets were brown and patterned, fresh out of the eighties, and wood chip covered the walls and ceilings.

'Who's that?' Mo mouthed to her as they passed the lounge.

'Oh that's Terry, don't worry about him. He's my fella. He looks tough but he has the heart of a kitten.'

The kitchen was small with a closed serving hatch to the lounge. Instead of cupboards, purple drapes, hung by a string, covered her pots and pans. They took a seat at a white round plastic table in the corner, which would've looked more fitting in the garden. Patio doors looked out onto a small paved yard which had washing hanging around a spinning line.

'I'd offer you a brew but I don't have any tea or coffee. Would you like a tinny?' She pointed to the crate of beers resting by the bins but Mo shook his head and smiled. 'What is you want then?'

'Well first of all I'm here to tell you formally that the case against The Predator Hunters is over, for now anyway.'

'Oh right,' Alison said but she didn't show any emotion.

'I wanted to tell you in person. And I wanted to check you were OK. I understand you haven't been around the boys much recently?'

'No, I've had to step away from all that.'

'Oh?' Mo tipped his head to the side and widened his eyes.

'There's just no point anymore, is there, Mo?'

'Why do you say that?'

'Well it's just all that work, stress and exhaustion. And for what? Just for them to get off anyway. I've been there time and time again and it just really got to me during the last one. We're out there showing the police and the world the absolute worst of society and they just don't seem to care. So I'm giving it all up. My work is pointless.'

'It's not pointless, Alison,' Mo replied. 'Look I don't agree with the way you always go about it, it's damn hard to defend, but what you guys do comes from a good place and you are making a difference.'

'News to me.' She laughed and sipped her beer.

'You really are. Just this week you have saved a young girl from being abused. Do you remember Rachel McCann, the lawyer who was suing you? The Predator Hunters exposed her partner as a predator and they told her just in time. He had her in a hotel at Alton Towers drugged up to the nines. He was going to harm her, Alison. And you guys stopped him. You exposed him just in the nick of time. Without you, Rachel's story would be very different. She would've still been suing you, yes, but I'm sure she's far more grateful for this outcome. Who knows what would've happened if you'd failed to expose that bastard.'

'Really?'

'Yes! And you guys should be really proud of that. I think maybe you need some processes and governance around what you do to ensure you don't end up in court again responsible for someone else's death, and maybe you could work in a way which doesn't lead to perverts getting off in court. I could even help you with all that, I'd be glad to support you guys if it meant keeping you out of court. But whatever you do, don't stop.'

'You really think I make a difference?'

'I think what you do is vital. I'm certainly glad you're around.'

Her eyes widened and she sat back.

'I mean for my daughter's safety!' Mo laughed. 'Don't worry, I'm not coming on to you.'

'Oh right.' She stared at her nails and picked them. 'I dunno, maybe.'

'You've got my card. Honestly, call me if you ever need any advice or representation. Whether it's for you and the boys, or just for you.'

'Why are you being you so nice to me, Mo?'

'I think I see someone who could've had everything but the world has been pretty unfair to her, meaning you haven't quite got out of life all the possibilities which would've been open to you in any other world. I don't know what the future for my daughter holds. I hope her mother and I are doing our best for her, but should anything knock her world upside down and I'm not around to support her, I hope someone is out there looking out for her. Which I'm sure somebody once wanted for you.'

'Nobody gives a shit about me, mate.'

'I know that's not true. Now I guess, for now, it's goodbye, but think about what I said. And whatever you decide, stay safe and good luck.'

'Thanks, Mo, I mean it. For a Paki, you're alright.'

'I'll try and take that as a compliment.' He smiled and left. As he turned around and glanced at the girl shutting the door, he wondered what the future held for this vulnerable being and found himself saddened that he was no longer responsible for her.

Chapter 24

To say it had been a rough few weeks would be an understatement. Rachel McCann spent the first few days on the couch, sobbing into a pillow, dressed in her sweaty pink pyjamas, only getting up to feed either her mother or her daughter. Thank God she had them to think about, she considered. As she had no other responsibility over those turbulent days, she wondered if she'd have lived to tell the tale without their neediness. Matilda was kept off school for the first week and Rachel lay beside her each night, following her everywhere she went in the house. She worried if she let her out of her sight even for a second that something would happen to her, which became overbearing for a confused little girl.

The police had interviewed both Rachel and her daughter several times. *No, they hadn't seen any inappropriate behaviour previously, no, he had been kind and considerate up until the Alton Towers trip.* Why the hell would she have left her daughter had he been anything other than that? She wondered how little they thought of her as a mother.

Despite their best efforts to ensure he was kept locked up, the police released Carl on bail. He was a copper; *he probably had connections*, Rachel assumed. He also had a bloody good lawyer. Rachel knew him from when she started out in law. Sylvester Crook, an ironic title for a criminal defence lawyer, was known for his underhand ways and using whatever means necessary to get his client off a charge. Carl might be able to roam the streets until his court case, but he had to keep three hundred metres away from Rachel and her family, and he was not allowed to have any unsupervised access to a child as part of his bail conditions.

As for explaining what had happened to Matilda, well that was a challenge in itself. She was naturally confused and upset; this man whom she'd grown to love and respect as the only father figure in her life, had suddenly disappeared. Everyone was talking about what a terrible man he was, and nobody was giving her an explanation as to why. She kept acting up, smashing plates and furiously calling her mother a *bitch* for leaving the only *'daddy'* she'd ever known. It didn't help that her forgetful grandmother kept asking where Carl was too.

Rachel decided to tell Matilda once and for all after a third explosive argument. She invited social services around for support, unsure of how to tell her little girl that the man who she thought the world of meant serious harm to her. It went beyond just explaining about his behaviour, they hadn't even had the discussion of boys or sex yet, although she'd heard enough about it in the playground to understand.

'Are you mad at me because your boyfriend fancied me, Mummy?'

'No!' Rachel cried, trying to force a smile for her little princess. 'I could never be mad at you. I'm angry at him. It was wrong for him to like you on so many levels, some of which you might only understand when you're older. He's not a nice person, but he won't tear us apart. We're a team just like we always have been. And I'm just so sorry I brought him into our lives.'

Rachel broke down, sobbing on her daughter's shoulder, clutching her as tightly as possible. The social services team sat a metre away, furiously writing on their notepads. Matilda gripped on to her mum, reassuring her that it was all OK. But how much damage it would lead to in the future was not something they could predict. Social services offered a number of support services and promised to keep in touch. They encouraged Rachel to ensure Matilda returned to school as soon as possible to restore some normality within her life, which she did a week later, mostly because Matilda became increasingly frustrated and bored with sitting around her depressed mother all day.

'When are you going back to work?' Dorothy bemoaned on one of her good days.

'What's the point, Mum?' Rachel replied. 'I'm a crap lawyer. I had one case which I lost. Imagine that on a billboard? We lose one hundred percent of our cases! When I can hold my head up high again, I'll call Ian and see if I can get my old job back at the law firm. God knows it's paid better; I had a pension, sick pay, security and private health care. My God, what did I land myself in leaving there in the first place?'

A surprise visitor arrived four weeks into her hibernation. It was Mohammed, dressed in more casual attire for a change. He wore a hoodie with a sports brand across the middle and jeans beneath. His beaming smile was just the welcome she needed.

'How are you?' he asked. She lifted her arms up and down, referring him to the sweaty pyjamas she'd embraced for several days and her hair, which hadn't seen shampoo or conditioner for over a week. She'd usually be rather embarrassed to see him in this state, but shame took second place to lethargy. 'Silly question, I know.'

'I just can't believe it's come to this, Mo. I let one man into my life and look what he does. I'm never ever putting Matilda at risk like that again.'

He nodded his head and rubbed her shoulder.

'It's so hard to say how I am. I'm feeling so many things at the moment. Anger at that bastard for ruining our lives. Guilt for putting my daughter at risk. And the worst thing about all of this is, I'm mourning my relationship with Carl. How sick is that?'

221

'That doesn't sound sick. No matter what he did, or what kind of monster he is, you clearly had feelings for him once. That doesn't just vanish overnight.'

'Oh don't worry, it's quickly transformed into hate. It's just, one minute he's the love of my life, the man who is taking care of me and my child. I'm thinking marriage, maybe more kids. And in a flash he's this person that can't be part of my life anymore. Don't get me wrong, I don't want him anymore, but I'm just so hurt. And I miss *him*. The person I *thought* he was. The person I was in love with has gone and I've not even been able to have it out with him.'

'That sounds normal. Well as normal as these situations can be.'

'Anyway, it is what it is. Pointless moping over it. Why are you visiting the competition anyway?' She raised an eyebrow and switched on the kettle, shutting the door to the lounge, allowing her mum to nap in her chair in peace. 'It's hardly kosher.'

'Well you're no longer the competition, but seeing you'd decided to make up your own visiting rules, particularly around my clients, I thought what the hell!' He chuckled and she smiled for what must have been the first time in a month.

'Hey, I have no regrets on that score, believe me.'

'I'm sure you don't.'

'Milk?' She raised the carton and he nodded.

'So you've left Karen in the lurch.'

'Come on, I could hardly carry on suing the gang who exposed my boyfriend and saved my daughter, could I? What a sorry state of affairs that would've been. The press certainly lapped it up. I just can't go back to that.'

'Why not?'

'I don't think I need to answer that. It would be ridiculous.'

'You still could, you know. Let the dust settle. You were really getting somewhere. And between us, I believe you had a strong case.'

'Mohammed Iqbal!' Rachel shoved him. 'Breaking a few ethical codes there, aren't we?'

'I'm not telling you anything you don't already know. Come on, we're lawyers, we could argue either side of this case.'

'And I can tell you my ex-boyfriend gave your side a lot more leverage. Any lawyer in the world would be sensible not touch your clients after this.'

'But you're not just any lawyer now, are you?' He raised his eyebrows and winked.

'No, I'm certainly not sensible as you can see from my mess of a life. Up the duff in my teens, quit a six-figure salary job to go out on my own and failed my first case. What an inspirational woman I've turned out to be.'

'I think you're amazing.'

'I think we should change this subject.'

They talked about university, the people they studied alongside and where they had ended up since graduating. A few had achieved great careers, while others had disappeared. They discussed the tutors they loved, and those they loathed, impersonating the latter with their catchphrases and silly voices. They discussed the people they dated back in their halls of residence, the embarrassing walks of shame and the ones that got away.

'I really had a thing for you back then, you know?' Mo said.

'Yeah, I had a thing for you too.' Rachel grew red.

'Why didn't you say anything?'

'Why didn't *you*?' Rachel replied.

'I figured you had enough going on.'

'Like a baby.' She laughed and pushed his shoulder away from her. 'Don't you worry, you are more than off the hook for *that*. You didn't need that taking up your life back then. Besides you went on and found a wife and had a little one of your own. We can't look back and wonder what could've been. Although I clearly wouldn't have been left with a damaged daughter and a reputation for dating perverts.'

'I suppose not. Look, I know you're not going to be in a good place for a long time, but promise me you won't swear off men forever. Not all of us are bad, I assure you.'

'Well I don't know. Certainly not before Matilda's eighteen anyway. She's my priority. Maybe when she's moved out and I'm a lonely spinster with an empty nest, I'll find myself a toy-boy for some company.'

'On that note I'm going to leave. But please consider coming back to the trial. You're a brilliant lawyer with a strong case. And I for one would be honoured to fight you in court.'

'That's the strangest proposal I've ever had, Mo. But thank you, I mean it. If anything it'll encourage me to go back to work. God knows we need the money. Thank you for being a friend, I haven't had one of those in a very long time.'

'Any time.'

He kissed her cheek and left. As he drove off out of her drive, she stared at his personalised number plate on his special addition executive car, and looked what she could have had in her life if only she had put in a little more effort at work.

The next day, she walked downstairs in her suit, with her hair washed and brushed and her make-up complete. Matilda and Dorothy glanced up in surprise at the transformation she'd undertaken in less than twenty-four hours. She grabbed her files and walked towards the front door. 'What?' she asked as she strutted out to her vehicle.

Her first day was fairly uneventful. She spent it putting files in order and reading newspapers. She read through the news articles highlighting car crashes and disputes over land to see where she could begin to start building a client list. She considered the ambulance chasers, who she worked alongside when she first began her career in law and wondered if she could lower her standards and begin hanging around hospital waiting rooms once again, convincing loved ones to use her services.

A call at three in the afternoon from the school came as some surprise as Matilda had settled surprisingly well in her first few weeks. She'd even checked in with her teacher and ensured she visited the school psychologist, but all reports so far had been delightfully normal.

'Mrs McCann?' The head teacher's recognisable voice was on the other end.

'It's Miss,' Rachel reminded her.

'Of course, it's Mrs Dahl here from St Peter's. I need you to come in urgently.'

Half an hour later, Rachel was in the head teacher's office. She'd already passed Matilda outside in the corridor looking rather glum, but she was called in before she had a chance to ask her what had happened.

'She's been disruptive again today and when we sent her outside, she threw a book at Mrs Selby and hit another pupil.'

'I'm so sorry about this. She's been through so much recently, which is really my fault, but I assure you this isn't *her.*'

'Can I remind you that this isn't her first incident? We excluded her only a couple of months ago. And now we have this very serious event of her assaulting a teacher. I'm sorry, Miss McCann, but I have no option other than to expel her from the school, permanently.'

'But please, Mrs Dahl. She's been so upset recently with everything that has happened. She needs normality, she needs her friends and she needs this school.'

'I'm sorry, Miss McCann, but that's not our problem. I am sorry, truly I am, but we have other pupils and our staff to consider and your daughter is not only a hindrance to their education, but she's also a serious risk to their safety. We will of course continue to offer our support. And we'll help you find another school or a pupil referral unit maybe?''

'A pupil referral unit? No, forget that! I'll teach her myself if I have to. I'm so shocked you'd abandon her like this. Do you know what that poor girl has been through?'

'We're at the end of the road, Miss McCann. We've done all we can for her. We truly have. But we can carry on no more. She's disruptive, abusive and quite frankly a very unkind and disturbed individual, which this school is not equipped to support.'

'Fine. Screw you and screw your school,' Rachel snapped and stood up.

'Well I see where she gets her attitude from,' Mrs Dahl replied with a judgemental tone.

Rachel strutted out of the office and slammed the door behind her. She looked to her daughter, sitting on a chair in the corridor, cross-legged and rocking back and forth. Matilda hung her head in shame.

'Am I in trouble, Mummy?'

'No. You're not in trouble, darling. Come on. Let's go home.'

Chapter 25

'Are you ready?' Stephen asked as Simon left the bathroom. They were in matching outfits, a Union Jack shirt and denim knee-length shorts. Their faces were painted with the St George Flag, a red cross in the centre and the rest coated in white.

'As I'll ever be.' Simon picked up his placard, resting on the floor. In bold letters it said *"Send Terrorists Home!"* Stephen had his resting against the front door, which had a print of Sir Winston Churchill and *"Give Our Country Back!"* stamped beneath.

They departed the flat. It was a sunny day, perfect for the march they were about to embark upon. They'd attended these events before but the North West's infamous weather had put a damper on the day previously. As they descended in the lift, their multi-cultural neighbours glanced at their signs and bowed their heads, escaping their presence as soon as the doors opened. The boys weren't fazed, standing proud as if they were going onto the battlefield.

In the reception, Alison was waiting for the lifts. She double-took as she saw her friends step out looking like they were on a stag party in Benidorm. They were equally surprised by her appearance. She'd washed and straightened her hair, and she'd lost the tracksuit and replaced it with a pair of dark jeans, a yellow top and a cardigan. The lobby was dark with a blinking bulb to lead residents to the fire exit. Posters lined the dirty-cream walls warning residents not to smoke in the public areas, to keep noise down after eleven at night and to stop clogging up the rubbish chute; none of these rules were ever followed and there was little authority around to enforce it.

'Fuckin' hell,' Simon said. 'What spat you out, M&S?'

She blew a raspberry and replied, 'Primark actually. My God, you two look like you've been shat out of a tourist gift shop. What are you doing?'

'It's the anti-immigration march today in Manchester, I thought you were coming?'

'I can't. I don't....' Alison mumbled before pulling herself together. 'I came over because I want to start up The Predator Hunters team again.'

'Again? We didn't stop, Ali, you were the one who fucked off. We carried on.'

'Properly this time.' Alison swallowed, took a deep breath and continued. 'We were getting it all wrong before. We were putting vulnerable people in danger and we were allowing guilty people to get off in court. If this is to be a business, then we should treat it as such. We need processes and policies. And I want Mo involved. He can keep us legal.'

'Mo's gone, Ali,' Stephen said. 'He's no longer representing us. The case is over.'

'He's willing to help me...' she replied before stuttering, 'I mean, *us*!'

'Is he your boyfriend?' Simon said in a childish voice.

'No it's not like that, he's just kind, that's all.'

'Well come round tomorrow when we're in. Are you coming with us on this march or not?'

Alison looked them both up and down and read their signs. She thought of the people they were fighting against, including the man who was trying to protect them.

'No, I don't do that anymore.'

'Fine, see you tomorrow, come on, we're going to miss our train.'

They arrived in Manchester an hour later. They received a few disapproving looks on the train and a hippy from Preston told them that their placards offended him. Simon stood up and clenched his fist, but a calm Stephen pulled him back. 'It's not worth it,' he said.

The march formed in Piccadilly Gardens. A fountain sat in the centre of the green space and large concrete boulders surrounded them. Behind, coffee shops and restaurants came to a halt as their inhabitants watched the commotion unfold outside.

Police surrounded the area, where the protesters were penned in until the proceedings began. Fifty people were on the protest; a mixture of white and blue shirts were their attire. Sixties men with bald heads and white beards along with big beer guts made up the majority of the crowd. The younger generation had skinheads or short hair gelled forward with a few spikes around the fringe and they wore tracksuits. They all carried a look of anger in their eyes, until they were moved closer together where they celebrated with a can of lager and sang the National Anthem. There were few women amongst them. Anyone walking by would think there was an England football match on, until they read the signs indicating their agenda floating past.

A man by the name of Tommy walked out with a megaphone and addressed the crowd before him whilst standing on a makeshift stage, made out of a crate. He wore a white t-shirt and black shorts. On his left leg he had an electronic tag.

'Patriots!' Tommy called and the crowd cheered. 'We are here today to show our government that the white working class will not be overlooked. We will not let these people come into our country and steal our jobs, terrorise our streets and rape our children!'

The crowd roared. The police shuffled in and made a circle around them. Tommy lifted his hand and began to direct people down Portland Street, passing bars and large hotels. They sang songs and chanted in harmony. The traffic was cut off. Hundreds of people swarmed to the pavements and booed the passing crowd.

'What do we want?'

'Our Country Back!'

'When do we want it?'

'Now!'

'Here's our island, here's our home. We won't stop 'til they go home!'

An object flew through the air from Simon's right and cracked against his head. A cold running liquid ran down the side of his ear.

'Oh my God, is it blood?' Simon panicked, placing his hand over the liquid.

'It's egg,' Stephen replied, wiping the shell and its interior off his friend. Simon's face grew red and he began to shake.

'Who did this?' He turned to his right and saw two lads in yellow Manchester Metropolitan University hoodies pointing and laughing. They looked like freshers with their long fringes and pierced lips. Simon leaped towards them and punched the shorter one in the face. Blood gushed from his nose. The taller of the pair retaliated which led to a brawl. Stephen ran over and tried to pull Simon away. He felt a blow to his stomach and he fell down, leaving him nauseous and rolling around on the concrete floor.

He didn't have much time to recover. A police officer dragged him up and threw him into the back of a van. Cuffed together, Simon and Stephen landed on the floor, and the light went out as the doors closed.

'Great work, Simon,' Stephen groaned.

'Hey, that guy attacked me!'

'It was a bloody egg!'

In the station, they were left in an interview room while the police hurried about. They were allowed to make a phone call each, which Stephen took advantage of when they arrived. Forty-five minutes later, the door opened and Mohammed walked in, suited and booted, and as usual with his satchel in hand. The room was cosy with just a small table and four chairs in the centre. A blue light hovered over them and a camera hung in the corner. White brick walls surrounded them and a recording machine sat to their right.

'What have you got yourselves into now, boys?'

'Thanks for coming, Mo,' Stephen said, shaking his hand. 'We need your help.'

'I don't know why I bothered. I'm no longer responsible for either of you. I don't represent you anymore, but out of the goodness of my heart, here I am. Why did you call *me* anyway?'

'You're the only lawyer we know,' Simon replied.

'Bullshit. You wanted an Asian to help get you off a racism charge.'

'Well that's not technically why we're here. It's assault actually. We just happened to be at an anti-immigration march. It wasn't about race.'

Mo shook his head and read over his notes. He looked at the pair, who were smiling and seemed to have little remorse for their actions. He closed his notepad and took a deep breath.

'The good news is I've got you off this charge. As the other lad attacked you first, I've managed to call it self-defence and said if he presses charges, then we will too. So you're off the hook, for now.'

The boys' shoulders relaxed. They turned to each other and grinned. The paint on their faces had now begun to fade and the red cross had smudged.

'However, I want to tell you something before I go. This is over between us. I am no longer your representative. I can't represent anyone who has such strong feelings towards people like me.'

'Mo!' Stephen butted in. 'We've nothing against *you*. You're alright.'

'The people you are protesting against *are* me! You just don't know them yet. They're my parents, they're my friends, my neighbours and they're my children. They're the teachers who gave me my education. They're the judges who ensured access to my child. And for *you*? One day an immigrant, or a Muslim, or whatever way you want to argue this about, might just protect you, or they might just save your life. They might even represent you in court. But not me. Not anymore. I'm done with the pair of you.'

Mo collected his belongings and walked out of the room. The boys sat in silence for a few minutes, each contemplating what their lawyer had advised. They were now free to go, but they were now on their own, without representation from their lawyer.

'Fine, screw him. I don't want that muzzie around us anyway.' Simon grumbled.

'Oh shut the fuck up, Simon,' Stephen replied. Simon looked up, appalled. 'No seriously, shut up. It's always *you* that gets us in trouble. It was you who dragged Charlie into our car. It was you who chased him out. It was you who caused a fight today. It's always you who takes things too far and fucks up everything for The Predator Hunters. Well no more.'

'What you saying, mate?'

'I'm saying I don't want you to be part of us anymore. You're out.'

Stephen stood up and left the interview room, slamming the door behind him.

Chapter 26

The first few days of Matilda's expulsion was fairly uneventful. Rachel took time off work and tried to read up on the syllabus of a girl of her age online, but she had to admit, she wasn't a teacher. To ensure she continued to learn, she found some exercises online but Matilda continued to struggle with them, despite them being for her age group. As an experiment, she tried one year below, which Matilda continued to find tough.

Realising her own weaknesses, Rachel decided to approach a tutor. She looked online and realised quite quickly how expensive a private teacher would be, and without a proper income coming in, she was stretched to be able to fund a full-time education for her daughter. They had explored other local schools, but due to her expulsion, they were unwilling to accept Matilda into their fold. One afternoon, they visited a Pupil Referral Unit, but they didn't get past the front gates before reversing and leaving. There were fights breaking out in the yard and Rachel just couldn't face putting her little girl in that environment.

A light-bulb moment occurred when Rachel read through the local newspaper. At first she was frustrated that the newspapers continued to cover her involvement (or lack thereof) in the Charlie Irvine case, while her ex-boyfriend had been exposed by the very group she'd tried to sue. The paper went into great detail about how she'd managed to have his cause of death overturned, and gave a background into Charlie Irvine's childhood, mentioning Nick, the classroom assistant who had diagnosed his autism and had been a witness in court. Rachel remembered Karen talking about what a great tutor he was to Charlie, and how he'd since retired.

Rachel had his details. She'd kept the files and the list of witnesses they'd asked to present at the previous consultation surrounding Charlie's cause of death and the upcoming case against The Predator Hunter group. She'd kept everything in case Karen wanted her to pass the case over to another solicitor, but to date she hadn't heard back from her former client. Within the list of witnesses was Nick's name and his contact details. A phone call later and they'd agreed an arrangement for him to come over three times a week to support Matilda's education.

It was their first session and Rachel was still a little nervous about leaving her daughter in the hands of a man alone, especially one she knew little about. They sat together at the table and worked through some of the exercises which Nick had brought with him. Matilda winced as she read through the questions he'd set her and became grumpy as he pressed her for an answer.

'I've got a headache, I can't do this!' Matilda snapped and stormed off.

'Come back here, Matilda!' Rachel called.

'No! I don't want to.' Matilda grabbed a glass and threw it on the floor, smashing it into tiny pieces.

'Matilda!' Rachel yelled, rising from her seat.

Nick put up his hand and lowered it, encouraging Rachel to sit down.

'Just wait,' he whispered before turning to his pupil. 'Matilda, why don't you come back and sit with your mum and me? I just want to try something. If you still can't answer the question, then I promise you we'll call it quits for today and try something different tomorrow. How does that sound?'

'OK.' Matilda returned and sat beside Nick. He lifted out of his rucksack a blue transparent plastic sheet and placed it over the A4 paper which the questions were written on.

'Right, can you try and read this to me now?'

Her eyes adjusted and she browsed over the questions. She turned to her tutor and smiled. 'A violin is a musical instrument. Thursday comes before Friday and her hip operation was cancelled at the last minute.'

'Well done!' Nick called with a celebratory tone. 'I knew you had it in you. Now why don't you go and sit down and watch television as a treat for half an hour while I speak to your mummy.'

Matilda ran off and switched over to the cartoon channel on the television. Rachel's shoulders relaxed. She turned to the tutor and placed a hand on his wrist. 'Thank you so much! I don't know how you did that. It's absolutely astonishing. Karen was right, you are good.'

'Rachel,' Nick said with an air of concern. 'I think I know what the issue has been with Matilda. The coloured sheet of plastic I put over her questions is a typical solution for a child struggling with dyslexia.'

'You think Matilda is dyslexic?' Rachel's mouth dropped and her eyes widened. Nick nodded. 'I can't believe it. No one's picked it up before.'

'It would explain a lot of her behaviour. She gets so frustrated and angry, she's upset that she can't answer basic questions which her peers can, and she doesn't understand why. But let's get this confirmed, I don't want to assume. And don't worry if she is dyslexic, there's so much help out there these days. If we know that's the issue then we can get her back on track pretty quickly.'

Over the following days, Rachel contacted the Dyslexia Foundation who supported her in receiving a free test. They quickly confirmed that Matilda's previous issues were the result of her dyslexia, just as Nick had suspected. While unsettling at first, it soon came as some relief to Rachel, who had blamed herself for her daughter's delinquent behaviour, and was now confident that Matilda could get back on track at school.

With the results in hand, she arranged a meeting with Mrs Dahl at Matilda's former school, St Peter's. Rachel explained the situation, giddily sure that this would revoke her expulsion. However her optimism was short-lived.

'I'm sorry, Miss McCann. Whether she had dyslexia or not, Matilda's behaviour was not acceptable. Therefore we cannot allow her to return to school. She's disruptive.'

'But it's because she hadn't been diagnosed. She was frustrated!' Rachel pleaded. 'Please, Mrs Dahl, please understand.'

'As I said to you last time, Miss McCann, we cannot accept her back. What sort of message would that be to the rest of the pupils? She is remembered as a troublesome child and the parents will just not be happy about their children socialising with her.'

'So what you're saying is that shit sticks?'

'I wouldn't have put it so bluntly but essentially yes.'

Rachel's head spun and her eyes lit up. 'Just like Charlie.'

'Who?'

'Nothing. I've got to go. Balls to your school. It's quite embarrassing that you didn't diagnose Matilda's dyslexia. You know what, I wouldn't put her in such an inadequate institution anyway. And I'll be putting in a complaint, ensuring a formal investigation into the conduct of the system here is completed too.' Rachel smiled and strutted out of the room. 'Don't mess with lawyers, Mrs Dahl! Bye!'

She giddily strutted out of the school and as she reached her car, she picked up her mobile phone and scanned her contacts. She found Karen's name and dialled. On the fifth ring, she answered.

'Rachel, this is unexpected.'

'Karen, I get it. I'm so sorry. This isn't about The Predator Hunters. This is about justice for your Charlie. If you'll still have me, I'd love to connect and get this case back on the road.'

Chapter 27

Karen Irving put down the phone. She couldn't believe it. That glimmer of hope had not been completely snuffed out. It had been a lonely few weeks. She'd lost everyone and anyone whom she once counted on for support.

Sylvia had abandoned her after she revealed her true thoughts on her son's guilt and subsequently Karen had blurted out a reminder of Sylvia's most painful attribute that she couldn't have children. She no longer visited the chapel; instead she prayed at home in the comfort and safety of her own home, which became dustier by the day as her lethargy took over.

Work had also become challenging. Her manager, Stanley, had taken a secondment to a new store which he'd been challenged to open, and his replacement was a team leader on some leadership course within the business and was trying to find her feet. She wasn't equipped to deal with Karen's problem and there were no policies in place to help her. While previously she could seek solace in her colleagues, Karen's peers in the shop were part-time students, who barely did four hours a week. There were fresh faces in the store nearly every day, all half her age and all nudging each other's arms when they clocked that she was the woman from the newspapers with the dodgy son.

Josh ended all contact with her as soon as she confirmed that the case was over; he sounded relieved that he was no longer having to fund what was becoming an expensive trial. His wife, Jennifer, followed up with a call to ease Karen's mind that she was still working on her husband's stubborn ways.

Rachel was the only true support she'd had remaining in her life. She brought her out of her shell and gave her confidence. More than anything, she'd had somebody to talk to. She was more than a lawyer, she'd become a friend. On that dreadful night when she returned home and announced that she was no longer going to represent her, suddenly that illusion of friendship revealed itself to be simply a contractual relationship, which came to an abrupt end. The days after the bust-up, Karen had ridden the change curve like it was the *Big One* at Blackpool Pleasure Beach. From anger, to resentment, to devastation, and finally to acceptance that not only was she going to be on her own from then on, she had to accept that people weren't going to change their minds about her dear Charlie.

A shimmer of support presented itself a week later when she was walking through town and bumped into Nick, Charlie's former tutor. She thanked him for his support in court where together they successfully changed her son's cause of death. They went for a coffee and talked about Charlie. Clasping on to the stories he shared from Charlie's schooldays, Nick offered snippets of her son that she'd never come across before. She only saw the grumpy teenager who hid in his room for his later years in the comfort of his own home. She was suddenly made aware of the kind Charlie, the articulate Charlie and the creative Charlie. Nick brought him back to life, if only for a few hours as they consumed enough lattes to fill a Nero.

But even he found a way to let her down. He revealed over lunch one day that he'd be busy during the week from then on as he'd be supporting Matilda; the daughter of the lawyer who betrayed her. The tears and the *'how could you'* pleas did little to change his mind. Nick wanted to visit his brother in Australia and needed some extra money to get the flight. And as a former assistant teacher, he struggled to turn down the opportunity to support a child, especially a vulnerable one. She threw him out of her house and told him never to contact her again.

Now, as she reconnected with Rachel, she wondered if she'd been a little harsh on Nick. On any of them. On Rachel.

And on Sylvia. She'd carried so much anger since Charlie's death. People only knew what they knew. Their assumptions and feelings were all based on what they see and hear. Only academics truly looked around the corner. She'd turned her back on a woman who had just found out her daughter had been in serious danger. How would she have reacted if that was Charlie? Well, she had an inkling, look how she treated Sylvia when she dared question Charlie's intentions. Reminding her that she couldn't have children. No wonder they hadn't spoken since. Wow, she knew how to burn someone in the frostiest of conditions.

She picked up a photograph of Charlie. It was one of the only ones she had of him smiling. It was taken in junior school. She placed her fingertips over his green jumper and rubbed the picture, wishing she could hold him one more time. She kissed her index finger and patted the tip on his cheek.

'We'll get justice for you, my love, I promise.'

She put on her waterproof and stepped out into the rain, pacing up the high street, and danced across the puddles in her path. The florist was hurriedly carrying in her displays and Karen gave her a hand, breathing in the fresh scent of lilies. The aroma brought back memories of her last visit to the shop, when Rachel ran around the corner and announced her desire to represent her, determined to get justice for Charlie. Now she was back to where they had started. But now she wanted to make amends.

'I'll take these,' Karen said, handing the daffodils over to the keeper. 'For delivery, please.'

'Who should I make the card out to?'

'Sylvia.'

*

Mo clicked the end of his pen repeatedly. It was the end of the day and he had less than an hour to write up his response to a claim made against a client, but his brain just wasn't functioning the same as it would in the morning. As a son of a shop-keeper, he was born and raised as an early bird and that hadn't changed thirty years on. He was in at six and tried to leave by four, on the rare occasion that he could.

The door to his office opened and his secretary, Thomas, stepped in with his headset hanging off his neck. He wore a stripy white shirt and jeans, despite Mo's protest that he should smarten up if they had clients visiting. Thomas appeared worn out; it seemed Mo wasn't the only one who was ready to go home.

'You have a visitor who is determined to see you. I tried to make your excuses but he's insistent.'

'Who is it?' Mo asked, stroking his five o'clock shadow.

'Stephen Fletcher.'

'Send him in,' Mo said with an air of intrigue.

Stephen followed behind. He'd spruced up in what appeared to be a freshly ironed shirt, but his tracksuit continued to take up the bottom half. *Thank Christ we didn't get to court,* Mo considered with relief.

'Mr Fletcher, I thought I told you not to contact me again.'

'I need your help, Mohammed. The case is back on. The Irvines are suing us.'

'And?' Mo shrugged. 'What do you want me to do about it? I'm no longer your solicitor. I'll happily pass on my paperwork to your new representative if you pass me their details.'

'Please, I need you. You're the best.'

'And why should I represent a racist little shit like you?' Mo placed his feet up on his desk and folded his arms. His black loafers scuffed the white plastic top.

'I'm done with all that, I promise. And Simon, he's gone. He's out. I've told him I don't want anything to do with him anymore. That day in Manchester, it was him who started the fight. I was trying to break them up.'

'You were still there, Stephen, fighting to end the rights for people who are just like me.'

Stephen looked down at the floor and anxiously rubbed his knee. He took a deep breath and exhaled, scratching his head as he searched for his response.

'We grew up in different backgrounds, Mohammed.'

'We certainly did.'

'You grew up in a family where you were encouraged to be your best. You were told you could be anything. I grew up in a world where I was told by rich white people that I was poor because my family were lazy. So we all tried to get jobs. And there weren't any. So we went back and told the rich white people just that. And you know what they told us? They said we couldn't get jobs because the immigrants took them all. And they were to blame for our poverty.'

Mo sighed and sympathetically tilted his head.

'I'm sorry if I naturally view immigrants as the enemy,' Stephen continued. 'It was my upbringing. You were smart; you got a degree and were taught to look outside the box. I was told to *shut up and listen* in big letters by the tabloids while they explain to me that *you're* the issue. They said if I am lucky to get an interview at one of these big establishments, *you'd* get priority because *you're* a minority. In school they tried to encourage us to be kind and love our neighbour, but then 9/11 came and I was told *you* were a terrorist. Then Alison came along and I'm told *you* raped kids. And then we had Brexit. And they said *you're* a drain on the NHS and that's why my nan died because the beds were taken up by *you*. That *you've* spent seventy years fuckin' things over for us. How can I not be angry when I'm living in a shit-hole while the rest of the world moves on? I'm not saying it's specifically *you*, Mo, but I'm saying this is what I was told about you all my life.'

'Do you see people like me in positions of power?' Mo asked.

'No. But here you are in a suit when I'm sat here in hand-me-downs.'

'Stephen, those rich white guys are trying to convince people like me that you're the reason I'm not richer. That you're a drain on my taxes. But I don't see you any different. I'm here to help everyone. Meanwhile, they're convincing people like you that I've taken away the jobs you could've applied for. We're in this together, believe it or not.'

'Very easy to say that from a position of privilege.'

'But I didn't grow up that way, Stephen. My parents were poor. They finally got enough money to buy a shop after years of working three jobs at a time, and they built up an empire but they had to do that *in spite* of the inherent racism which was surrounding us then. Despite all the setbacks we pushed through to better ourselves.'

'So what does that say about my family?' Stephen snapped.

'You were let down. By lots of people. You could've had everything I had. But you were told to give up and blame others, instead of trying to work hard and progress. The rich don't want you to make a success of yourself, but I certainly do.'

'I need you, bruv. I know you can't stand the sight of me right now. But I promise, I'm a changed man and what's more is I think you believe in our case.'

'I can't deny that.'

'Alison needs you too, mate. So how's about two fellas from the block take on the world?' Stephen put forward his hand towards Mo and smiled. His lawyer took it and shook.

Stephen left the office and Mo looked out of the window and smiled. Thomas ran back into the room with a panicked look on his face.

'I'm so sorry about that, Mo. I won't let it happen again.'

'No, honestly, thank you, it was good to see him. Get his file out of the drawer. And ring Rachel McCann and tell her we're back in business. Tell her I look forward to seeing her in court.'

Chapter 28

The leaves poured down on a windswept Bolton. Autumn had arrived and blown its scatterings across the court steps. Rachel and Karen arrived in matching blue suits and sunglasses covered their eyes, despite the sun being nowhere in sight. The shades offered protection instead from the flashes of the paparazzi keen to witness one of the most controversial cases in the town's eight-hundred-year history.

Behind, Mohammed walked in with Stephen, whom he'd taken shopping for a suit in Manchester a day earlier. On his arm was Alison, who wore a black trouser suit and a velvet hairband on her freshly dyed now brown hair. Mohammed felt a shiver of glee as he'd made them appear presentable; unfortunately he couldn't speak on their behalf in court. God knows what they would come out with, despite significant preparation over the previous weeks.

Judge Judith Miller walked in and took her seat. She browsed over her notes and reacquainted herself with the case. Before her were two tables. On the left, Rachel sat beside Karen. Papers filled their table, all labelled and scribbled with highlighter pen. To their right was Mohammed with his clients. His notes were hidden within a blue Filofax; he wasn't allowing anyone to capture a glimpse of his strategy.

'So I believe it has taken a while for us to be here for various reasons. Miss McCann, I see you're back on the case. I'd like opening statements please and make it to the point. No waffling. We'd all like to make a decision on this matter and go home. Thank you.'

Rachel stood up and looked around her. The back of the room was made up of local journalists relentlessly taking down notes as she spoke. A herd of retired ladies sat at the back and nibbled on crisps, looking ready to watch an Oscar-winning blockbuster. An older gentleman sat behind them. He had thick white combed-over hair and big blue eyes, which had lines forming beneath them. He'd arrived casually in a red jumper and jeans, with a beige overcoat drooped over his shoulders. Rachel recognised him immediately. It was Professor Price from the University of Manchester. He'd taught both lawyers in the case today and he had a look of pride as his former students took the stand, competing against each other. He reminisced about the debate classes he held many years before; now they were going to recreate those scenes with a real case. Beside him, he'd brought a selection of students in tow who were furiously taking notes. No doubt he'd be watching them in a few years' time taking to the stand themselves.

'Your Honour, today I'm going to ask you to decide on whether Mr Fletcher and Miss Sharples here are responsible for the death of Charles Irvine, known to his friends and family as Charlie, which is how I'll address him in this case going forward. Now I don't for a second believe they deliberately killed Charlie. That would be unfair. However the actions they took last year led to his death. The pair have a non-profit organisation, The Predator Hunters, who operate a scheme to entrap people on the internet and expose them as child abusers. In the past they've had some success, but in this case, they enticed a young and vulnerable person, but most importantly an innocent person.'

'Charlie Irvine was autistic,' Rachel continued. 'They lured him into a false sense of security and exposed him online as a predator. If that wasn't enough, they kidnapped him, held him hostage and caused him significant distress, so much so that when he managed to escape, they chased after him. He had no choice but to run out into oncoming traffic, leading to his death. Charlie Irvine would still be here today if this group had employed more honourable procedures to ensure the safeguarding of a very vulnerable person and hadn't committed the very illegal practice of keeping him from leaving a dangerous and frightening environment, against his will. They assaulted him and he died trying to escape. Your Honour, at the end of this trial, I'm going to ask you to award my client a bereavement payment, charged to the people who are responsible for his death, which is The Predator Hunters gang which you see sat before you today.'

Rachel nodded her head and took to her seat. She looked over to Karen who whispered a *thank you* in her ear. To their right, Mohammed stood up and cleared his throat before beginning his opening statement.

'Your Honour, Miss McCann here is going to present to you the theory that Charlie's autism exonerated him from the law, something which I personally find quite offensive. She's going to try and excuse Charlie's behaviour based on a development disorder, claiming he wasn't responsible for his actions. It's completely distasteful and quite frankly dishonourable to the seven hundred thousand people in this country who have autism. She's also going to present to you a supposedly innocent person. But I'm going to show to you in this court that Charlie Irvine was a child predator and my clients took significant steps to ensure that he didn't harm any children.

'Were their actions considered to be conventional?' Mo continued. 'Maybe not. However they did what they had to do to keep our children safe. Even their own lawyer, Miss McCann's child, has been personally saved from abuse due to this group. I'm going to show you that Charlie Irvine was someone who regularly met young children on the internet and viewed illegal images on the internet. And what's more, Charlie Irvine had violent tendencies and attacked my client with a hammer leading to serious injuries and a loss of earnings for my client. Therefore at the end of this case, Your Honour, I'll not only be asking you to exonerate my client from the horrendous claims, which Miss

McCann here is making, but to also award Stephen Fletcher financial compensation for the injuries sustained from Charlie Irvine's actions.'

Mohammed sat down and the judge jotted some notes down before looking up at the pair and smiling. 'I thought I said to keep it short and direct.' The crowd behind them giggled, before she waved her hand to silence them. 'Right, let's begin. Miss McCann, if you can proceed with your case.'

Rachel collated her notes and walked to the front of the court. A television stood on a trolley, which was wheeled before them. The lawyer turned on the screen and pressed play. The footage showed the video from The Predator Hunters' Facebook page, showing the initial conversations between Charlie and the girl he believed to be Anna, who was thirteen, discussing their favourite ice creams, before he met her at the cinema in Farnworth. The video showed him being thrown into a car and forced into the garage at Alison's home. Karen winced and shut her eyes as once again she had to watch the footage of her son escaping the house and ultimately being hit by a lorry. The crowd behind them gasped. The judge pushed her glasses from the edge of her nose up towards her eyes, before looking away to write further notes.

'Your Honour, as you can see, Charlie was duped into a conversation with this gang. The conversation he and the supposed *Anna* had was actually very innocent. Child-like if anything. He went to meet what he believed to be a friend, someone he could actually relate to in many ways. When Alison and Stephen here approached him, he became very confused and scared. They forced him into their car and, against his will, kept him in their garage. As you can see, Stephen and the other person in the video, who is Simon, who isn't here today for reasons I don't know, are seen looking for duct tape to tie my client's son down. If he wasn't there against his will, I ask you today why duct tape was required. Charlie Irvine was so frightened, he used whatever force he could to free himself from this very frightening situation and ran away as fast as he could, even if it meant running into oncoming traffic just to get away. Your Honour, the defence will try to tell you Charlie isn't innocent, that he knew what he was doing and that he was trying to commit suicide to free himself from the backlash to what would obviously become a social media nightmare. I'll give you the backstory to Charlie as a person to show you who he really was. My first witness is Nick Pugh.'

A sweaty Nick took to the stand, wiping back his damp ginger hair. He appeared whiter than normal and his hand trembled as he found his place in the box. He glanced over at Karen, who bowed her head, avoiding eye contact with the man she'd told to get out of her house weeks earlier after he, in her eyes, betrayed her. Nick recounted working as an assistant teacher, how he'd worked with Charlie and recognised quite early that he wasn't like other children. He recounted the story of how he ran away when another child touched him, having panicked and simply focused on getting the hell out of a frightening situation. The TA told stories about Charlie's kindness and his innocence towards the world. When he finished, Rachel smiled, thanked him and she returned to her seat.

Mohammed stood up and read over his research on the former tutor, before approaching the bench.

'Mr Pugh, are you a qualified teacher?'

'No, I'm an assistant.'

'And are you a psychologist?' Mo grilled.

'No.' Nick gulped, glancing back to Rachel who nodded her head with encouragement.

'So you don't really know what Charlie was like. You saw the person he presented himself to you in school.'

'My experience after twenty-five years with young people makes me have a good indication.'

'That may be the case, Mr Pugh, but you are not qualified to give a psychological assessment of a child. You don't know the real Charlie any more than anyone else. He allowed you to see this innocent and vulnerable person. But you can't say for sure really that he didn't possess the behaviours of a predator because you just simply don't know, do you, Nick?'

'No, I suppose I can't really be sure.'

Rachel and Karen bowed their heads, frustrated that their key witness to who Charlie was had been tarnished by the simple case that his qualifications didn't make him a credible character witness.

'Tell me more about Charlie, Mr Pugh. I'm particularly interested to know if he was ever violent.'

'*Ever*...?' Nick replied.

'Violent, Mr Pugh. Did he ever hurt other children?'

'No.'

'No? You never witnessed him ever be violent, never hit anyone?' Mo grilled. 'And remember you're in a court of law so don't lie, Mr Pugh. Remember you're under oath.'

'Well, on occasion if other kids teased him or touched him, or moved his things, he would shove them.'

'Did he ever hit them, Mr Pugh?'

'I did see him hit other children, it was rare, but yes I did see that. He was so young though.'

'Thank you, Mr Pugh. Your Honour, I show you today the real Charlie Irvine, who presented to everyone this loving and kind, almost innocent person, but he couldn't always hide the real person. This is someone who had a history of violence and he attacked these children, just like he attacked my client. Thank you, Mr Pugh, you're free to go.'

Mohammed sat down and smiled at Stephen, who patted his lawyer on the back. Rachel glared at Mo, who stared down, avoiding his friend's dismay.

'Miss McCann, who is your next witness?' asked the judge.

'Well, seeing Mr Iqbal wants to hear from a qualified psychologist, he's in luck as that's exactly who I'm bringing on next. I call Dr Fatima Panchal.'

A large Asian lady took to the stand. She had a thick Indian accent and a serious expression on her face. She had a black jacket, purple skirt and a gold brooch upon her breast pocket. She sat with her shoulders high with a straight posture and stared towards the lawyer, ready for her grilling.

'Dr Panchal, how long have you been a psychologist?' Rachel began.

'Nearly thirty years.'

'And during that time can you give me the scope of your expertise?'

'I started out in couples' therapy but then developed into criminal psychology and then finally became a child specialist.'

'And you saw Charlie a few times, didn't you?'

'Yes, I had to dig deep into the notes but yes, I went into his school and assessed him and I determined that he had autism.'

'What traits gave you that indication?' Rachel asked.

'Well from what I could see during our sessions, he had repetitive behaviour, my report showed he experienced anger, he struggled to interact socially, and he clearly had anxiety and cognitive distortion which is an inability to determine between accurate and inaccurate thoughts. He struggled to have empathy and he was clearly very lonely.'

'Would you say his development was delayed?'

'Yes, psychologically. He was very young, even for his age which was ten when I saw him. I thought I'd met a five-year-old at the time, but then he stood up and I saw how tall he was. It's quite normal for this sort of severe case to carry on into adulthood.'

'And in terms of this inability to form social interactions, would you say it was normal for an adult with severe autism to seek out friendship in children?'

'They'd seek it out anywhere they could. It's very lonely and it's hard for people to understand. Children hold no judgement and so I could understand somebody who really wanted to connect with someone that they would meet whoever could offer that friendship.'

'I've shown you the notes of the chat which Charlie had online with the girl he believed was thirteen. What did you determine from that conversation?'

Fatima read over the notes which Rachel handed to her. She held up her glasses and placed the papers under the light before turning to the lawyer.

'I'd assume it was a child, but then again if you told me it was an adult, I'd say it was someone who has a significant development disorder who is seeking out a friendship online.'

'Do you ever witness violence as a trait of someone with this condition?' asked Rachel.

'Well, if they feel threatened, they may act out, certainly, but in my experience it wouldn't be unfounded. They're usually quite calm and distant, unless they feel they are in harm's way. This can be if someone touches them if they don't like to be touched.'

'So if someone tied them to a chair or locked them in a garage, you'd expect them to exhibit some sort of violent tendencies?'

'Then I'd expect them to lash out as they'd be fearful, but I'd expect that of most human beings to be honest in that situation, Miss McCann.'

Rachel browsed through Fatima's CV and the notes which she'd made upon it.

'You said you've dealt with criminal psychology, have you dealt with people who are child abusers?'

'Yes, there's very few people I've not come across. Murderers, rapists, you name it, I've seen it,' Fatima replied.

'And in your experience, have people with autism typically become child abusers?'

'No,' Fatima said firmly. 'In my experience, the autistic person is usually the victim of this type of crime rather than the perpetrator. People take advantage of children with development disorders as they're an easy target. Reaching out and talking doesn't come easy to them, so that's very easy to manipulate.'

'Thank you, Dr Panchal. That's all my questions.'

Rachel sat down and her competition rose up, leaping over to the stand.

'Dr Panchal, thank you so much for coming here today. It was fantastic to hear all about your history and you've got quite a lot of credentials.'

'Thank you, Mr Iqbal.' For the first time since she entered the court, she smiled as she absorbed his compliment.

'You said earlier that psychologically Charlie and other people with this development disorder may act younger than what they really are.'

'That's correct.'

'How about their physical bodies?' Mo quizzed.

'What about them?' she asked with a surprised voice.

'Well, do their bodies struggle to develop, or is it just their mind?'

'In my experience, their bodies grow naturally like anyone else.'

'And in which case, a nineteen-year-old man, regardless whether he had autism or not, would typically have sexual urges.'

'Yes as long as there were no other physical development issues, I'd expect him to have a healthy sexual interest. Whether he could make a connection with someone to understand that, would be something else altogether.'

'Therefore isn't it highly possible that Charlie might be meeting young children for a social interaction but actually his sexual appetite would still be present?'

'Without a full psychological evaluation, I wouldn't be able to say.'

'But it isn't impossible?'

'I wouldn't completely rule it out, no.'

'Just finally, Dr Panchal, you said you've met lots of sexual predators in your time as a psychologist. Would you describe to me the typical traits of someone who was a child abuser?'

'Erm...' Fatima scratched her head, rolling her eyes up to the ceiling, before returning to Mohammed. 'Well, I typically used to see low self-esteem, antisocial behaviour, personality problems, lack of remorse or empathy and interpersonal hostility.'

'Sounds very similar to the traits you described Charlie as having. Thank you, Dr Panchal, no more questions, Your Honour.'

Mo sat down and shook his client's hand. Rachel bowed her head and sighed, listening to the mutterings behind her. She had no doubt that the people who were staring at the back of her neck believed Charlie to be guilty and she only had a limited selection of witnesses left to convince them otherwise. In the seat before her, Judge Judith held her poker face and continued to jot down notes.

'Who is your next witness, Miss McCann?' the judge turned to Rachel.

'Charlie's mother, Karen Irvine.'

Karen grew pale and felt her arms glued to her seat. Rachel turned to her client and glared at her, nodding her head towards the stand. *'Come on,'* she mouthed, but Karen sat still and shook her head.

'I can't, I'm too scared.'

'Miss McCann,' the judge called. Rachel held up her index finger before pulling at her client's arm.

'You have to do this,' Rachel said between gritted teeth. 'Remember when we were at Snowdon and despite all your fear you did it. You went back to that belly fire you had when you used to dance at Coyotes. I need you to get that belly fire back, Karen, and I need it now. Remember what your boss said? Nothing matters. Picture them all naked.'

Karen took deep breaths and closed her eyes. Her shoulders bounced up and down while she tried to maintain a rhythm. The judge stared on with dismay, while those behind were astonished by what they were witnessing.

'Miss McCann?'

'Your Honour, I may need to wrap things up....'

'I'm coming,' Karen shouted. 'I'll take the stand. Sorry, Your Honour, last minute nerves. I was never good at public speaking.'

Karen lifted herself up slowly and hobbled over to the stand. She was shaking and her lips trembled. One shaky hand covered her mouth and the other lifted out a tissue and wiped a tear away. Rachel eased her in by asking her about Charlie's upbringing, his personality and his struggle to connect. They discussed his joy when he found the internet and the time he spent on chat rooms, which was a relief to her that he was finally talking to *someone*. Karen said that he rarely left the house and he spent most of his life on the internet playing games. They relived the day he died and Karen broke down in tears as she spoke about the emptiness she now felt now he was no longer alive.

'I know Charlie died petrified, so afraid and alone, and that kills me. And what's worse is I'm mourning him alone as this awful group not only caused his death, but they released this awful video on the internet and made him out to be something he's not. People hate my son but he did nothing wrong.'

'Thank you, Karen.' Rachel nodded and winked at her client as she took her seat. She was surprised to see Mohammed stand up and approach the poor grieving mother. *What now? Hasn't he destroyed enough of my witnesses today?*

'Ms Irvine, did you ever see what your son looked at on the internet?'

'No, he was very protective about his things.'

'So you don't know what he was looking at, or who he talking to?' Mo asked.

'No, and I had no reason to be worried at the time.' Karen gulped.

'Did he ever leave the house?'

'Yes, occasionally.'

'And where would he go?'

'I don't know.' Karen's eyes watered. 'I know it sounds terrible, but I was just glad he was getting fresh air.'

'Would you ask him where he went?' Mo grilled.

'Yes, he'd just say he was going to the park or to a friend's. I never really knew. But I knew he'd never go far, I don't think he'd really know how.'

'You say he wouldn't go far, but on this day he managed to get to Farnworth.'

'Yes it was a surprise, oh and he also called me up from Manchester once. I don't know how he knew how to get there or what he did when he got there, but that was Charlie, always a surprise.'

'So he could've been doing anything while he was away from home?'

'I suppose yes.' Karen nodded.

'Even abusing children?' Mohammed's voice turned to a dark and grim tone.

'No! He wouldn't do that,' Karen screamed.

'You make him out to be this wonderful and innocent boy, however he stole the money out of your bag on the day he died, so that he could go and meet what he believed to be a thirteen-year-old girl. Would you say stealing was something an innocent person would do?'

'That's not fair.'

'Answer the question, Ms Irvine, would an innocent person steal?'

'No,' Karen sobbed.

'No more questions, Your Honour.'

Karen returned to her seat where a distraught Rachel embraced her and gave her a seat. She asked for a break and the judge agreed a ten-minute recess while Karen had a drink of water and recuperated before the case continued.

'My last witness today, Your Honour, is a digital forensic consultant. I call Richard Vixon.'

A mid-twenties man was called and made his way to the stand. He had long brown hair and thick square glasses. A moustache slithered across his top lip. He wore a suit with a waistcoat beneath and a bright yellow tie. He smiled as he looked at Rachel who began the questioning.

'Mr Vixon, you reviewed Charlie Irvine's computer, is this correct?'

'That's right, Miss McCann.'

'Please give me an overview of your findings.'

'Well, it was normal for a nineteen-year-old boy, I suppose. He played lots of games, watched porn, which from my report you will see was adult porn with no concerns. He didn't access any illegal items from the dark web, or anything typical of what I'd find on a predator's computer.'

'And the porn he did access, this was all above board?' asked Rachel.

'Yes, he used a fairly common website, XXXWeb, which anyone would find in the top three items of a Google search.'

'And his web chats?'

'Yes, he was quite child-like, really. He generally discussed his favourite ice cream or his favourite games. Nothing I would consider sinister but I'm not a psychologist, I look for facts.'

'Thank you. Your Honour, the full report is available for you to read.'

Mohammed took Rachel's place with his report and a remote in hand.

'Mr Vixon, in your report you said there was one image where you couldn't verify whether the models or actresses, whatever you may call them, were of legal age or not.'

'That's right but it didn't fall into a pattern of predatory behaviour. It was one image out of hundreds.'

'I wonder if this was the image you were referring to.'

Mohammed pressed play on the screen of the television, which was used for presenting evidence earlier in the case. On the screen, two pale girls with black long hair tied up in pigtails made out, dressed in school uniforms. When they did break away from kissing for just a second, they spoke in Russian. Mohammed paused the footage before they began to take their clothes off. The

265

crowd behind them gasped and the judge hid her eyes behind her hand.

'Is that the image you were referring to, Mr Vixon?'

'Ahem, that is the footage in question, yes.'

'Regardless of what the rest of your report says, Mr Vixon, would you not expect young girls who look below the legal age, dressed in school uniform, to be exactly the sort of file you'd see on a predator's computer?'

'Well possibly but as per my report, the rest of his search history wasn't typically…'

'Mr Vixon, answer my question. Is this, or is this not, yes or no, exactly the sort of thing you'd find on a predator's computer?'

'Well, I suppose when you put it like that, the answer has to be yes.'

Chapter 29

Their fingers clasped on to the arms of their chairs, the crowd before Mr Vixon were on the edge of their seats as they took in the nature of the images, which the supposedly innocent Charlie Irvine had looked at, on the television screen before them. The judge hurriedly wrote down her notes while the lawyers consulted with their clients. They were surrounded by white walls and above the judge the crest sat proudly in the middle of the wall above a clock, its ticks getting louder as a shocked silence filled the court.

'Your Honour, I need to challenge this image.' Rachel marched towards the bench.

'And why is this?' Judge Judith replied with a raised eyebrow.

'Because one, this is the first time I've seen this image. Why wasn't this submitted to me as part of the evidence pack? Secondly, that video does not show an age, therefore, regardless of what it can be translated as, we can't determine that this *is* an illegal image. I think my client deserves the opportunity to defend the image therefore it's only fair that we recess while we investigate it.'

'You've had plenty of time already, you all had access to the report and this was listed in the appendix. To be honest I don't even see how any of this is relevant. This is to determine whether two people had a hand in someone's death, not a trial of an alleged predator.'

'With all due respect, Your Honour, this whole case is based around the fact that The Predator Hunters kidnapped a vulnerable and innocent man while they attempted to try to sell him to the public as a child molester. They've made some very

267

damaging claims in this court and I feel it's only right that I can defend this.'

The judge sighed and looked at her watch, before shrugging her shoulders.

'Fine, we'll recess. You have one week to review this. Regardless of what comes back we're proceeding again next Monday. You have seven days, Miss McCann. Thank you, Mr Iqbal, your clients may leave the court for the time being.'

Rachel sighed with relief and turned towards Karen who was sobbing. She ran over to her and placed her arms round her, ensuring her that they would sort out the mess which had presented itself. Furious with this new information, the lawyer stormed out of the court. On the steps outside, Nick stood waiting for Karen. She ran over and cried into his shoulder.

'Hi, Karen. I didn't know if you'd want to see me after everything that has happened recently but I had to see if you were OK after that.'

'Thank you for your support, Nick, I just can't believe they're saying these things about my Charlie.'

'Karen,' Rachel butted in. 'I need to run to the office and begin this background check as soon as possible on the girls in the video so we can quickly get this over with. I can run you home but it might delay us and I only have a week to turn it around.'

'I'll take her home,' said Nick. Karen looked up at him and whimpered a *thank you* before burying her head back in his chest.

Rachel returned to her office and with the help of the report began to search for the video. She wondered if searching for it herself would incriminate her but she figured it was the only way to find out. The report gave a very specific link, which brought her to XXXweb. She watched the video all the way through to see how damaging it would be if it turned out the models were underage. It was pretty graphic, with little left to the imagination.

Underneath the video, it stated that fourteen thousand people had watched the video, three thousand had rated it as their top video and three hundred had left reviews. If the video was illegal, that was a lot of people to consider as predators, she considered. She clicked on the *'About Us'* link at the bottom of the page and found a contact number for the company. She dialled and heard a range of options from online payments and membership, to advertising and complaints. Selecting the option to speak to an advisor, she waited in a queue for fifteen minutes before someone finally answered.

'Hi, XXXWeb, how can I direct your call today?'

'I'm looking to verify the ages of two models who feature on a video on your site.'

'I'm afraid we don't own any of the content. All of our videos are uploaded by either other companies or individuals. We're basically like YouTube but for porn.'

'OK well I can see this was uploaded by a particular member and has the branding of a company called *RussianXEntertainment* therefore can you give me their details?'

'I'm afraid that's all confidential,' replied the operator.

'How would you like it if I told the press that your website was implicated in sharing illegal images online?' Rachel replied with a firm tone.

'We have a clear process for this. Our website is self-managed by the viewers. They can report any video to us by a click of a button and we will not only remove the item but it'll also be sent to the police. I'm guessing you're talking about a video which is currently live on our website, by all means, feel

269

free to report it. The website is self-managed by our users, who we trust to make a decision themselves on whether an image is legal or not.'

'It's been up for two years,' Rachel said, scanning over the date of the upload.

'Well then I guess the public don't find it offensive.'

The operator hung up and Rachel sighed, frustrated with the red tape she had to get past to find out information, especially when vulnerable people could potentially be at risk. When she scanned the internet for the name of the video creator, *RussianXEntertainment*, the search engine came back with zero results. She watched the video again to see if it would give any clues. The Russian accents reminded her of a connection that she had to the country.

Timothy Jenkins had studied alongside her at Manchester. They took several law modules together, before he went on to study a master's in politics at Oxford. From the alumni magazine sent to her on an annual basis, she discovered he'd gone on to become the official Advisor to the Russian Ambassador and now lived in Moscow.

She scanned her Facebook friends and found his details. There he was; a little older, a little balder, but much smarter than the hooded hooligan she hung out with at university. He stood proudly between the Prime Minister and the Ambassador of Russia. She sent him a private message and within an hour they were on Skype, talking like old friends. After reminiscing about their uni days, she updated him on her situation.

'No worries, I can get someone on this,' Jenkins said as she pleaded for his support.

'I need it looked into really fast. I only have a week.'

'I'll have it by tonight, I'll just threaten Putin's Federal Security Service on the company. It's the Russian MI5. You might remember it as the KGB. No one who creates adult content here wants them looking into their work. These companies might put out legal content on official channels but they usually feed into the dark web too. They create snuff videos and all sorts, you'd never believe the shit that goes on here behind closed doors. And if they're not doing any of that, I'm sure a search on their tax returns will put the fear of God in them.'

'Thanks, Tim. I can't believe you'd do this for me. To be honest, I contacted you on a whim today, I didn't expect you'd be able to do anything for me, or would want to in the first place.'

'For you, I'd do anything. I'll never forget you staying up until three AM helping me with my dissertation. I got a first because of you. I never got the chance to make it up to you. So here it is.'

'Well it was obviously worth it, look at you now. And it paid off as now you're able to help me.'

They hung up. Rachel knew it was out of her hands but decided to continue to review the website. She browsed the reviews and the people who had shared the video in question on other platforms. She kept notes and took screenshots of her findings, searching for breadcrumbs in case Timothy couldn't deliver on his promise.

Three hours later, an email pinged into her inbox. She opened it and saw a message from the Ambassador's official account. Attached were two PDF Files. She opened each one. Enclosed were photocopies of Russian passports, each with an image of the girls she recognised from the films. The dates of birth put them at the age of twenty, which covered the site for the two years which they'd had the video streaming online. They were just eighteen when they made the films. Rachel sighed with relief, lay back on her sofa and wiped the sweat off her forehead. She couldn't help fearing that this would be the future for her own daughter in eight years' time if she didn't get her back on track soon.

A week later, they returned to court. Rachel strolled in with a smug smile on her face, knowing full well that Mohammed could not touch her evidence. The images were legal, end of discussion. Regardless, he challenged her anyway.

'Whether they're legal or not, Miss McCann, he was watching girls who looked barely legal in school uniforms,' Mohammed responded to her claim. 'That's surely a man who gets a thrill from looking at young girls.'

'Oh, Mr Iqbal. Fourteen thousand people watched that video and not one person reported it. Are you saying that fourteen thousand people are paedophiles?'

'Well... yes,' Mo replied.

'Even your own client?' Rachel smiled and glanced towards Stephen.

'What do you mean?'

'You see, on this website, you have to be a member. They do it to ensure those watching the video are of the legal age of consent. These people's identities are kept private in the back of the system. However people can create profiles and *like* videos, give them a rating and even leave reviews. Most people have blank profiles with a random image of a cartoon or a cat. However, your client, Mr Stephen Fletcher, quite proudly shows his name and even his photograph. And while I was reading the reviews for the video you claim could only be enjoyed by child predators, who did I spot that had left a review, but Stephen Fletcher himself.'

Rachel reached into her folder, pulled out two prints of a screenshot she'd taken the previous week and slammed one onto the judge's desk and handed the second to her competitor.

'I wonder if Stephen protests too much by hunting down these predators. He's clearly enjoying images like this himself, therefore he must be a predator himself, if we're going by your reckoning, Mr Iqbal. Mr Fletcher described this video as *"hot, tasty and can't wait to see more from this director."* So I'll ask you again, Mr Iqbal, do you still believe this image would only be enjoyed by a predator?'

'No.' Mohammed bowed his head, knowing full well that his argument had crumbled. He returned to his desk with his tail between his legs and grumbled at Stephen for not telling him sooner. They'd all viewed the video together prior to the case and not once had Stephen held his hand up and said he'd seen the video himself. Beside Stephen, Alison couldn't stop giggling and shoved her friend in the arm, calling him an idiot.

'No more questions, Your Honour.'

Chapter 30

After a rough day in court, Karen took Nick out to a local Italian restaurant for dinner as a thank you for his contribution to the case and the lift home from Bolton Court. The restaurant was built inside a former terraced house with just a handful of tables taking up what was once the sitting room. They dined on pizza and pasta, while they were still dressed in their court attire. They shared a bottle of Pinot, which they brought with them as the restaurant didn't have a licence.

'I really appreciate you being there today, Nick.' Karen sipped her wine and gave her friend a warm smile. 'And I'm sorry for falling out with you over the whole Matilda-gate thing. I was just so angry and you were the only person I had left who I could count on.'

'Water under the bridge,' Nick replied.

They paid up and he walked her to her house just around the corner, giving her a kiss on the cheek as they reached the front door. She waved him off and ran upstairs to get into her pyjamas and white fluffy dressing gown, before returning to the kitchen. She poured herself what was left of the wine which she'd brought home from the restaurant.

A knock at the door disturbed the peace. She instantly thought of Nick; had he forgotten something? Maybe he'd returned to give her a second kiss? She smiled, tightened up her robe and opened the door. Behind it a scruffy twenty-something with a pierced lip and large holes in his ear-lobes stood smoking a rolled-up cigarette, which Karen suspected had more than just tobacco in it. He wore a black suit and a white shirt, which was now unpinned at the collar.

'Mr Fletcher,' she said; his formal title being how he'd been addressed throughout the proceedings. 'What the hell are you doing here?'

'I wanted to talk,' Stephen replied.

'How did you get my address?'

'You read it out in court last week.'

Karen raised her head and closed her eyes as she relived having to expose her personal details to everyone as she gave evidence. She opened her eyes and glared at the man who was responsible for her son's death.

'I don't think this is appropriate, I want you to go away.'

'Please,' Stephen replied with his hands together as if in prayer. 'I really need to talk to you. You've already given your evidence, the trial is nearly over. I just really needed to come and meet you, and explain.'

'You get that opportunity tomorrow.'

'That's all the formal shit. I wanna see the whites of your eyes. If we'd talked sooner maybe we could have worked this out long ago.'

Karen stood back and nodded her head in towards her hallway. She walked into the kitchen, picked up her phone and keyed a few buttons. She slipped the device into her robe pocket and returned to the lounge where Stephen was sitting in an armchair.

'That's where *he* sat,' Karen said, glancing over at a framed photograph beside him. He turned to his left and picked up the picture and stroked the face of Charlie Irvine.

'From what I heard in court, he sounds like a nice guy.'

'He *was*,' Karen said, a tear duct bursting in the corner of her eye.

'Things got really fucked up that day, Karen,' Stephen said. 'I don't know what happened. We hadn't done it that way before. But Charlie was so keen to get away. Simon, the other guy in our group, wanted to take a lead on this target. Well let's just say he made a pig's ear of it. Forcing Charlie into a car, then wanting to tie him up. Fuck knows what we'd have done when the police arrived.'

'So you admit you made a mistake.'

'I do. I should never have let it get that far. Looking back, I can see all the tell-tale signs that he wasn't like the usual lot we expose. I said to both Simon and Alison that he was too easy. I thought we were the ones being entrapped, not him. I thought some angry paedo was coming to get us, so I said we had to go as a three just to ensure we were all safe.'

'Why didn't you just let him go?'

'Because at the time I was angry. Angry that some knob-head adult could think he could come and meet a little girl and have his way with her, like. I know that's not what he was like now. But at the time I was furious. We couldn't tell that he was autistic. He looked just like us.'

'And then you put him all over the internet! As if I hadn't been through enough; now everyone talks about me like I'm some sort of monster mother, and my son's honour is ruined forever. You ran after my son, chasing him into oncoming traffic. He died needlessly and you then had to humiliate him and me.'

'I'm sorry.' Stephen's voice broke. 'Listen, the way we went about things that day, we were worried we might be arrested for kidnapping or for chasing after him. The best thing we could do was put that video on so the public would be in our favour and not Charlie's. Without the video, Charlie was some disabled teenager who we locked up. With it, he was a predator who we stopped from hurting people's kids. For anyone watching, he was a guilty man killing himself before someone else did it for him.'

'Do you have any idea what you have done to me and my family?' Karen wept. 'I don't know how anyone can be so monstrous. All this and for what? We've done nothing to you.'

'You haven't, Ms Irving, but lots of bad people have. You didn't grow up like me. You didn't see what I saw.'

'I don't care if you've had a rough upbringing. It doesn't mean you can go round terrorising the streets. Charlie and I struggled and we didn't turn to a life of hurting others. And you think you're some do-gooder vigilante? You're not bloody Batman! I'm sorry you had it rough but it's no excuse.'

'*Rough?* You think what I lived through was rough?' Stephen growled. 'I can live without a nice house or holidays. I can even live with the second-hand uniform I got at school. Sure, that's rough. But what I couldn't live with is having my stepdad abuse me.'

Silence filled the room as Karen soaked in Stephen's story. Her shoulders relaxed and she sat back, taking deep breaths as she endured the reality of his past.

'He was such a nice guy,' Stephen continued. 'He took me everywhere. I bloody loved him. Then he'd want to take photos of me swimming, sometimes in even less. Then he'd touch me. Tell me he loved me. What's worse is that I loved him too! And then I grew up and I was deemed too old for him. He'd moved on to my brother. And that's when I realised what he did was wrong.'

'What happened to him?' Karen asked, reaching out a hand to place on his knee, but he waved it away.

'I told my mum and she confronted him. He beat her black and blue for even suggesting it and then he came after me. Then she caught him with my brother. She picked up a knife and stabbed him. She just didn't stop.' Stephen took a deep breath and retched as he relived the story. 'There was blood everywhere. They arrested her and she couldn't face telling the police what happened to us. She didn't want us to have to go to court or to have to relive the whole thing. So she said it was domestic. She went to prison. She received a life sentence. Then me and my brother were put into care. He was adopted as he was still young. Nobody wanted me. I was too old and too troubled. So I lived life in the system until they kicked me out at eighteen and ended up in a council flat without a penny to my name. And I was so fuckin' angry, Karen!

'And then I met Alison on a march after all that kicked off in Rotherham,' Stephen continued with his story. 'I finally found mates. I met people who'd been through what I'd been through. She was passed around like a bloody doobie when she was younger. We were so pent-up after the march, we went home and went on this chat room, pretended to be a kid and arranged to meet some perv. We battered him when he turned up. It never came back to us, luckily. But then we thought well, we've not stopped him doing it again really, have we? I was so close to cutting his fuckin' balls off but figured I didn't want to spend the rest of my life in prison. Not just to save what, one, two kids? So we thought about how to do it legally and how we could expose as many of these fuckers as possible, once and for all. And so we formed The Predator Hunters group. Simon joined later when he saw our work on Facebook, but he's always been a wanker. He was always heavy-handed; he loved coming to the immigration marches and kicking off. He just wanted some violence. God knows what's up with him. He's gone now. He's no longer one of us.'

'What happened to your brother?' Karen gulped and wiped her eyes.

'No idea. I've tried finding him but I've had little luck. I wrote a couple of times and asked them to put it away in his file for when he's ready to review it, but they won't tell me where he is and he's never written back. I hope he's happy anyway and with a nice family. Maybe I'll go on that *Long Lost Family* show on TV sometime. He'd be eighteen by now.'

'I'm so sorry this happened to you, Stephen. I really am. It does make sense though. It doesn't make me any less angry with you but I at least understand why you go to such great lengths with these schemes.'

'I know I fucked up that day, Karen. We'll never be able to bring you your lad back. But I just wanted to reach out to you and say outside of court, whatever happens tomorrow, that I am truly sorry for what happened to him that day. It shouldn't have happened.'

He reached his hand out and she took his. They forced a small smile to each other and nodded their heads, before hugging each other. He then made his excuses to leave. She thanked him for coming and saw him out the door, watching him walk without his usual swagger down the road, his head lowered.

She clutched her chest and walked inside and took out her phone. She read the earlier message which she'd sent to Nick asking him to come round if he hadn't heard from her within the hour. He had sent urgent replies asking if she was OK, and even tried calling but she'd put the device on aeroplane mode to prevent any calls coming in. She replied *'It's all good, don't worry. See you tomorrow x.'*

Chapter 31

Warren Watkins couldn't believe his luck. Despite losing his large house in the divorce, as well as his job as a head teacher at a prestigious school, he had his freedom, something he'd come very close to losing. The stress of the trial had made him lose a little weight too. Unfortunately any interested ladies wouldn't be too impressed when they turned up at his house to find out he was living with his mother, but hey, it was better than the forced shower fun he'd have anticipated had he been made a resident of HMP Forest Bank.

Whilst he couldn't return to teaching, he had found a role as a consultant for the education system, supporting universities with their finances. It wasn't what he dreamed of doing with his career but it meant he could get back on his feet and hopefully move out of his mother's house soon enough.

Having found a new job, he decided to go out and celebrate. He drove out to a pub in Chorley town centre and sat on a wooden stool at the bar, talking to the landlord. Locally brewed ales covered the pumps within the beach-hut themed bar. The staff wore coconut bras and had grass skirts wrapped around their waists. Warren downed several pints before moving on to spirits. At eleven, the landlord said he'd had enough after he got a bit handsy with one of the bar staff, and Warren returned to his car, sure that he could make it home safely without being stopped. It was only a ten-minute drive down a straight empty road, therefore what would be the harm?

As he reached his car, a puddle of doubt entered his mind and considered the possibility that if he was stopped, the police officer would smell the fumes on his breath. A bulb lit up as he remembered he had mouthwash and aftershave in the boot. He opened it, stroking the side of his Mercedes, his pride and joy; the one thing he'd got to keep after his divorce from Shelley.

'Hey.' A voice came from behind as he reached for the aftershave. He turned around and saw a large man in a white tank top, thick waist and towering figure. His arms were nearly as wide as his neck, which had rolled at the top.

'Can I help you?' Warren replied.

'You're Warren Watkins, aren't you?'

'Yes, that's right.' Warren pulled on his own collar and a dribble of sweat poured down his forehead.

'But some might call you Pete?'

'Oh you read that in the paper probably or saw it online, I presume. Just so you know, I was let go. It was all a trap. The courts found me an innocent man.'

'But you're not though, are you, Warren?'

'I am, I promise.'

The angry-eyed beast before him grabbed Warren's keys and threw him in the boot. It was dark and Warren couldn't see a thing. Remembering a trick he'd heard about cars having an escape latch, he felt around for a lever, but he failed to find a way to get out of the vehicle. The car was in motion for some time and he rolled around in the back with every sharp turn. Eventually it came to a sliding stop and Warren jerked as he came to a halt. The boot opened; the tank-topped thug lifted him out of the boot and pulled him by the scruff of his neck into a wood. It was beginning to rain and his charcoal suit and shoes were splashed with mud as they walked over the puddled path.

'Please, I'll do anything. Do you want money? You can have the car. Anything!'

'Shut up. I don't want anything from you.'

The route became darker and darker, lit up only by his kidnapper's torch. He stopped beside a hole, large enough to be his grave. A pile of soil lay to the side. Trees surrounded them. Warren swallowed hard and began to cry. He fell down onto his knees, clutched on to his captor and begged him to let him go. The man lifted off the ground a spade, lying next to the damp hole.

'This is for every child you've ever harmed.'

The spade was lifted up and swung down hard on Warren's temple. He silently fell back into the hole and lay there, blood pouring from the side of his head. He opened his eyes, dazed and confused and looked up towards his attacker, who began to fill the hole with the remaining soil. His world went black and he could taste the soil piling on top of him. His airways became blocked and he panicked until peace eventually arrived.

Up above, the attacker looked around and was confident that he was alone. He took the car and drove off, dumping it in a nearby river. As he watched the Mercedes drift off, another car pulled up, a Ford Fiesta. Inside, a woman with dark long hair and a piercing through her lip, smiled and opened the door for him.

'It's done,' he said as he entered the passenger seat.

'Thank you.' She kissed his cheek and took to the wheel.

'That's the last favour I'm doing for you, Alison. You're on your own now.'

'That's all I need.'

She smiled and drove off into the night.

Chapter 32

The court proceedings recommenced the following morning. Mo stood up to introduce his defence for his client, The Predator Hunters group. Behind him, Alison and Stephen sat in their seats, dressed in their off-the-peg suits, which he was just glad they'd agreed to wear after taking them shopping. They'd made enough noise in the Trafford Centre. Alison had dark shadows around her eyes and Mo wondered if she had struggled to sleep as she relived some of her own horrors as they replayed the abuse others had received.

He began by introducing the video which Rachel McCann had gone through the previous week. He told a different story with the same footage. He showed Charlie's conversations as predatory, eager to meet a young girl, and displayed the nude photographs he'd sent her. He talked through his attempt to run away, not from the gang, but their threat of the police. Mo took particular time showing and replaying the footage of Charlie attacking Stephen with a hammer. Finally, the lawyer moved to the final scene, replaying the video of Charlie running in front of the lorry.

'A coroner may have established this as misadventure, however another coroner had determined Charlie's death as suicide. Had Charlie wanted to escape, he could have run left, or right, instead he went straight on into the traffic. Charlie wanted to escape this world, not the gang, and therefore the only responsibility they have for his death is revealing to the world that he was a monster, which he couldn't accept and so he decided to leave us. Had he still been here, we'd have been at Charlie's trial right now and not The Predator Hunters' trial, who have done absolutely nothing wrong.'

Mohammed then introduced his first witness. Stephen took to the stand and talked about his experiences with the group. He talked about the people they'd caught, the predators they'd put in prison and the children they'd kept from harm, reminding the court that the claimant's own lawyer had been saved from losing her daughter to a predatory monster because of the vigilante group. Stephen discussed Charlie's attack on him with a hammer, how it had meant he couldn't work and had caused him significant pain, bringing along with him the notes from the hospital. Once Mohammed was happy with his client's testimony, he sat down and allowed Rachel to take over.

'Mr Fletcher.' Rachel walked up to the defendant and placed her hand on the stand. 'You're clearly well versed in how predators operate, how they manipulate children and influence them to come and meet them, aren't you?'

'I'd say so,' Stephen said confidently.

'Charlie's conversations were quite different to the other predators you've mentioned this morning. There was no *slow burn* as you described it earlier, or weeks of discussions. He simply came out with it and asked to meet. The language he used was completely different to the language you described by predators too. Did this not raise any questions that this person might not be in fact a predator, but possibly someone with a condition?'

'I thought he came across as an inexperienced horny teenager. All paedos start somewhere.'

'You've discussed this morning how your group operate and yet not once did you mention kidnapping the people you approach. Why was it different the day you met Charlie Irvine?' Rachel grilled.

'He was really twitchy and eager to get away. We didn't know where he lived and we wanted to ensure the police got him as quickly as possible. We performed a citizen's arrest which you can't hear on the tape because of a scuffle. That's perfectly within our rights.'

'Tying someone to a chair in a locked garage isn't though, is it, Mr Fletcher?'

'We didn't manage to do that. If he wanted to leave, he could've done,' Stephen defended himself.

'It doesn't look that way to me. Mr Fletcher, there's usually a third person with you, a Mr Simon Jenkins, who appears to be missing from your case today, and yet he's been an integral part of the group for around two years now. Where is he?'

'Mr Jenkins no longer operates with us. We decided to go different ways.'

'Nothing to do with him messing up that day you met Charlie then?' Rachel replied with a raised eyebrow.

'No.'

'Or would it be because he's quite violent as we recently saw at an anti-immigration march? He had a tendency to turn to violence, didn't he, like he was with Charlie.'

'We had a disagreement but it had nothing to do with Charlie. If you think Simon was out of order, you have to take it up with him, not me.'

'But it's your organisation, Mr Fletcher. It's set up with you as the director. You're responsible as director for your staff, which technically, no matter how loosely you call this not-for-profit company, is still a company, and Simon was your employee.'

'That's not how it works,' Stephen assured her.

'I'm afraid in the eyes of the law it is, Mr Fletcher.'

'I have nothing to say on that matter.' Stephen gulped and looked to his lawyer who shook his head.

'Mr Fletcher, do you have any regrets from the day Charlie died?'

'No,' Stephen replied.

'Oh, that's strange. It's not what you said last night to my client. You turned up at Ms Irvine's door and apologised. You said you'd made fatal errors of judgement.'

Mohammed stood up and slammed his fist down on the table. 'Your Honour, there is no evidence for this, this is just Ms Irvine's word against Mr Fletcher's.'

'That's what a witness statement is, Mr Iqbal. Proceed, Miss McCann,' the judge replied and Mohammed retreated with embarrassment.

'Mr Fletcher?' Rachel looked to Stephen.

'She's lying,' Stephen said.

'Your Honour, what you're about to hear is a recording, made by my client on her phone last night. Ms Irvine felt quite threatened when Stephen turned up unannounced at her door so she made sure she captured everything.'

The recording played. The court heard how Stephen had been abused by his stepfather, his admission that Charlie was most likely innocent, his fallout with Simon and those damning words, claiming he had made mistakes on that day, which had led to Charlie's death. The crowd behind them gasped. Stephen turned to Karen, who bowed her head and whispered, *'I'm sorry.'*

'Do you have anything to say to that, Mr Fletcher?'

'No.' Stephen folded his arms and sat back.

'No more questions, Your Honour.'

*

After lunch, Mohammed brought his final witness to the stand. An attractive gentleman in his forties entered the court. Beneath his shirt and jacket he had a trim figure and Rachel double-took at the handsome stranger.

'Please state your name,' Mohammed said.

'It's Benjamin Graham,' he confirmed.

'Mr Graham, tell us what happened on May 3rd, 2019.'

'My daughter, Becky, said she was going to meet a friend at the park, someone called Charlie she said. I thought he was someone her age, she'd been talking about him for a little while. My mother-in-law had become sick and had been rushed to hospital. I had to quickly pick Becky up from the park and take our family to the hospital. When I got to the park, she was sitting on the swings with a man.'

'And that man was Charlie Irvine?'

'The very same.'

'What did you think when you saw Charlie with your daughter?'

'Naturally the worst. I thought he was a predator,' Benjamin replied.

'And you say she'd mentioned him several times, even met him?'

'She talked about him all the time. I think Becky even said he was her boyfriend, I thought it was innocent, until I saw who Charlie was.'

'And how old is Becky, Mr Graham?'

'Thirteen.' The crowd behind them gasped. Karen turned to her lawyer, who appeared as surprised as she did, unsure of where Mohammed was going with his questioning.

'Thank you, no more questions, Your Honour.'

Rachel turned to Karen who appeared terrified. Rachel whispered to her, telling her not to worry, before walking over to the stand.

'Mr Graham, thank you for coming here today and telling us all about Becky's relationship with Charlie. Tell me, Mr Graham, where would Becky and Charlie meet when they were together?'

'It was always at the park,' he replied.

'How are you so sure?' Rachel asked, swinging her arms in the air.

'I have a tracker on her phone, I always know where she is,' Benjamin confidently replied.

'Did you ever see her location deviate from the local park?'

'No,' Benjamin said, squinting his eyes with curiosity.

'And how many times would you say they met?' asked Rachel.

'A handful, five or six times maybe.'

'Did you never worry about her being in a park alone with a boy?' Rachel replied sceptically.

'Well no!' Benjamin said with a raised voice. 'I thought this boy was the same age. I'm not a rubbish dad, you know?'

'I never said you were, Mr Graham, but even so, even if Charlie was let's say a thirteen-year-old boy, with all that testosterone forming, I wouldn't want them alone too long with my daughter, I'll tell you that for free. Were you not concerned at all?'

'Well I would have been…' Benjamin responded.

'But…' Rachel said, anticipating Benjamin was holding back.

'Well, this little park, it's tiny and it's by a road. It's a square bit of grass with a swing and a slide on it. There's nowhere really to hide away. I know they couldn't do anything there without being in sight of someone.'

'I see. Mr Graham, from what you've said Charlie Irvine met your daughter five to six times, in a public park, in sight of everyone, and didn't once leave the vicinity. In which case, Charlie Irvine couldn't possibly have been inappropriate with your daughter, could he, without anyone seeing them?'

'I would call their friendship inappropriate, he was a grown man.'

'But nothing sexual could have happened,' Rachel replied.

'Well, I guess, no.' Benjamin gulped and tightened his tie.

'If I told you Charlie Irvine had severe autism and had the feelings and thoughts of someone much younger, would you feel the same direction of anger towards him?'

'Well, I didn't know that he had.' Benjamin stroked his chin.

'Well he did, Mr Graham, so does this change anything?'

'I don't know, I didn't know him.'

'I assume seeing your daughter was put at such high risk and you didn't know what happened to her, that you'd have put her through some form of counselling? Or ensured she got professional support?'

'Well...' Benjamin stuttered and sipped his water. 'I didn't at first, I suppose I didn't want it all to be real. I buried my head in the sand for a long time. But when Mohammed Iqbal came and told me about Charlie and the case against The Predator Hunters, he offered me a psychological assessment of Becky.'

'And did you accept it?' Rachel asked.

'Yes, of course.'

'So where are the results?' Rachel held out her palm to Benjamin, who bowed his head.

'I don't have them with me.'

'But I'm assuming my learned colleague, Mr Iqbal here, would have ensured they were part of the evidence here today had there been anything damaging towards Charlie in there?' She turned to Mo, who bowed his head. 'What did that report say, Mr Graham?'

'It said she was a happy girl and that they couldn't find anything to suggest that she'd been abused.'

'Thank you, Mr Graham,' she replied before turning to Mo. 'Mr Iqbal, I'm surprised, I thought better of you. No more questions, Your Honour.'

Rachel returned to her seat and Mohammed informed the judge that he had no further witnesses. The judge read over the notes before asking the lawyers to make their final statements.

'Your Honour, over the past week and a half, I've shown you that Charlie was an innocent man with childish tendencies due to the conditions that he had.' Rachel began her closing

292

statement. 'He was a desperately lonely person who simply wanted a friend. I've shown you that Charlie had no predator traits; a look at his internet history showed nothing unusual for a typical teenage boy. So much so, even Mr Iqbal's client had looked at the same images! Charlie Irvine decided to go online one day and met someone he connected with, for friendship and nothing more, discussing something as innocent as his favourite ice cream flavours. They decided to meet. He arrived at their agreed meeting point and he was approached by The Predator Hunters gang, and I call them a *gang* because they behave as such. This gang kidnapped him, threw him in a garage and attempted to tie him up.

'Charlie managed to escape their lair, but in fear for his life, ran out into oncoming traffic, scared of what they would do to him,' Rachel continued. 'Charlie died because of The Predator Hunters. Your Honour, I feel it is only right that you acknowledge their part in Charlie's death and award his mother a bereavement payment and relevant funeral costs. She's a struggling single woman who works part time in a shop and the money would not only support her, but would be a recognition that her son is innocent and she can move on from this horrible situation. Had The Predator Hunters not kidnapped Charlie that day, he'd still be here today and no one can doubt that.'

Rachel sat down and turned to Mo who took the stand for the final time.

'Your Honour, over the last week we've seen Rachel try to convince you that Charlie was this innocent boy with a condition which made him somehow above the law. The fact is he was a grown man with adult feelings and tendencies. Regardless if he was, shall we say, immature, he was still a grown man luring children over the internet to come and meet him. And he was successful on at least one occasion. I've even shown you through the psychologist, which my colleague brought along to defend

Charlie's honour, that he had the psychological traits of a child abuser.

'Charlie got unlucky,' Mo continued. 'He was met by The Predator Hunters where they performed a citizen's arrest on him, which they're entitled to do by law. They were in the process of calling the police when they took him to a house out in Chorley. I ask, why would they kidnap him and tie him up if they were calling the police? They'd have landed in prison themselves. They were about to expose this man to the world as a predator, and Charlie, whether he was autistic or not, was about to be arrested for predatory behaviour. So he stood up and attacked my client with a hammer, causing serious injury before running off and ending his own life. Your Honour, I believe you should exonerate my client from being responsible for Charlie's death. Charlie caused his own death, whether it be by misadventure, or whether it was suicide. Charlie knew the police were on their way, and he was running from *them*, not The Predator Hunters.'

The judge thanked the lawyers and left the court. Outside, Mohammed grilled Stephen on his visit to the claimant's house, while Rachel stood nervously by with Karen, who was shivering. Nick stood by her side, holding her hand. They had no doubt put across a good case, but so had Mohammed, and Rachel couldn't see which way Judge Miller would turn. They didn't have to wait long. They were called back into the court nearly an hour later where Judge Judith entered and gave her verdict.

'Thank you to both of you for submitting this very complex case. I've read through all the evidence and listened to what you both had to say. I believe Charlie knew what he was doing that day, I believe he acted in a calculated manner in trying to meet what he believed to be a young girl, as he had done it once before as Mr Iqbal has pointed out...'

Rachel and Karen bowed their heads and sighed.

'But what did he meet those girls for? Friendship. We've heard that Charlie was a lonely person who struggled to find connections in this world and was desperate to meet someone, anyone, who would be willing to listen to and spend time with him without judgement. Children very often like that. I'm not saying parents shouldn't be concerned or shouldn't keep a check on anyone associating with someone like Charlie, as after all, he was still an adult with adult feelings, but I believe Charlie in this case at least was harmless.'

The girls smiled at each other, grateful for this confirmation of his innocence in a public and legal forum. Rachel began to rub her hands and shot a smug look towards Mohammed, who appeared resigned across from her.

'And it is with this that I believe The Predator Hunters did what they do best; they approached someone who *they* believed to be a predator. A job I hear they do very well. They clearly completed a citizen's arrest and somewhere along the way they made some mistakes, but most of this I put down to someone who isn't even here today; Simon Jenkins. However, I believe they made it very clear to Charlie that the police were on their way, therefore that should have eliminated any danger to Charlie if he was at all scared. Their due diligence was undertaken and it wasn't their fault that Charlie's mind didn't act like yours or mine.'

The two lawyers looked at each other, unsure of where the judge was going.

'Which brings me to the attack itself. Charlie's condition meant that he acted in a way which was natural to him. He couldn't connect the dots. Was that The Predator Hunters' fault? No. But neither was it Charlie's fault either. He ran and ran because he was scared, but as we've heard in this court, we heard he had done this before when someone touched him at school, and not necessarily because he felt he was under attack.'

'This is a very sad case but I think it's a mainly blameless one,' the judge continued. 'Therefore I assign neither of you an award, and neither of you any money. Now I do judge The Predator Hunters for putting this awful imagery on the internet, allowing the world to believe innocent people are monsters. Had Charlie survived the accident, I have no doubt that his life would've been ruined by the public. I think you have done a brilliant job of keeping our street's safe, but allowing a person's trial to be undertaken by the media, is something we simply cannot allow to happen. I encourage you to rethink about your actions in future and to hand over your footage to the police, rather than to Facebook. I've made my decision and that is the order of this court.'

The judge banged her gavel and left the court, as the usher called, 'All rise!' Those remaining stood in an unsettling mood of both relief and fury. The lawyers met privately with their clients in quiet corners of the corridors, while the media outside waited for the results.

'I'm sorry I didn't win your case, Karen,' Rachel replied. 'Maybe if we hadn't fallen out for those few weeks and I hadn't let my personal situation interfere with this case we'd have stood a better chance. I don't know. But I'm sorry I didn't get us an award.'

'Rachel.' Karen placed her hand on her lawyer's. 'That judge exonerated my son of any wrongdoing today in a court of law. That's all I came here for. I don't need any money for that. I just want people to stop thinking my son is a predator. This alone allows me to be able to talk about him and celebrate his life without people judging me. That was the biggest win for me.'

They smiled at each other and began to write a statement. Once they had chosen the perfect words to honour Charlie, Karen asked if she could borrow Rachel's laptop. Together they formed a plan and walked out of court, hand-in-hand towards the flashing lights from the local press. Rachel got out her notebook and read a statement.

'My client may not have got the reward money we sought out today, or justice for her son in regards to pinpointing those who were responsible for his death. However, the judge acknowledged that Charlie Irvine was an innocent man who did no wrong. Charlie had severe autism and simply wanted friendship and in this case, the only way he could find friends, was through children online. He meant nothing sinister or sexual through it, and the judge completely exonerated him of that claim. This legal and public statement is a clear message to the world that Charlie Irvine should now be allowed to rest in peace and his family should be offered the respect which they've long deserved but not been given.

'Judge Miller also heavily criticized The Predator Hunters group for allowing the media to be Charlie's judge, rather than a court of law, by putting the video of his misfortune on Facebook,' Rachel continued. 'We have just launched a petition online to ask our government to prevent vigilantes like The Predator Hunters from putting these dangerous videos online before a court case can be undertaken, which can lead to innocent people being hurt unnecessarily. We need one hundred thousand signatures to get in front of The House of Commons. Until we get there, Ms Irvine in the meantime would like some time to grieve for her son now, which will be for the first time she's been allowed to since he died. I'd ask the media to respect her privacy. Thank you.'

Rachel walked off with her client with Nick to the right of Karen arm in arm, and stepped into Rachel's Qashqai. They drove off out of Bolton towards Horwich, relieved that Charlie's name could no longer be tarnished within the town. Rachel dropped the pair off at their respective houses before heading back to hers. There was a bottle of bubbly in the fridge which she'd saved for if she'd won the case. Whilst she hadn't won it per se, she'd got what she wanted for her client, and that was just as good as a win, even if it meant a cost to Karen, or even her ex-boyfriend Josh. Regardless, she was ready for a drink and she stepped out of her car and rushed to the front door.

But something wasn't right.

The door was ajar. She sighed, wondering if her mother had gone walkabout again. Pushing open the door, she stepped in and called out to Dorothy, but there was no response. She threw down her handbag by the door and stepped into the lounge. In her mother's chair, sat a man with a baseball cap on, dressed in a black hoodie and jeans.

'Hello, Rachel,' he said. Her heart raced as she was faced with her former boyfriend once again.

'Hello, Carl.'

Chapter 33

Rachel froze as she came face to face with the man who had planned to abuse her daughter. She glanced carefully around the room for Matilda and Dorothy, but they were nowhere to be seen.

'How did you get in?' asked Rachel.

'Dorothy's such a dear, isn't she? Thick as old shit though.'

'Where is my mother, Carl?' Rachel said with a lump in her throat.

'She's upstairs in her room,' he replied in a sinister tone.

'And my daughter?'

'She's also upstairs.'

'If you dare hurt a hair on her head, Carl….' Rachel spoke through gritted teeth.

'Nobody needs to get hurt, Rachel, I'm just here to talk.' He held out his hand and offered her a seat, which she took. She felt around her suit for her mobile phone but punched her palm when she remembered it was in her bag, which was by the front door.

They sat across from each other, facing each other for the first time since his arrest. The last time they'd spoken, she was waving him off as he took her daughter to Alton Towers.

'What do you want with me, Carl?'

'I want you to tell the police to end any claims against me. I want you to end all this shit right now. My life is in tatters, my family hate me and I've been suspended from work.'

'Carl, you know I can't do that. The police caught you red-handed. You drugged my daughter.'

'You can make this stop,' Carl replied.

'Even if I could, I wouldn't. You need to rot in jail, you monstrous pig.'

'You were in love with me.'

'Not anymore.' A tear sprung from Rachel's nervous eyes. Her face lost all colour. She looked over this man who just a few weeks before she'd found sexually attractive. Now he made her nauseous. 'Why did you do this to us, Carl?'

'It's not my fault.'

'What do you mean it's not your fault? You drugged a child and intended to have sex with her. How can that possibly not be your fault?'

'I have a mental illness, Rachel. I can't help what I do. *Paedophilic Disorder*, it's called. I thought you'd understand seeing you were currently representing someone who had a mental health disorder themselves.'

'He was autistic, that's very different to you. You hurt children and you manipulate people. You take vulnerable kids and...' Rachel couldn't even finish her sentence as she burst into tears.

'I'm mentally ill.'

'Then do something about it!' Rachel yelled. 'Don't go round screwing up other people's lives. Go to a doctor or to the police. Get chemically castrated. Kill yourself, I don't care. But don't start dating single parents and using them to get to young kids. You're sick. You're a freak. And you should not be in this house!'

'I was abused myself, you know.'

'Oh, classic. The abused who became the abuser. You know as part of my job I've had to meet people who've been through the same thing. Real victims, Carl, they get help. They don't let it turn them into predators themselves.'

'I was so young. It was a neighbour. She used to look after me while my mum was at home lying on the couch drunk. She'd hit me, force me to do things to her and to others.'

'You are just as bad as *her.*'

Carl stood up and walked over to her chair and slapped Rachel across the face. Her head flung to the left and a red patch grew across her cheek. She quickly grabbed her cheek and hid her face away.

'Don't you dare say that! I'm nothing like her!'

'Let me and my family go, Carl,' Rachel pleaded.

'I thought we had a good little unit, you and I. We had a nice life. You were even suing The Predator Hunters. I thought we were on the same page.'

Rachel turned back to her attacker and her jaw dropped. 'Are you saying you thought I was a predator too?'

He shrugged.

'You can think again. I'm a lawyer, I defend people who have been wronged. And if you thought I was like *you*, even for a second, you should've said so and I could've thrown you out sooner. Instead you manipulated all of us and you ruined our lives.'

'You were just as liable for all of this. You left your daughter with a strange man.'

'I loved you! You were a police officer! I didn't think you would hurt her!' Rachel replied. 'Christ, if I can't trust someone I loved who worked on behalf of the law, then who can I trust? You broke my trust, Carl. Never ever put this on me. You came into our lives and you hurt my daughter.'

'I would never hurt her, I love her. She wouldn't have known.'

'And you think that makes it right? You are despicable,' Rachel yelled.

'If I'm going down, you're going down with me.'

'And how do you think you're gonna do that, Carl?' Rachel folded her arms.

'Well look at you. You left your daughter with a strange man alone. You defend predators. And you have CCTV all over your house with footage going directly to both of our phones with Matilda undressing in the videos. You were complicit in all of this.'

'*You* suggested that, Carl! To keep our family safe, you said. It was after that fire started in my house,' Rachel said, before stroking her chin. Her eyes widened. 'You started the fire didn't you? And you killed Matilda's dog!'

'Maybe,' Carl smirked.

'You let me blame my sister, you sick freak!' Rachel cried.

'*You* came to that conclusion when we saw her on CCTV spray painting messages on the house.'

'And you let me think that she would be so evil as to harm her niece. What is wrong with you? You purposely bought my daughter a dog just to kill it, so she'd run to you. And you made me distance myself from my daughter and fall out with my sister.

My God, you've completely isolated me. I have no one in my life and it's all because of you!'

'You didn't really have anyone before, did you, Rachel?'

'I'm going to ask you once again, Carl, what do you want from me?'

'If you can't change the charges, I want you and Matilda to run away with me.'

'You think I want to run away with *you*? I would never allow my daughter to be near you ever again.'

'Come on, we were in love. If you love your daughter and want her to remain with you, the only way is this way.'

'And what about my mother?' Rachel asked. 'How the hell are we supposed to run off with an elderly woman with dementia?'

'I've already sorted her out.'

'What do you mean?' Rachel raised a shaking hand over her mouth.

'I put her out of her misery, and yours.'

Rachel sat in silence, her mouth wide open as tears poured from her eyes. She heard a rustling from upstairs and felt her heart pound. She stood up and ran towards the stairs. As she reached the bottom step, she felt a tug on her shoulder. She fell back and met the hard cold surface and smacked her head. When she opened her eyes, Carl was standing over her with his foot on her chest.

'Mattie!' Rachel cried. 'Carl, get off me, let me go, please!'

'Never, it's all of us, or none of us. You decide.' He climbed on top of her and forced a kiss on her lips. She bit his lip, causing him to bleed. 'Oh you want it to be like that do you?'

Carl lifted into his pocket and lifted out a penknife and held it to Rachel's throat. She could feel his breath on his face and his tongue smelt like it hadn't met the face of a toothbrush for some time. She felt the cold face of the blade against her and the sharp edge nipped at her skin.

'I have some good news for you, Rachel,' Carl said, stroking the knife around her neck. 'I won't kill Mattie. Once I've got rid of you, I'm going to take her away and she'll be all mine and there won't be anything you can do about it. Say goodnight, Rachel.'

He lifted up his hand to carve her throat. As the knife began to glide across her skin, she heard a thud. Carl's eyes widened and his head came crashing down on hers. The impact caused her nose to crack. She tried to move but Carl lay floppy on top of her. Moving his head away from hers, she found Mo standing with Matilda's trophy from her school netball team. It had stood proudly on the mantel since her recent award ceremony and weighed a ton.

'Oh my God, Rachel. What happened?' Mo asked, moving Carl's body off her. Carl lay on the floor, covered in blood, pouring from his head, his eyes wide open and staring forward towards his killer. Mo checked his pulse but failed to find one. 'He's dead. Are you alright?'

'I am all the better for seeing you here. Call the police. What are you doing here anyway? Not that I'm not relieved.'

'I came round to see how you were after the case and the door was open. I slipped in and heard a commotion. I'm glad I came!' Mo picked up his mobile phone and began to dial.

'Me too!' Rachel shouted as she ran up the stairs. She ran into each room. The first was her mother's bedroom. Dorothy was in bed, her eyes closed. An empty glass beside her and empty pill packets scattered across the floor. She placed her hand over her mother's and felt it was ice cold. She kissed her mum's hand and cried, but a murmuring distracted her moment of grief.

She ran to Matilda's room, where she found her daughter tied to a chair and tape covering her mouth. She ripped it off, untied her and held her. Matilda was dressed innocently in her Disney's *Frozen* pyjamas and her hair was tied up in pigtails. *How anyone could do this to an innocent child,* Rachel thought as she gripped on to the love of her life.

'Oh, Matilda!'

'Mummy! It was so scary! Carl's so horrible!'

'Did he do anything to you?' Rachel asked, her heart pounding. She wiped the tears from her daughter's cheeks and grabbed her arms.

'No. He just tied me up and then he heard your car pull up, so he went downstairs. Is Grandma OK?'

'I'm afraid not, my love, Grandma has died.'

Outside the police sirens grew nearer and commotion filled the house as the law enforcers stormed the building. Rachel and Matilda lay together in each other's arms, waiting for safety.

Chapter 34

In the House of Commons, the Members of Parliament sat down for the usual Prime Minister's Questions. Green benches lined each side of a wooden bench in the centre. A mace sat on top. The government and its opposition took turns in debating Brexit, the Middle East and how they could ensure affordable homes for young people.

Above in the public galleries, Karen Irvine watched in anticipation as the two sides went into battle over the matters which meant most to their constituents. The Speaker shouted *'order'* and everyone took to their seats while he read out a petition which had been completed online. For several weeks, the petition had done the rounds on social media, and Karen had stood outside social clubs and universities gaining signatures from passers-by.

'We have a petition which has received one hundred thousand signatures therefore under UK law we have to debate it. The petition asks us to review the current use of social media platforms to share videos which may allow the public to determine that an individual is a criminal, before they have time to represent themselves in a court of law.'

'I know exactly where this comes from and I have to agree, Mr Speaker.' The Leader of the Opposition stood up and spoke into the microphone. He had white hair and a matching beard, and was dressed in a black suit, white shirt and a red tie. 'This follows a very public case in which a vigilante group called The Predator Hunters catfish potential paedophiles on the internet and expose them all over social networks. It can lead to innocent people being put at very serious risk. The public should not be our judge, especially on social media, and even those who are potentially guilty deserve their day in court. Vigilante groups like this should be banned altogether.'

The Prime Minister stood up and took the stand. He had white floppy hair which hadn't seen the face of a brush that morning, he was circular in shape and spoke with a quintessentially British accent like he'd fallen out of an Emily Bronte book. He dressed in a designer suit and a blue tie.

'Well I have to say I've seen these groups work and hear they're quite effective myself. If our police are struggling to find these predators, then these people deserve our support in ensuring our streets remain safe. Carry on, I say.'

'Well if you supplied enough police, Prime Minister, we wouldn't need vigilante groups. Why won't you step in, up our police support and ban these people who are not qualified to take the law into their own hands?'

'Is the Right Honourable Gentleman suggesting we allow children to remain unsafe online? In my eyes, they should be rewarded, not punished. I say keep them! And as for posting videos online and the public being our judge, I ask him what on earth he thinks a jury is, if it isn't the general public? I vote to keep our streets and our children safe. It is not our job to police the internet and as soon as we ban this, we ban free speech!'

They had a show of hands and it was resounding in the favour of keeping The Predator Hunters live with their full support for sharing the content online. Up above, Karen sighed as she lost a second battle against the people who took down her son.

Chapter 35

It had been a rough few weeks for Rachel. Her daughter had been placed in danger for a second time. Her heart broke as she untangled Matilda from the chair and handed her over to the police and social services to review. She questioned herself whether she deserved Matilda back home after everything she'd put her through, but having heard what the system had done to people like Stephen Fletcher, she more than anything wanted her daughter home to ensure her protection, determined never to allow a man to enter her life again.

Once social services returned her home, confident that she was safest with her mother, Matilda found a local school which was briefed on the challenges she'd faced over the previous year. The school had special programmes to support children with dyslexia, allowing her once again to shine, and a team of school psychologists, who were working round the clock to undo the damage that Carl had inflicted on their family.

She'd also lost her mother. Dorothy McCann died peacefully in her sleep after Carl Packer gave her a lethal overdose of her medication. At least she didn't suffer, Rachel considered, as she waited for probate. As soon as it was through, she sold the house. There were too many painful memories and she wanted to move on, for her, and her daughter.

Carl was laid to rest a week later with nobody but the undertaker at his funeral. The police took no further action against Mohammed, assessing the attack as a clear attempt to save Rachel's life. While she was frustrated that Carl would never face repercussions for his actions, she was grateful he was no longer around to hurt her little girl, or any child for that matter.

After confirmation from Carl that he was the one who torched the house and killed their dog, Rachel made amends with her sister, Lisa. Since their mother's death, they began to meet up again and rebuilt the relationship which they'd lost all those years before. They began to get on so well that Rachel offered to buy a barn on Lisa's farmland and converted it into a house for her and her daughter. There was lots of land for Matilda to run around and she loved the animals, especially the alpacas. Their weekends were spent walking the creatures across the fields, talking to each other about the previous months and coming to terms with what had happened to them.

On one of their Sunday strolls, Matilda turned to her mother and asked about their family. Rachel talked about her parents, their careers and who they were as people before they began to lose their memories. She talked about her own grandparents who served in the Second World War.

'Now it's just us two,' Mattie said.

'Well and Aunty Lisa of course.'

'Yes, her too. Our family just feels a bit small. My friends at school have grandparents and daddies and I don't have anything like that. I just feel a bit lonely.'

Rachel looked at her daughter. Her beautiful biracial little girl and how lost she must feel in a world where few people already looked like her in the local village. There was no one who even looked like her in her own family. Rachel thought about Matilda's father and where he was now, and how she could somehow bring him back to life for her.

'Now that Carl has gone, you don't seem very happy, Mummy.'

'Mattie, I'm very happy Carl has gone. If I'm sad, it's because I let you down.'

'Do you think you'll get another boyfriend?' Matilda asked.

'Not for a long time, my love. My focus is on you now,' Rachel replied, wrapping her arm around her daughter.

'You should find someone, I'd certainly like a boyfriend.'

'Well let's make a deal that neither of us have one until you're at least eighteen!'

'I can't wait that long!' Matilda stropped. 'Besides not *all* men are bad, Mummy. Look at that Mohammed who saved us. He seems nice.'

'He does, doesn't he?' Rachel smiled.

The following weekend they took a trip to Manchester Southern Cemetery and found the grave of a young man named Liam Holloway, who died suddenly ten years before, leaving behind grieving parents and siblings. There was no mention of the child he'd left behind because nobody knew that he had. Rachel hadn't told him he was a father before he took his own life. She looked to the photograph in the corner of the stone in a gold frame and saw the spit of her daughter in his smile.

'This is your daddy, Matilda,' Rachel said, stroking the top of the marble. Matilda lay down yellow tulips on the ground before the grave and blew a kiss towards the photograph.

'What was he like?'

'He was wonderful. Kind. And he'd have loved you so very much had he known about you. He was also deeply sad. Unfortunately he couldn't find the words to tell any of us. I wish he could have, he could have been here today to meet you.'

A short woman with a black curly weave shuffled up the path towards them. She had bags drooping beneath her big brown eyes, which carried the weight of sorrow within them. The lady was dressed in a black cardigan and a purple shirt beneath. A baggy skirt hung from her waist. As she reached closer to Liam's gravestone, she looked at the two girls laying flowers and squinted.

'Do you know Liam?' the lady asked.

'He's my daddy,' Matilda replied with a beaming smile. The lady's eyes widened and she staggered back, covering her beaming white teeth. Moisture coated her gleaming eyes.

'Oh my, yes I can see it,' she replied with a subtle Jamaican twang. She stroked the little girl's cheek and smiled. 'I'm Liam's mother.'

'You're my grandma?' Matilda asked, her jaw hanging from her face.

'It seems so.' She looked up at Rachel, who was perplexed. 'I always hoped I'd meet you.'

'You knew?' Rachel asked.

'It was in his note which he wrote before he left us. He didn't give us any details, just that he had a child.'

'Oh,' Rachel said with an air of guilt.

'Oh no, don't worry, my love. You did the right thing. The weight of the world was on his shoulders. He couldn't have coped with a child on top of everything else. I don't think any of us could have saved him in the end. He was so broken. But I've spent years being angry and upset. I can't have that pain anymore. We need to live for the future and for what he left behind. And for this little girl. May I?'

She held out her arms and Rachel nodded. Matilda jumped into her grandmother's arms and embraced her, joyful that her little family was beginning to grow.

*

The tower blocks in Chorley had begun some major reconstruction. The tiles outside of the building were being replaced with an inflammable alternative, and inside the reception areas were facing a lick of paint. Notices around the building offered council grants to provide new kitchens and bathrooms to all residents, along with a selection of free paint and new carpets for the apartments.

Stephen had put his time and energy into a new project, which was with the local neighbourhood watch. He took a stand against the local drug dealers in the apartments and slowly but surely began to make the living space a much more habitable place to live for the families surrounding him. He was glad to be out of his suit and returned to his tracksuit, but he'd let his hair grow longer; leaving behind his skinhead days. Unfortunately he'd noticed the early signs of male-pattered baldness and wondered how long he'd be able to keep his new look.

The Predator Hunters had taken a break from their operation while they let the dust settle on the Irvine case. They'd been left with a damaged reputation following Charlie's posthumous exoneration.

A surprise visitor tapped him on the shoulder as he placed fresh flowers in the hallway one day. Behind him, Karen Irvine stood timidly with a nervous look on her face. He jumped back, cautious of her visit. She was much brighter than their previous meeting; the bags had gone from under her eyes, she wore a bright pink top and white trousers, and her hair had been freshly dyed and styled following a morning visit to her hairdresser. The biggest change was her smile. He'd never seen that on her before.

'What do you want?' Stephen said.

'I came to apologise. It was unfair of me to give that recording to Rachel. It wasn't my intention to upset you. I recorded you in case you, well, attacked me or something, I didn't know what you were going to do. I told Rachel about our meeting after you left and she asked to hear the recording. She persuaded me to let her use it in court. I felt terrible about it all, really I did. That was your story to tell, not mine. And I stitched you right up with the case when all you did was come round to apologise.'

'It didn't get you very far anyway, did it?' Stephen relaxed his shoulders and shot Karen a resigned look. 'What's done is done. We both got what we wanted out of it in the end though, didn't we? You got your son's legacy back and well, I didn't have to pay through the nose.'

'And you don't have to live with the fact that you're responsible for anyone's death. The judge made up her mind. By law you are completely exonerated of any responsibility.'

'I'll still live with the responsibility, Karen. Every day.'

'I haven't seen many videos from The Predator Hunters recently. I joined Facebook and followed your page. It's gone very quiet.'

'We've taken a break. Alison has her own stuff going on at the moment and I haven't spoken to Simon for a long time.'

'Oh that's a shame. I wanted to help you guys out.'

'Help out?' Stephen replied with a look of suspicion. 'Why the hell would you do that?'

'I agreed with the judge's point of view on your group. You *do* do a lot of good in the area. And had I had a little boy or girl right now, I'd be wanting you around to protect them from predators too. I do however have an issue with how you go about

314

it. So I wondered if I could possibly get involved. I could add a little human touch to the proceedings.'

'Ms Irvine, you certainly are a surprise.' He smiled and gave the formerly timid lady, who'd suddenly grown in confidence, a hug. 'Come on, I'll show you how it all works.'

*

Down the road in Preston, Mohammed had also received a surprise visitor. Thomas opened the door to his office and nodded out towards the reception.

'The chavvy one is here,' he whispered through the door. Mo waved his hand towards him and Thomas moved out of the way after calling the visitor through. Alison stood proudly in the doorway. She'd kept her lip piercing but had dyed her hair and dressed as if she was attending a job interview in a grey tartan skirt and white shirt.

'Well this is a surprise.'

'You said I could come and see you anytime.' She held up his business card.

'Of course, how can I help?'

'You're an amazing lawyer, Mr Iqbal.'

'Thank you. You know I lost your case, don't you?'

'That's not entirely true.' Alison shrugged. 'You did a brilliant job and I want you on my side while I go after my next target.'

'You've not catfished some TV presenter have you?'

'No.' Alison chuckled. 'I told you about my past. Those men who attacked me. I've found one of them on Facebook. They're tagged in teenage girls' photographs and I can see the same pattern again. Fuelling them with booze and free takeaway food. They've moved away but they've not changed. I know I have to tell my story to stop them from hurting others. Will you represent me?'

'Of course. Are you not tempted to use your mates to get them on a chat room or something?'

'No, I want this done properly. I'm not risking them getting away with this.' They sat down together for two hours and hashed out a plan, and Alison informed Mo of everything she knew about her abuser.

'OK, well let's get them.' He pressed a button and Thomas replied on an intercom. 'Tom, clear my diary for the next month. And find everything you can on Tahir's Taxis in Sheffield.'

Chapter 36

As Valentine's Day approached, Rachel was surprised by how much she was bothered by all the love hearts and reminders that she was single. She struggled to determine if it was because she felt lonely or whether it was because her last relationship was a complete failure.

She waved off Matilda to a disco, hosted by her new school. The now eleven-year-old was talking about boys and she was determined to get an eight PM kiss before Cinderella had to return home and go to bed so she was ready for school the next morning.

Alone and frustrated by the number of romcoms the TV had scheduled on nearly every channel, Rachel walked out to the nearest pub so she could get herself a drink. Matilda was getting a lift home with a friend so she didn't need to worry about driving anytime soon. Unfortunately the local pub also served as a restaurant and was offering two-for-one Valentine's special meals. Red ribbons filled the room, streamers poured down from the ceiling and she had to force her way through heart-shaped balloons to get to the bar.

In the far corner, she spotted a table by the window, with two very familiar faces. Nick and Karen were sitting holding hands, looking fondly into each other's eyes. Karen looked to her side and spotted Rachel and waved. Rachel smiled and waved back, before hiding behind the drinks menu to avoid intruding on their romantic meal. She ordered a rhubarb gin and ginger ale, which was served in what could only be described as a goldfish bowl, and read over her emails on her phone. A few new clients had come through following the publicity she'd received in the news after Charlie's exoneration and she was keen to get stuck in and earn some money at last.

After downing her first gin, she ordered another and ran to the toilet, leaving her coat to reserve her seat. As she walked past the entrance, an Asian man walked in, dressed finely in a blue suit. To his left, a beautiful blonde bombshell with legs up to her elbows joined him. Rachel recognised the man as Mohammed and tried to sneak past him as he asked the waiter for a table.

'Oh, Rachel,' Mo called as she inconspicuously ran past.

'Hi, Mo! Lovely to see you!' she awkwardly replied, pretending she hadn't already spotted him.

'What are you doing out on Valentine's night? With anyone special?'

'Sure,' Rachel lied, forcefully smiling. She couldn't face the humiliation of being alone. 'But he's stuck in traffic so I've just said I'd meet him at his place instead.'

'I see.' Mo laughed before turning to his dinner date. 'Hey, Lois, why don't you go and get the table.'

'Who is she? She's gorgeous,' Rachel whispered.

'Jealous?' Mo replied.

'No!' Rachel gave him a gentle shove and laughed. 'Just nosey.'

'She's my new partner.'

'I see, lucky man.' Rachel winked. 'She's beautiful.'

'No, I mean she's a new partner at work. She's bought into the business. This is a celebratory dinner. We forgot it was Valentine's night. Her husband nearly killed her when he found out! But here we are. There's nothing going on by the way.'

'I wouldn't care if there was.' Rachel shrugged.

'That's a shame. Well...' He picked out a rose from a basket next to the plinth with the restaurant's reservations listed. 'Have this, from me, and if you ever want to meet for dinner yourself sometime, you have my number. And I don't mean to discuss business, if you get what I mean.'

'OK, how about Saturday?'

'I've got my daughter on Saturday.' He punched the air with frustration. 'I shouldn't complain. I finally have regular access after all this time. But why don't you come along? Bring Mattie?'

'A play-date? That sounds nice.'

'I'll see you there.'

Rachel left the building feeling something which she hadn't felt in a long time; joy.

*

In a large house in the hills, Josh Simmonds watched the sun go down while having dinner with his wife and two children. Jennifer poured them both a glass of Merlot and gave her husband a nudging look. He'd just returned home from a trip to Los Angeles and was wearing the same charcoal suit he'd been flying in, but he loosened his tie and threw off the jacket. Jennifer's long flowing red hair lay immaculately over her black designer dress despite her having worked from home all day.

'Molly, Seb, I have something important to talk to you about.'

'Oh, Dad, we've got to go to the Valentine's Ball! Please don't delay this meal,' Seb moaned. He had a black t-shirt on with

319

the logo of his favourite band and his jeans were so baggy he tripped as he walked across the lounge. He had long scruffy hair, which infuriated his perfect parents.

'It's important, kids,' Jennifer said and shot them both a stern stare. They sat upright and nodded towards their father.

'You see, before your mother and I married, I was with another lady, named Karen. Things didn't quite work out between Karen and me, but what did happen was very wonderful. She had a child. And his name was Charlie.'

Jennifer lifted out a box from under the table and passed the photographs sent to them every year on Charlie's birthday from Karen, all up to his nineteenth year. He gently explained how he was no longer here.

'Why didn't we get to meet him, Daddy?' asked Molly. She was dressed up ready for the ball in a pink dress. Her strawberry blonde hair was curly and hung down to her shoulders.

He choked up, trying to find the right words which made him look anything other than selfish.

'Your dad was busy ensuring you two had the best life, and he knew that Karen was providing the best life for Charlie.' Jennifer saved her husband, who was stuttering as he tried to articulate himself. He smiled and nodded a small *thank you* towards her.

'Can we go and visit his grave?' asked Seb.

'Of course, that would be nice. There's just one problem with that but I think we can fix it.'

*

Karen stepped out of her house in her Sunday attire, a red coat with a faux-fur hood, and a dark blue dress underneath. It was a cold day, so she had her hood up and leather gloves on. Outside, a red Qashqai continued to beep. Karen waved her hand.

'OK, OK, I'm here. What's with the rush?' she said as she locked the door and threw her keys into her handbag whilst juggling a bouquet of flowers.

'We're going to miss Mass,' Rachel replied through the open car window. Karen walked around to the passenger door and stepped into the car.

'I don't plan on going to Mass. We're just going to lay these flowers for Charlie and go. I don't think I can face anyone at church again. They all hate me.'

'It's his birthday, Karen, you need to light a candle for your son's memory.'

'I suppose but please can we avoid Mass?'

'Very well.' Rachel started the engine and drove them to the chapel.

'Did you see the papers?' Karen said woefully.

'I did, I'm sorry it wasn't what you were hoping for,' Rachel replied.

The day after Charlie's exoneration, Karen rushed to the shops eager to see the headlines. She expected quite a spectacle after the amount of journalists waiting outside the court once the judge had delivered her verdict. She had visions of photographs of her son with 'Innocent' stamped across the front page. However Charlie's vindication barely made a quarter of page five. One paper didn't even mention the judge's comments on his innocence, while another put it as a final line at the end of the article, focusing instead on The Predator Hunters' success in court against the cruel lawyer who tried (and failed) to bring them down.

'Maybe I was little naïve. It is the press after all. I don't think anyone will really ever believe Charlie is innocent. They've already made up their minds, no matter what a judge says.'

It was a cold but sunny day and they got a clear view of Rivington and the surrounding villages. They walked to the back of the church towards the space where they last joined together to pay their respects to Charlie nearly a year before.

Something was different.

The flat rectangle of grass with a flowerpot had been disturbed. In its a place, a marble gravestone stood. Karen stopped and held her hand to her mouth.

'They haven't filled his space already, have they? He's still there! They can't just give it up to someone else! I have the right mind to tell the priest!'

'No of course not, you need a court order for that! Come on, let's just go see what it is before we complain.'

Rachel grabbed Karen by the arm and pulled her towards the front of the stone. Upon it, Charlie's name stood proudly, with a small photograph of him in the corner.

'Oh my!' Karen gasped and clung on to her lawyer. 'Did you do this?'

'No, Josh did it.'

'And who are these flowers from?' She lifted up the tulips and read the card. *Love Molly and Seb.* She lifted up a tissue and dabbed her eye. 'His brother and sister.'

They stood for five minutes and had a quiet moment of contemplation. A bong from the church bell disrupted their tranquillity. They jumped and made their way to the entrance of the church. The doors were closed. Rachel jiggled the knob and opened the door, before stepping out of the way to let Karen through.

The church was filled to the rafters. Old friends and family were piled into the available seats and a few faces she didn't recognise stood at the back. A red carpet ran from the door to the front of the chapel. Before the altar, a wooden stand held a large photograph of Charlie, wrapped with flowers around the edges. Karen gasped and turned to Rachel, who smiled and offered an encouraging nod towards her. As she took a step forward, the crowd around her applauded as 'Somewhere Only We Know' by Keane began to play.

'He loved this song,' Karen said, wiping a tear away from her eye, as she walked down the aisle. She smiled at those who she knew and grabbed the hands of Josh and Jennifer as she passed them, blowing a kiss towards their two children. '*Thank you,*' she mouthed.

School friends and teachers from Charlie's school, the ladies from her support group at church and Stanley, her old manager from the convenience store, all waved as she past. Alison and Stephen stood proudly at the back. Even Mrs Butcher, the rude old woman who approached her at work when Charlie's story hit the press, had made an appearance; she offered a pleading stare as Karen passed. As she reached her seat, she spotted Nick who turned and smiled. She batted her hand towards him and kissed his cheek. 'Oh, you!'

And behind Nick was Sylvia. Wearing a beaming smile, a sight she hadn't seen from her friend for months. The lack of contact and animosity suddenly disappeared as she reached her and they embraced.

'What is this?' Karen asked.

'You never got to give Charlie a proper goodbye back then. So here we are,' Sylvia replied.

Karen nodded and gripped on to her pals, old and new, and turned towards the priest, who began the ceremony. As she looked around the church towards those who had made a special effort to attend the ceremony, Karen realised that it didn't matter what the papers said. She could rest assured with the fact that her dear son, Charlie Irvine, was not only vindicated of all wrongdoing. What is more, he was loved.

Note from the Author

Trial by media is becoming more and more prevalent every day, especially in an era where social media forms an integral part of our lives. It is so easy now to have stories thrust in our faces day after day and we begin to believe what we're told if we scroll past the headline enough times; some would argue that's what swung the latest American election. And we only have to look towards the late Caroline Flack to understand just how damaging this can be.

The Catfish was inspired by a Channel 4 documentary in which a vigilante group enticed suspected predators online. They filmed their humiliation before presenting their work on social media. It would be unusual for anyone who has been on Facebook not to have seen at least one of these videos as they're shared hundreds of thousands of times. And there have been occasions when innocent people have been approached and later committed suicide despite being cleared of any wrongdoing. How could anyone return to society and live their lives after such a scandal? There isn't a court in the land who would stand up against the fierce gaze of social justice. Charlie Irvine's story is a very real one; a man with a development disorder was approached and humiliated online on a national scale before anyone had the chance to defend him.

This is one of the hardest books I've had to write. It took a lot of research and a lot of emotional motivation to get through it, but it's the one I'm probably proudest of. I felt it was a really important story to tell, especially in 2020, where facts and questioning what we read online is becoming sadly lost. I've started to realise I'm naturally drawn to controversial subjects. But The Predator Hunters' involvement in the book is simply a backdrop to a story of a dedicated mother trying to fight her way through a world she is unfamiliar with, where she will stop at nothing to support her son. I know this book wouldn't have been any easier to read than it was to write but I thank you for sticking by it; I do hope you enjoyed it.

I just wanted to say a huge thank you to everyone who has taken the time to read my books, left reviews and told their friends. I couldn't have done any of this without you.

Best Wishes

David Hatton

With Thanks

I'd like to thank the following people:

- My parents for their constant support and being the best sales reps for my books.
- My partner, David, who loses out on sunny adventures on weekends when I'm inside writing away.
- Julia for your constructive criticism which developed the book.
- To anyone who has read my books, written a review, told their friends and promoted it on social media! Thank You!

About The Author

David Hatton was born in Preston, Lancashire where his love of writing began. He's lived in Leeds, Manchester and Chicago, but today he resides in the town of Horwich, which this book is set in. He enjoys long walks in the Riverton Hills with his partner, also called David, and a pint down at the Bank Top Brewery. David has written two other books; *The Return* and *The Medium* and has spoken at Literary Events in Lancashire.

Did you enjoy this book?
Please leave a review on
Amazon or Good Reads!

Please feel free to tell your
friends too!

Other Books by David Hatton

The Return

Beverly Hahn has the fright of her life when her husband, Marty, knocks on her door....ten years after he was declared dead in the 9/11 terrorist attacks in New York. With a race against time before the world discovers her sinister secret, how will Beverly tell her children? And how will she face those who supported her through the grief she had no right to feel.

Feedback for The Return from Amazon & Good Reads

"The Return perfectly captures the emotional turmoil of a family devastated by the 9/11 attacks. A decade on their loyalty to one another is tested to the limit in a turn of events not one of them could have foreseen."

"

"Utterly compelling, the novel is notable for its authentic representation of the patriotism of a nation to ensure justice will always prevail."

"In light of the backdrop that surrounds the story, David Hatton was compassionate and respectful to the devastation caused to so many on that fateful day."

"A real page turner. I am very much looking forward to reading more by this author."

"Enjoyed the book from start to finish."

"Highly recommended... A gripping and original storyline, plenty of twists and turns, a real page turner. David Hatton is one of those natural story tellers who keeps you guessing what's coming next. Can't wait to read more from this author."

"Grab your seats for the ride of a lifetime!"

"If you're looking for a lot of suspense/thriller/mystery for your dollar, this one pretty much has it all.

The Return by David Hatton – Available on Amazon © 2018

Other Books by David Hatton

The Medium

When Michael Walker is approached by a psychic medium claiming to know the whereabouts of his missing wife, he has to choose between his belief in science and the desire to find the love of his life. Is the psychic all that she seems?

Feedback for The Return from Amazon & Good Reads

"As the suspense builds, each chapter manages to intricately draw the reader deeper into the twists and turns of the plot, which made for exciting reading."

"I loved David Hatton's first novel, The Return, but in my opinion The Medium is even better!"

"The characterisation is rich, layered, and trickled through to the reader just enough to keep you guessing, and I loved the way the descriptions of the places I know well- Manchester, the Lake District, Stratford- provide setting and atmosphere to the plot by almost being characters in their own right."

"The medium is just as much of a page turner. It has so many twists and turns that even Jackie Wallace couldn't predict what was going to happen next!"

"As with every good suspenseful mystery, everyone has a secret and they often set themselves up to look guilty. This is a really interesting portrayal of grief, hope, and the ends some will go to hide their secrets."

The Medium by David Hatton – Available on Amazon © 2019

Coming Soon!

The Exhumation

1n 1876, a plot to steal President Lincoln's body in exchange for ransom was foiled. Over 130 years later, the body has been snatched once again. Detective Darnell Jackson is on the case to find the former President's body. As Jackson becomes more emotionally involved in the case, he discovers the secrets that America has hidden away from their citizens for far too long. Should Detective Jackson reveal the darkest secrets of their former leader?

Coming soon to Amazon! Follow David Hatton on Social Media to keep up to date with his book releases!

Keep in Touch

For all the latest news on new novels and to contact David:

Email: davidhattonbooks@gmail.com

Facebook: fb.com/dhattonbooks

Twitter: @davidhattonbook

Instagram: davidhattonbooks

Amazon: Search David Hatton Books

Good Reads:
https://www.goodreads.com/author/show/1362999.David_Hatton

Printed in Great Britain
by Amazon